# A. E. VAN VOGT

"is always read compellingly, he is fascinating, and one gains a sensation of having had one's brain exercised.

"I find van Vogt always unusual. No two works of his are ever quite alike and no one can possibly tell in advance each new twist of the toboggan slide. He embodies all the phases of the cosmic future. His stories span all time and all space."

—Donald Wollheim in *THE UNIVERSE MAKERS*

*OTHER PAPERBACK LIBRARY BOOKS*

*BY A. E. VAN VOGT*

THE PROXY INTELLIGENCE AND
OTHER MIND BENDERS

THE BOOK OF PTATH

THE HOUSE THAT STOOD STILL

MONSTERS

# M 33 IN ANDROMEDA

by

## A. E. VAN VOGT

PAPERBACK LIBRARY

New York

PAPERBACK LIBRARY EDITION
First Printing: April, 1971

Copyright © 1971 by A. E. van Vogt
All rights reserved

"Siege of the Unseen" was originally published as "The Chronicler" in *Astounding Science-Fiction*. Copyright © 1946 by Street and Smith Publications, Inc. (now Condé Nast Publications, Inc.) tions, Inc. (now Condé Nast Publications, Inc.)

"The Expendables" was originally published in *If* Magazine. Copyright © 1963 by Galaxy Publishing Corp.

"M 33 in Andromeda" was originally published in *Astounding Science-Fiction*. Copyright © 1943 by Street and Smith Publications, Inc. (now Condé Nast Publications, Inc.)

"Discord in Scarlet" was originally published in *Astounding Science-Fiction*. Copyright © 1939 by Street and Smith Publications, Inc. (now Condé Nast Publications, Inc.)

"Heir Unapparent" was originally published as "Heir Apparent" in *Astounding Science-Fiction*. Copyright © 1945 by Street and Smith Publications, Inc. (now Condé Nast Publications, Inc.)

"The Weapon Shop" was originally published in *Astounding Science-Fiction*. Copyright © 1942 by Street and Smith Publications, Inc. (now Condé Nast Publications, Inc.

This Paperback Library Edition is published by arrangement with Forrest J Ackerman, 915 So. Sherbourne Drive, Los Angeles, California 90035.

Paperback Library is a division of Coronet Communications, Inc. Its trademark, consisting of the words "Paperback Library" accompanied by an open book, is registered in the United States Patent Office. *Coronet Communications, Inc., 315 Park Avenue South, New York, N.Y. 10010.*

# CONTENTS

# SIEGE OF THE UNSEEN

## CHAPTER I.

### BEFORE THE CORONER'S JURY
### STATEMENT OF THOMAS BARRON

MY NAME is Thomas Barron. For nine years I have been a partner in the brokerage firm of Slade & Barron. I never suspected Michael Slade was abnormal. He was a strong character, and I always thought him rather a superior individual.

I saw him a dozen times after the car accident that precipitated events, mostly in connection with my purchase of his share of the business. He gave me no inkling of anything wrong, and I have no idea what actually happened.

The crash was over, the car neatly turned on its top. Slade sprawled dizzily on his back, conscious that he had lost his glasses. Something warm trickled from his forehead into his left eye.

He wiped it away, and saw with a start that it was blood. He mustered a smile for his wife, who was sitting up. He said:

"Well, we survived. I don't know what happened. The steering gear broke, I think."

He stopped, Miriam was close enough for his near-sighted eyes, even without glasses, to see that she was gazing at him in mixed horror and alarm.

"Michael, your forehead—the soft spot! It's torn, bleeding, and—*Michael, it's an eye.*"

Slade felt blank. Almost automatically, he bent towards the rearview mirror, tilting it upwards to catch his head. The skin was torn raggedly starting about an inch from the hairline, and coming down about two inches.

A third eye was plainly visible.

The eyelid of it was closed by a surplus of sticky matter, but abruptly he grew aware that it was pulsing with a vague perception of light.

It began to hurt.

## LOCAL MAN HAS THREE EYES

A car accident, which tore a layer of skin from the forehead of Michale Slade yesterday revealed that the young business executive has three eyes. Mr. Slade, when interviewed in the hospital, where he was taken by a passing motorist, seemed in good spirits, but could offer no reason for his possession of a third eye. "I always had that soft spot in my forehead," he said. "The eye itself seems to be a thoroughly useless appendage. I can't imagine Nature's purpose."

He admitted that it was very likely that he would have the skin grafted into place again. "People," he said, "go to sideshows to see freaks. Otherwise they don't like to look at them."

The discovery of a three-eyed man in this small city caused a buzz of interest in local scientific circles. At Technical High, Mr. Arthur Trainor, biology teacher, suggested that it was either a mutation, or else that a third eye was once common to human beings, and this is a retrogression. He felt, however, that the latter possibility was controverted by the fact that two eyes were normal throughout the entire animal world. There was, of course, the gland known as the pineal eye.

Dr. Joseph McIver, eye specialist, thought that it would be an interesting experiment to bring all three eyes back to perfect vision. He agreed that this would be difficult, since Mr. Slade's third eye has a bare perception of light, and also because the famous eye training systems now in existence have a hard enough time getting two imperfect eyes back to focus together and work perfectly.

"Nevertheless," Dr. McIver concluded, "the human

brain is a strange and wonderful machine. When it is relaxed, everything balances. But when it is tensed for any reason, eye, ear, stomach and other organic troubles begin."

Mrs. Slade, whom our reporter tried to interview, could not be reached.

## BEFORE THE CORONER'S JURY
## STATEMENT OF MRS. M. SLADE

My name is Miriam Leona Crenshaw. I am the former Mrs. Michael Slade. I divorced Mr. Slade and have legal right to use my maiden name. I met Michael Slade about six years ago, and had no suspicion that he was anything but a normal individual.

I saw my husband only twice after the car accident that revealed his abnormality. The first time it was to plead with him to change his mind about keeping all his three eyes visible. But he had been profoundly influenced by a comment in the press by a local eye specialist concerning the possibility that he might recover the vision of his three eyes. And he felt that publicity had then been so widespread that any attempt at deception was useless.

This determination was the sole reason for our separation, and it was to sign the separation papers that I saw him the second time.

I know nothing special of subsequent events. I did not even look at the body. Its crushed condition having been described to me, I refused to view it.

Slade sat palming and glancing at the Snellen charts, waiting for the eye specialist.

The sun was shining down on the chart, but he himself was in shadow, and comfortably ensconced in an easy-chair. Relaxation, that was the secret.

Only, after nearly three months of doing it on his own from books, his progress had been comparatively tiny.

Footsteps crunched on the walk. Slade looked up at the eye specialist curiously. Dr. McIver was a tall gray-haired man of fifty-five or so; that much was visible to Slade without glasses.

The doctor said: "Your man told me I would find you here."

He did not wait for a reply, but stood at ease, looking across the lawn at the three charts, respectively five, ten and twenty feet from the chair in which Slade sat.

"Well," he said, "I see you're familiar with the principles of eye training. I wish a billion more people would realize how satisfactory it is to have a light of ten thousand candlepower shining from the sky into their back yards. I think," he confided, "before I die I shall become a sun worshiper!"

Slade found himself warming to the man. He had been a little doubtful, when he had phoned Dr. McIver, about inviting even a specialist into his problem. But his doubts began to fade.

He explained his trouble. After nearly three months his third eye could see the ten-foot line at one foot, but with each additional foot that he drew back from the chart, its vision became worse out of all proportion to the extra distance. At three feet he could barely see the two hundred foot C.

"In other words," Dr. McIver said, "it's largely mental now. Your mind is suppressing images with which it is familiar, and you can be almost certain that it is suppressing them because it has been in the habit of doing so."

He turned, and began to unpack his bag. "Let's see," he said confidently, "if we can't persuade it to give in."

Slade could literally feel himself relaxing before the glowing positivities of this man. This was what he needed. For long now, tensions must have been building up inside him. Unconsciously he must be resenting his slow progress.

"A few questions first," said Dr. McIver, straightening with a retinoscope in his hand: "Have you been reading fine print every day? Can you 'swing' the letters? Have you accustomed your eyes to direct sunlight? O.K.! Let's begin with the right eye without palming."

Slade was able to read at twenty feet the line that should have been visible at fifty. He was aware of McIver standing eight feet away studying his eye through the retinoscope. The eye specialist nodded finally.

"Vision of right eye 20/50. Astigmatism of two diopters." He added; "Do you practice looking at dominoes?"

Slade nodded. Up to a point he had made considerable progress with the muscle imbalance that caused the astigmatism which affected all three of his eyes.

"Left eye next," said Dr. McIver. And a little later: "Vision 20/70, astigmatism of 3 diopters."

"Center eye, vision 3/200, astigmatism of 11 diopters. Now palm."

Palming produced long flashes of 20/20 vision in his right and left eyes, and a bare instant of 5/70 vision in his center eye.

"I think," said Dr. McIver, "we shall start by trying for a better illusion of black. What you see may seem black to your imagination, but you're fooling yourself. Afterwards, we'll do some whipping and shifting, and bounce a few tennis balls."

He fumbled in his bag, and came up with a roll of black materials. Slade recognized a black fur piece, black wool, black cotton, a square of black cardboard, black silk, a piece of black metal, a hand-engraved ebony ornament, and a variety of familiar black items including a plastic fountain pen, a bow tie, and a small book with a black cover.

"Look them over," McIver said. "The mind cannot remember any shade of black more than a few seconds. Palm, and switch your imagination from one to the other of these items."

After half an hour, Slade had improved noticeably the vision of each eye. He could see the large C with his third eye at twenty feet, and the R and B below it were recognizable blurs. But perfect vision was still a long, long way off.

"Again, palm," said Dr. McIver. This time he went on talking softly as Slade closed his eyes. "Black is black is black. There is no black but black. Black, pure, unadulterated black is black black."

It was nonsense with a pattern of reason in it. Slade found himself smiling, as he visualized the black in the various articles that McIver had placed on his lap. Black, he thought, black, wherefore art thou, black?

11

As simply as that it came. Black as black as the black of a moonless, starless night, black as printer's ink, black as all the black that the mind of man ever conceived. The black.

He opened his center eye, and saw the ten line on the twenty-foot chart. He blinked, but it was still there as bright and black as the print itself. Startled, he opened the other two eyes. And still there was no blurring. With 20/10 vision in all three of his eyes he looked around his back yard.

He *saw!*

At first, the fence and the other residences and the charts and all the shrubbery remained as a part of the scene. It was like looking at two pictures, with one super-imposed upon the other, like two images coming through two different sets of eyes. But images of different scenes.

The familiar one—his own back yard, and the hill to the right and the rooftops of his neighbors that made up his horizon—had the effect of blurring the other, stranger scene.

Gradually, however, its outlines pushed through. To his left, where the house fell away into a large shallow depression, was an enormous expanse of marsh, thick with brilliant growth. To his right, where the hill had always hidden his view, were scores of caves with fires burning at their openings.

The smoke from the fires rose up in curling tongues of black and gray, and intensified the blur that already half hid the Morton and Gladwander mansions, which dominated the hill. They kept fading, fading. And now, Slade saw that the hill with the caves was somewhat higher and steeper than the hill with the houses. There was a wide ledge that ran along in front of the caves. And it was on this ledge that he suddenly noticed something else.

Human beings! They moved around, now bending over pots that hung above the fires, now adding wood to the fires, or disappearing into the caves, and then emerging again. There were not many, and most of them had long hair characteristic of woman, or else they

12

were small and childlike. Their primitive clothes—clearly visible even at this distance—made the reality of them unnatural.

Slade sat there. He had a remote impulse to get up, but it was too soon yet for reaction or even understanding. At last memory came that this was happening as a result of improvement in his vision; and the lightning thought followed: What in the name of sanity had happened?

It was too vague as yet, the tugging amazement, and besides there was still the scene of the cave dwellers becoming clearer and clearer to his vision. The houses and his own yard were just shimmering images, like fading mirages, like things dimly seen through an all-enveloping haze.

For the first time Slade realized that his eyes had been straining to hold those two scenes, but that the strain was lessening, as the second one took stronger and stronger hold of his attention.

The paralysis left him. Quite automatically, he stood up.

He noted, with enormous and developing interest, that, where the marsh ended, a rolling meadow began, spotted here and there with bright splashes of gigantic flowering shrubs, and in the distance trees that looked amazingly tall.

Everything was as clear and bright as a summer sun could make it. A warm, glowing wilderness, almost untouched by man, spread before him. It was like a fairy land, and he stared and stared.

At last, with wondering delight, he turned to look at the other horizon—and the girl must have started the same instant around the tree that was there.

She was tall and very straight. She must have been intending to swim in the stream that babbled into the marsh a few yards away because, except for a rather ornamental silvery belt around her waist, she had no clothes on.

She had three eyes, and all three of them appraised Slade with amazement but without a shade of embarrassment. There was something else in her manner that was not so prepossessing, even a little repellent. It was the

13

dominating look of a woman accustomed to think only of herself. He had time to realize that she was older than she looked.

The woman's eyes were narrowing. She spoke in a violin-toned contralto, meaningless words, but offensively sharp in tone.

She began to fade. The trees, the great marsh, the hill, partly visible to his left now, faded perceptibly. A house showed through her body, and all around, the earth as he had known it for years took swift form.

Suddenly, there was the yard, and himself standing beside his chair. There was Dr. McIver, his back to Slade, peering around the corner of the house. The eye specialist turned, and his face lighted as he saw Slade.

"Where did you go?" he asked. "I turn my back, and you're off without a word."

Slade made no immediate reply. The pain in his eyes was like a fire.

It burned and burned.


BEFORE THE CORONER'S JURY
STATEMENT OF DR. McIVER

I had personal contact with Michael Slade over a period of about two and a half months. For an hour a day I assisted him with his eye training. It was a slow process, as, after apparently recovering the first day, he had an unusually sharp retrogression.

When I asked him about any particular effects he had observed during his brief spell of good vision he hesitated a long time, and then shook his head.

At the end of ten weeks his third eye had a normal vision of only 10/400. He decided then that he was going to take a holiday on his farm at Canonville, in the hope that his childhood surroundings would relax his mind, and so effect a cure.

I understand he later returned to his home, but I did not see him again until I was called to identify his smashed body in the morgue.

# CHAPTER II.

THE FIRST day on the farm! It was distinctly cooler. A September breeze was blowing over the pasture, when Slade settled down with his eye charts. He glanced at the sun, already low in the west, for he had arrived late. And he sighed. The day was almost gone.

It had to be today. That feeling was strong in him. This afternoon he was still convinced that it would be easy to recall the relaxed days of his childhood on the farm. By tomorrow, if he failed today, the tension of doubt would have set in.

Then, too, there had been the anxious feeling way in the back of his mind about the cave dwellers. He was just a little reluctant to appear within a stone's throw of a primitive tribe. Here, on this prairie, it was different. It was very unlikely that any inhabitants of that obviously sparsely settled world would be anywhere in the vicinity.

*What the mind wants to see,* Slade thought, *it will see if it is there to see.* He was creating conditions where his mind would again want to see.

He palmed, and then looked at the chart with his center eye. He could see the big C at twenty feet; the R and B below it were a blur, and the T F P a blotch of gray. As an improvement it was practically worthless.

He palmed again. The eyeball, according to the eye training theorists, was a round organ, which elongated for near vision, and flattened for distance vision. Some of the practitioners were willing to concede the possibility that the ciliary muscles did, in addition, change to some extent the shape of the lens.

But whatever the explanation behind the reality that the system worked, if the muscles pulled disproportionately, vision was poor. The fact that those muscles were controlled by the imagination, a difficult part of the mind to train, made the problem all the more intricate for people who had long worn glasses or had eye trouble.

*The solution,* Slade thought, *is in me. I have got rid of all the astigmatism in my right or left eye, yet my center*

15

*eye persists in being astigmatic, sometimes to the point of blindness.*

It was of the mind, his trouble. His eye had proved that it was able to function normally.

About an hour before sundown, his brain was still refusing to work with the third eye.

*Perhaps,* Slade thought, *if I went to the various spots, of which I have particularly vivid childhood memories, I'd be able to recapture the mood and—*

First, the creek beside which he had hidden so often in the brush, and watched the cars go by to their remote and wonderful destinations.

The grass had grown deep where he had once worn it down with his small body. He knelt, and the scent was a tang in his nostrils. He pressed his face to the cool, green softness of it, and he lay quiet, conscious of his weariness and of the sustained effort he had made during the past months.

*Am I a fool?* he wondered. *Did I turn my wife against me, break off with my friends, all in order to follow a will-o'-the wisp?*

And had he really seen that other world, or was that some fantastic illusion which his mind had experienced during a profound organic readjustment?

His mood of depression intensified. The sun went down, and twilight was yielding to darkness when he finally started back along the bank of the creek towards the farmhouse.

In the darkness he couldn't find the path, and so he struck across the pasture, stumbling once in a while through thicker patches of grass. He could see the light of the end window of the farmhouse, but it seemed farther away than he remembered. The first alarm came with that realization, but it wasn't until five minutes later that a far more telling fear struck into him. The fence! He should have come to the fence long ago.

The light seemed to be only a few hundred feet from where he stopped short.

Slade sank slowly down onto the grass. He swallowed hard, and then he thought: *This is ridiculous. I'm imagining things.*

16

But there was an empty sensation in the pit of his stomach, as he strove to penetrate the intense darkness all around him. There was no moon, and clouds must have been heavy overhead, for not a single star showed. The light in the near distance glowed with a hazy but bright steadiness. It failed, however, to illuminate the building from which it came.

Slade blinked at it with a gathering fascination, his tenseness draining before the consciousness that it would probably be easy to get back to Earth. After all, he had *thought* himself here. He should be able to get back without too much trouble.

He climbed to his feet, and began to walk forward. As the light drew nearer, it seemed to him that it was coming from inside a doorway. Vaguely, he could make out that the doorway was inset under a curving sweep of metal, that bulged far out. The metal gleamed dully, and then merged with the general blackness without leaving a hint of the shape of the whole structure.

Slade hesitated about a hundred feet from the entrance. He was even more fascinated than he had been, but his desire to investigate was dwindling. Not now, in this dark night of a strange plane of existence. Wait till morning. And yet he had the uneasy conviction that before dawn the tensions would have reasserted in his mind.

*One knock at the door,* he thought, *one look inside. And then off into the darkness.* The door was metal, and so solid that his knuckles made only the vaguest sound. He had some silver coins in his pocket, and they tinged with a sharp sound as he used them. Instantly, he stepped back, and waited.

The silence grew tremendous, like a pall pushing at him. Dark and silent night in a primitive land inhabited by cavemen and—

And what? This was no caveman's residence. Was it possible he had come to a plane of Earth entirely separate from that of the nude girl he had seen?

He retreated into the shadows away from the light. He stumbled, barking his shins. On one knee, he felt the object over which he had nearly fallen. Metal. That brought a thrill of real interest. Cautiously, he pressed the button of his flashlight, but it wouldn't light. Slade

17

cursed under his breath, and tugged at the metal thing in the ground. That was the trouble. It was in the ground. And held hard.

It seemed to be a wheel attached to a boxing of some kind. He was still fumbling over it, tugging tentatively, when it began to rain. That sent him to the nearest brush for cover. But the rain grew heavier, until finally the bush poured water on him. Slade accepted his fate, and headed back for the doorway. He tried the latch, and pushed. The door opened immediately.

The interior was brightly lighted, a long, high wide corridor of dully shining metal. About a hundred feet away, the massive hallway ended in a cross corridor. There were three doorways on each side of the corridor.

He tried the doors one after another. The first one opened into a long, narrow room that was all shiny blue mirror. At least it looked like a mirror. Then he grew aware that stars were shining in its depth.

Slade closed the door hastily. It wasn't that he felt fear. But his mind had hesitated, unable to interpret what it was seeing. Its hold on this world was far too precarious for him to subject it to incomprehensible strangeness.

He moved across the hall to the first door on his left. It opened onto a long, narrow room half filled with case on case of goods. Some of them were open, their contents spilled out on the floor. Instruments glittered up at him, a quantity array of miscellaneous gadgets of all sizes. Some of the boxes were haphazardly pulled aside, as if a searcher had been looking for some specific item.

Slade closed that door too, puzzled but without any threatening strain this time. A storeroom was a recognizable thing, and his mind accepted it without there being any necessity for him to identify what was in the boxes.

The two middle doors revealed identical interiors. Massive machines that towered three quarters of the way to the ceiling. In spite of their size Slade recognized them for what they were. For more than a year American papers and magazines had shown pictures of the atomic engine developed at the University of Chicago for rocket ships. The design was slightly different, but the general tenor was unmistakable.

Slade closed each door in turn, hastily. And stood in

18

the hallway, dissatisfied with the situation. A spaceship settled on a lonely moor in an alien plane of existence brilliantly lighted inside, and a solitary light outside like a beacon in the night beckoning to wanderers like himself, offering surcease from the darkness—was that the reality?

Slade doubted it, and a grisly feeling came that he had willed himself into a nightmare, and that any instant he would wake up, perspiring, in his bed.

But the instants passed, and there was no waking. Gradually, his mind accepted the silence, the brief panic faded, and he tried the fifth door.

It opened into darkness. Slade stepped back hastily. His eyes grew accustomed to the shadows, and so after scant seconds he saw the shape. It was pressed against the darkest wall, and it watched him alertly from three eyes that gleamed brightly in the vaguely reflected light. One swift look Slade had, and then his mind refused the vision.

Instantly, the ship, the light, vanished. He fell about three feet to a grassy embankment. Half a mile away was a yellow glowing light. It turned out to be his own farmhouse.

He was back on Earth.

Slade remained on the farm, undecided. The vision of all three of his eyes had deteriorated this time, and besides he was a badly shaken man. It couldn't have been the same woman, he told himself. Standing there in the shadows of a corridor of an old, seemingly deserted spaceship, the same young woman—watching him.

And yet, the resemblance to the nude cave girl had been so apparent to his brain that he had instantly been under an abnormal strain. His mind proved that it recognized her by the speed with which it *rejected* the logic of her presence.

The question was, should he continue his exercises? For a whole month he walked the reaches of the farm, unable to make up his mind. And the main reason for his decision was his realization that his return to the two-eyed world had not been absolutely necessary.

Normal vision was a product of many balancing factors, not only mental but physical. Muscles weakened by glasses or by disuse lacked the endurance to resist the shudderingly swift impulses of the mind. Properly strengthened, they would withstand far greater shocks than he had experienced.

*A demonic woman,* he thought, *standing in the shadows of a shadow ship in a shadow land.* He was no longer sure he wanted to commit himself to that other plane of existence—to a woman who was aware of him, and who was trying to lure him.

After a month, the first snowfall whitened the foothills. Still undecided, Slade returned to the city.


## STATEMENT OF PROFESSOR GRAY

My name is Ernest Gray, and I am a professor of languages. Some time ago—I cannot remember the exact date—I received a visit from Michael Slade. It seems that he had been away on his farm, and that, on returning to his city home, he learned that, in his absence, a three-eyed woman had visited his home.

From the account Mr. Slade gave me, I understand that his manservant admitted the woman to the house— she seems to have been a very assured and dominating individual—and permitted her to remain five days as a guest. At the end of that time, the day before Mr. Slade's return, she departed leaving behind her nearly a score of phonograph records and a letter. Mr. Slade showed me the letter. Although it is to be shown to the jury as a separate exhibit, I am herewith including it in my statement to clarify my own account. The letter read as follows:

Dear Mr. Slade:

I want you to use the phonograph records to learn the language of Naze. The key record will dissolve in about two weeks after it is first played, but during that time it should have helped you to gain complete mastery of Nazia.

The situation on Naze is very simple, as you will discover, but it is also very dangerous. Here is what you must do. As soon as you have learned the language, drive to the plateau two miles west of the city of Smailes,

20

and park your car beside an abandoned granary several hundred yards from the road at midnight of any night.

In all your ventures on Naze, beware of Geean and the hunters of the city.

Leear.

By the time Mr. Slade brought the records to me, the key record had dissolved, but after listening to those that remained I am able to say without qualification that the language is a fraud, possibly an artificial creation of the three-eyed people for secret intercommunication.

I am assuming, now that a three-eyed woman has turned up, that there is more than one three-eyed freak in the world. My first reaction was that the name, Naze, might have some connection to the Nazi party, but the pronunciation of the word as given in the records, rhymes with faze and daze.

It is unfortunate that the key record was destroyed. Without such a key there can be no translation of a language which, in the ultimate issue, is nothing but a product of the imagination of three-eyed neurotics.

I am told that Mr. Slade's body was found near the city of Smailes, about a mile from the granary outhouse referred to in the letter of the woman Leear. But I know nothing about that, and did not myself see the body.


## CHAPTER III.

AT FIRST Slade sat in the car. But as midnight drew near, he climbed out and examined the granary with the probing beam of his flashlight. The bare, unpainted interior was as empty as it had been in the afternoon when he had driven out for an exploratory look.

The stubble field stretched off into darkness beyond the farthest ray of his flash. A quarter moon rode the eastern sky, and the stars shone with a pale radiance, but the resulting light failed to make his surroundings visible.

Slade glanced at his watch. And though he had known the hour was near, he felt a shock. 11:55. In five minutes, he thought shakily, *she* would come.

Not for the first time, he regretted his presence. Was he a fool, he wondered, to come here— risk himself on an abandoned farm, where his loudest shouts for help would merely echo mockingly from the near hills? He had a gun of course, but he knew that he would hesitate to use it.

He shook himself. She had been cunning, had the woman Leear, not naming a date for him to come. *Any* midnight, she had said. She must have known that that would work and work on the mind of the only three-eyed man of Earth. If she had named a time as well as a place, he could have made up his mind against it.

The indefiniteness nullified his resistance. Each day that passed brought the same problem: Would he go tonight? Or wouldn't he? Each day, the pro and con, with all its emotional overtone, racked his mind and body. And in the end he decided that she wouldn't have taught him the language of Naze in order to harm him in the night that he came to keep their rendezvous.

She was interested in him. What she wanted was something else again, but being what he was, a three-eyed man, he could not but be interested in her. If talking to her tonight would bring him information, then the risk was more than justified.

Here he was, for better or worse.

Slade put away his flash, and glanced at the illuminated dials of his watch. Once again, but even more tinglingly, the shock ran down his spine. It was exactly midnight.

The silence was intense. Not a sound penetrated the night. He had turned off the headlights of his car. Now, abruptly, it seemed to him that he had made a mistake. The lights should be on.

He started toward the car, and then stopped. What was the matter with him? This was no time to desert the shelter of the granary. He backed slowly until his body touched the wall. He stood there fingering his gun. He waited.

The sound that came to him there was almost not a sound at all. The air, which had been quiet, was suddenly gently agitated. But the breeze was not normal. It came from above.

*From above!* With a jerk, Slade looked up. But he saw nothing. Not a movement was visible against the dark dark-blue of the sky. He felt a thrill akin to fire, a sense

22

of the unknown stronger than anything he had ever experienced, and then—

"The important thing, Michael Slade," said the resonant, familiar voice of Leear from the air almost directly above him, "is for you to stay alive during the next twenty-four hours while you are in the city of Naze. Be cautious, sensible, and make no unnecessary admissions about what you do or do not know. Good luck."

There was a dazzling flash of light from about a dozen feet above. Slade blinked, and snatched his gun. Then he stood tensed, and looked around wildly.

The granary was gone, and his car, and the stubble field. He was on a city street. Buildings loomed darkly all around him, spirelike shapes that reared up towards a haze of violet light which half-hid the night sky beyond. The light spread like a great curving dome from an enormously high spire in the distance.

Slade saw those details in one flashing glance. Even as he looked, understanding came of what had happened. He had been transported to the city of Naze.

At first the street seemed deserted, the silence utter. But then, swiftly, his senses began to adjust. He heard a vague sound, as if somebody had whispered to somebody else. Far along the street, a shadowed figure raced across the road, and vanished into the darkness beside a spire.

It struck Slade with a pang that his position here in the center of the street put him at a disadvantage. He began to edge carefully towards the sidewalk to the right. The roadbed was uneven, and twice he stumbled and almost fell. The greater darkness under a tree enveloped him, and he had barely reached it when there was a human screech about fifty yards away.

The sound was jarring. With a spasmodic movement, Slade flung himself onto the ground, simultaneously raising his gun. He lay very still. He waited.

It took a moment for his brain to gather together. And several seconds passed before he could locate the direction of what was now a noisy struggle. Cries and groans and muffled shouts came from the darkness. They ended abruptly, and there followed a curious silence. It was as if the assailants had been worn out by their struggle and were now resting. Or—what was more likely—they were silently and greedily engaged in searching their victim.

Slade's brain had time to catch up with his reflexes. His first thought had in it a blank, amazed quality. What had he run into? He lay quiet, clutching his automatic tightly, and after a moment the second thought came: So this was the city of Naze.

Briefly, then, he felt overwhelmed. He thought, *How did she do it? How did she transfer me here?* There had been, he remembered, a flash of light. And instantly he was in Naze.

She must have used the same mechanical means as she had employed to transfer to the Earth plane. An instrument the light of which somehow affected the visual center behind each eye. There seemed no other logical explanation, and that logic, with the spaceship as an additional example, pointed to a highly develope science, that included a thorough understanding of th human nervous system.

The question was, would the effect of the light be permanent? Or would it wear off?

His thought was interrupted by a cry of rage. "Give us our share of the blood, you dirty—"

The words were shouted in the language of Naze, and Slade understood them all except the last one. It was that instantaneous, easy comprehension that thrilled him for a moment. Then the meaning penetrated also. Blood. Share of the blood.

Lying there, it seemed to Slade that he must have misunderstood. His doubt ended as another, even more furious cry came, this time from a second voice:

"The thief has a double-sized container. He got twice as much blood as the rest of us."

A third voice, obviously that of the accused, shouted, "It's a lie." The man must have recognized that his denial would not be accepted. Footsteps came racing along the street. A tall man, breathing hard, flung himself past Slade. Rushing after him, and strung out behind him, came four other men, all smaller than the first.

They charged past where Slade was lying, vague, manlike shapes that quickly vanished into the night.

24

For nearly a minute he could hear the noise their feet made, and once there was a loud curse.

The sound faded as had the sight. There was silence. Slade did not move. He was realizing the full import of what he had seen and heard. A dead man, drained of blood, must be lying on the street a few hundred feet away. Realizing—Naze at night was a city of vampires.

A minute, two minutes, dragged by. The thought came to Slade, *But what am I supposed to do? What am I here for?*

He recalled what the woman Leear had told him just before she flashed the light at him. "The important thing, Michael Slade, is for you to remain alive during the next twenty-four hours while you are in the city of Naze."

Twenty-four hours! Slade felt a chill. Was he expected to remain in Naze for an entire day and night with no other instructions but that he remain alive? No purpose, no place to go, nothing but—this!

If only there were street lights. But he could see none in any direction. Not that it was pitch dark. An alien shiningness glowed at him, different from the night-lit cities of Earth. The sky glowed palely where the violet haze trailed down from the central tower, and lights flickered from the slitted windows of a dozen spires that he could see.

It was definitely not pitch dark, and in a way that might be to his advantage. It seemed clear that he couldn't just continue to lie where he was. And darkness would provide protection for an uneasy explorer.

He climbed to his feet, and he was about to step from under the tree when a woman called softly to him from across the street:

"Mr. Slade."

Slade froze. Then he half turned. And then he recognized that he had been addressed by name. His relief left him weak.

"Here!" he whispered loudly. "Here!"

The woman came across the street. "I'm sorry I'm late," she whispered breathlessly, "but there are so many blood seekers abroad. Follow me." Her three eyes gleamed

25

at him. Then she turned, and headed rapidly up the street. And it was not until Slade was swinging along behind her that the startling realization came to him that this woman was not Leear.

Swiftly, he and his guide headed deeper into the city.

They climbed one of the darkest stairways Slade had ever seen, then paused before a door. The girl knocked, a measured knock. Three times slow, two fast, and then after a short interval, one.

The pause was long. While they waited, the girl said:

"Mr. Slade, we all want to thank you for coming—for the risks you are taking. We will do our best to familiarize you with Naze. Let us hope that this time the ship will be able to destroy the city."

"Uh!" said Slade.

The exclamation could have been a giveaway, but at the last instant he had an awareness of the danger of his surprise. He choked the sound down to a contorted whisper.

There was the click of a lock. The door creaked open. Light poured out into the hallway. It revealed a heavily built woman slowly making her way to a chair.

Inside, Slade examined his surroundings. The room was both long and wide. For its size, it was scantily furnished. There were three settees and two lounges, end tables, tables, chairs and rugs. The drapes could once have belonged to his divorced wife, Miriam.

Once? A very long time ago, Slade decided after a second glance. They looked as if they had originally cost a great deal. They were so shabby now that they actually seemed out of place.

Slade let the room recede into the background of his tired mind. He walked over, and sat down in a chair, facing the older woman; but it was the younger woman he looked at.

She had paused a few feet away, and was now standing smiling at him. She was a lean, olive-complexioned girl with a proud smile.

Slade said: "Thank you for the risks *you* took."

The girl shook her head with an easy smile. "You'll

26

be wanting to go to bed. But first I want you to meet Caldra, the Planner. Caldra, this is Slade of the ship."

There it was, definite, stated. *Of* the ship. He, Michael Slade! Leear was certainly taking a great deal for granted.

The older woman was looking at him with strange, slow eyes. The impression of slowness was so distinct that Slade looked at her sharply for the first time. Her eyes were the color of lead, her face colorless, pasty, unnatural. Lusterless, almost lifeless, she stared at him. And said in a dead slow voice:

"Mr. Slade, it is a pleasure."

It was not a pleasure to Slade. He had to strain to keep the repelled look off his face. Once, perhaps twice, before in his life, people had affected him like this, but neither of the other two had matched this creature for the unpleasant sensation they made him feel.

Slow thyroid, he analyzed. The identification made her presence more palatable to his soul. It freed his mind. Memory came of what the girl had called the other. His brain paused. Caldra, the Planner.

He relaxed slowly, and made a conscious concession. She might be very good at that. Slow brains could be extremely thorough.

His interest began to sink. The strain of his experiences weighed suddenly on him. In his teens and early twenties, he had been a night hound, a haunter of cocktail bars and clubs. At thirty he had started to go to bed at ten o'clock, much to Miriam's disgust. Midnight usually found him yawning and sleepy. And here it was—he glanced at his watch—five minutes to one. He glanced at the girl. He said:

"I can use that bed."

As the girl led him towards a corridor door, the older woman mumbled:

"Things are shaping up. Soon, the hour of decision will be upon us." Just as Slade went out the door, she said something else with the faintest suggestion of a laugh. It sounded like, "Don't get too near him, Amor. I felt it, too."

The words seemed meaningless. But he was surprised, the girl opened the bedroom door, to notice that the color in her cheeks was high. But all she said was:

"You're reasonably safe here. There is a very large group of us who believe in the destruction of Naze, and this is our part of the city."

In spite of his weariness, a gathering excitement kept Slade awake. He had been too tense to realize his situation. The thoughts that had come were simply the first unfoldings of his mind. But now, in bed, slowly relaxing, the tremendousness of what was happening penetrated.

He was in Naze. Outside the walls of this building was a fantastic city of another plane of existence. And tomorrow he would see that city in all its strangeness. Tomorrow!

He slept.

## CHAPTER IV

NAZE seen under a brilliant morning sun was a jarring spectacle. Slade walked beside Amor along a wide street. Shabby city, he thought, distressed. And old, oh, old!

He had realized the night before that Naze was ancient and decadent. But he hadn't grasped the extent of the disaster that had befallen the city. The buildings that he saw looked older than all his imaginings. Five hundred, perhaps even a thousand years had dragged by since those buildings were built.

For hundreds of thousands of days and nights, the city had rotated under its sun. Its streets and sidewalks had borne the load of daily living. The strangest building materials could not but be worn out after such a lapse of time. And they were.

The sidewalks were almost uniformly rubble, with only here and there a patch of smooth hardness to show what the original had been like. The streets were a little better, but they, too, were largely dust packed down by the pressures that had been put on them.

Not a single vehicle was visible anywhere, only people, people and more people. Evidently, all wheel machines had long ago been worn out.

What had happened? What *could* have happened? There was, of course, the war between the city and the ship—but why? He half-turned to the girl to ask the question, then abruptly remembered that it would be unwise to show ignorance. Leear had warned him to make no admissions.

The city that surrounded him, so obvious a relic of an ancient culture, drained the fever of that fire out of him. Never anywhere had he seen so many people on the streets of a metropolis. With this difference. These people weren't going anywhere. Men and women sat on the curbs, on the sidewalks and on the roads. They seemed unmindful of individuals who brushed past them. They sat, staring vaguely into nothingness. The mindlessness of it was awful to see.

A beggar fell into step beside Slade. He held up a metal cup:

"A few drops of your blood, mister," he whined. "I'll slit your throat if you don't give it to me."

Amor's whip lashed out, and struck the ghoulish thing in the face. The blow raised a welt on the man's face. Blood trickled from the welt.

"Drink your own blood!" the girl snapped.

Her color was high, Slade noticed, her face twisted with almost unnatural hatred.

"Those beasts," she said in a low, intense voice, "lurk in alleyways at night in gangs, and attack anybody who comes along. But, of course," she broke off, "you know all about that."

Slade made no comment. It was true that he knew of the night gangs, but what he didn't know would fill a book.

The continuing reality tore his mind from that very personal problem. The streets swarmed with people *who had nothing to do*. And again, and again and again, fingers plucked at Slade's sleeve, and avid voices whimpered:

"Your blood is strong, mister. You can spare a little, or else—"

Often and often, it was a woman's face that leered up at him.

Slade was silent. He was so appalled he could have spoken only with difficulty. He looked down side street after street, boiling with lecherous beings; and he saw

29

for the first time in his life what utter depravity was possible to the human animal.

This city must not continue to exist. It was clear now why Leear had lured him into the city. She wanted him to see, and she must believe the actuality would end any doubts in his mind. Doubts, for instance, about the reasons for the immeasurably horrible conditions—unquestionably due to the war betwen the ship and the city. Understanding the origin of a plague was a side issue.

The plague itself must be wiped out.

He had no doubts; so great was his horror. He felt sick with an absolute dismay. This, he thought, going on day after day, year after year, through centuries. It mustn't. The girl was speaking:

"For a while we thought if we could get the chemicalized cups away from them, we could end the blood craze. But—"

She stopped; she shrugged, finished: "Of course you know all about that. Except in rare cases, depravity only sinks to new depths; it does not rise."

There was nothing to say to that. It was easy to see that his NOT knowing "all about that" was going to be a handicap to his understanding of the details of hell. He didn't really need the details though; the overall hell was enough.

End it! Destroy it! Help the ship if he could, help these fifth columnists. But destroy Naze.

He grew calmer. He analyzed her words. Chemicalized cups! Then it wasn't the blood itself, but some chemical in the metal of the cup, that made it so intoxicatingly attractive.

Removal of the cup apparently had channeled the craving into something worse. What? Well, he was supposed to know.

Slade smiled wearily. "Let's go back," he said. "I've had enough for today."

The early part of the lunch was eaten in silence. Slade ate, thinking about the city, the ship and the cavemen, and of his own part in the affair. In a way he now knew the essentials of the situation. He had seen the ship, and he was seeing the city.

The question was, just what was he supposed to do?

30

He realized abruptly that Caldra, the slow, was about to speak.

The woman was laying down her fork. That movement alone required many seconds. Then she lifted her head It seemed to Slade that it took her eyes an unnaturally long time to focus upon him.

The next step was even more prolonged. She opened her mouth, sat considering her first sentence, and finally began to articulate the syllables. Over a period that seemed longer than it was, she said:

"Tonight, we raid Geean's central palace. Our forces can guarantee to get you to the fortieth level as agreed. The apparatus Leear asked for is already there, ready to ease you out of the window, so that you can focus your dissembler onto the controls of the barrier. You no doubt saw for yourself when you were out this morning that they are located at about the ninetieth level.

"We assume, of course, that the ship will rush in the moment the barrier is down."

Long before her measured words reached their end, Slade had grasped their import. He sat motionless, eyes half closed, startled. Tonight. But that was ridiculous. He couldn't be expected to rush into an attack as blindly as that.

His opinion of Leear went down a million miles. What was a dissembler anyway? Surely, he wasn't expected to learn how to operate an intricate mechanism during the heat of a battle. His consternation reached a peak as Caldra fell silent, and looked at him expectantly. Amor, too, he saw, was watching him with eager anticipation.

Slade parted his lips, and then closed them again, as another, greater realization struck him. The realization that he had been given an immense amount of information. It was all by implication, but the import was unmistakable.

The haze of light he had seen the night before, radiating from the skyscraper central tower—and which he recalled suddenly had been vaguely visible during his morning walk as a faint mist—that was the barrier. What kind of a barrier? Apparently, a barrier strong enough to keep the spaceship at bay. A barrier of energies potent beyond anything on Earth.

But that meant the city was under siege, and—judging from the decay—had been for hundreds of years.

Slade's mind poised. "This," he told himself, "is ridiculous. How would they live? Where would they get their food? They can't possibly be living on each other's blood."

He stared down at his plate, but there was very little left. The remnant looked like a vegetable, though it was covered by a sauce or gravy that hid the details. He looked up, a question about the food quivering in his throat—and realized that this was no time for such things. If he was going to prevent a major disaster, he had better say something, and fast. Before he could speak, Amor said:

"One bold surprise attack and"—she smiled with a savage excitement—"finish!"

For a moment, the play of emotions across her face held Slade's attention. She was quite a deadly creature herself, this tall girl who carried a whip for the vampires of Naze. It was the old story of environment of course. The mind shaped by its physical climate, and in turn shaping the body and the expression of the face, and setting fast the capabilities of the senses.

For the first time it struck him that, if he committed himself to this plane of Earth, here was a sample of the kind of girl he would eventually marry. He looked at her with interest, prepared to pursue the thought further. And then, once more he realized that his mind was striving to escape from its only immediate problem, the attack. Tonight! He said:

"I'm sorry to have to tell you that the ship will not be here tonight."

Amor was on her feet, her eyes widening. "But all our plans!" she gasped.

She seemed overcome. She sat down. Beside her, Caldra emerged from her stupor, and showed that Slade's words had finally penetrated.

"No ship!"

Slade said, "The ship was to signal me this morning." He felt as if he were sweating, but it was a mental sensation, not a physical one. He went on, "There was no signal."

It was not bad, he realized, for ad lib. He relaxed, in spite of not having solved his basic problem. He watched Armor head for the door. She paused on the threshold. "I'll have to call off the attack."

The door banged behind her, leaving, after a moment, silence.

Armor having failed to turn up, Caldra and Slade ate dinner shortly before dark.

It was late when Amor came in. She slumped into her chair, and began to pick absently at the food that Caldra set before her. Several times Slade caught her looking at him from under her lashes with speculation. And with something else. He couldn't quite decide what.

Slade decided not to let that disturb him. He walked over to the great window of the living room. He was aware of Amor joining him after a while, but she said nothing; and so he, too, held his peace. He looked out at Naze.

Shadowed Naze, night enveloped. Seen from the spire window, the city drifted quietly into darkness. It seemed almost to glide into the shadows that crept in from the east.

Slade gazed and gazed. At last except for the flickering lights and the almost invisible barrier, the darkness was complete.

Realizations came: His was surely the strangest adventure in the history of the human nervous system. Born in the foothills of western United States, brought up on a farm, quickly successful as a broker in a small western city. And now here! Here in this dark, doomed city of a planet the civilization of which was in desperate straits.

And yet it was not an alien planet; simply another plane revealed to his brain and body because he had three eyes instead of two.

The thrill of excitement that came was connected with his companion. She stood beside him, a woman of that world, young and strong, perhaps still unspoken for by any man.

It was possible. He was sure of that. The marriage

state was almost meaningless under present conditions.

It was some time since he had given serious thought to the subject of women. Now, he was fairly easy prey. During the afternoon he had thought of Amor in a very possessive fashion, and his previous realization—that IF he stayed, he would have to marry a girl of this world—had sharpened.

It was possible that there would be other women on this plane of existence more attractive than she was, but they were far away.

Slade said: "Amor."

No answer.

"Amor, what are you planning to do afterwards?"

The girl stirred. "I shall live in a cave, of course. That is what we must all do."

Slade hesitated, torn from his line of approach by the implications of her words—*Must* all do! Why? It had not struck him before that Amor and her group accepted the idea of a primitive existence.

He remembered that in a kind of a way, he was trying to make a girl.

"Amor."

"Slade."

She seemed not to have heard him, for her tone was not an answer, and showed no awareness that he had spoken.

Slade said, "What is it?"

"This will sound terrible to you, but I was once a blood drinker."

It seemed a futile confession. It brought no picture at first; the words themselves made him uneasy, however.

"And so was Caldra. And everybody. I don't think I'm exaggerating. There's never been anything like it."

A picture began to come. And thoughts. Slade licked his suddenly dry lips, repelled.

And still he had no idea what she was getting at.

"It was easier for me to break off," the girl said, "and to say off—until today . . . last night. Slade," her voice was tiny, "you have strong blood. I felt it all day."

Abruptly, he knew where she was heading. He thought of the men and women she had lashed with her whip hat morning. In a twisted fashion, those blows had been aimed at her own craving.

"You can't imagine," Amor was saying, "what a shock it was to Caldra and me when you said the attack was not tonight. It meant you would be around at least another day. Slade, that was terribly unfair. Leear knew our situation only too well."

The repulsion was greater. It seemed to Slade that in another moment he would be sick. He said in a low voice:

"You want some of my blood."

"Just a little." Her tone had the faintest whine in it. Enough to make vivid a picture of her begging on the streets. Slade felt mentally nauseated.

The thought came that he had no business making any remarks. But he was emotionally past that stage of common sense. This was the girl he had tentatively intended to offer marriage. He said harshly: "And you were the one who used a whip on the others this morning."

In the darkness of the room, he heard the sharp intake of her breath. There was a long silence. Then she turned, and her body was a slim, shadowed shape that disappeared into a corridor towards her bedroom.

And so the night that was to be long began.


## CHAPTER V

AFTER SEVERAL hours, Slade still couldn't sleep. He had been unfair to somebody he liked; and it was disturbing.

She had rescued him from almost death, restored his health; and, surely, surely, he could spare her a little of his blood. Out of all the people in this fantastic city, he and her group had fought hardest against the craving that had destroyed the soul of Naze.

It must have been a fight to make the very gods take pity. But he had had none. He, supermoralist Michael Slade, the perfect man, had cast stones and created pain.

Actually, the true explanation was worse than that,

rooted as it was in his own physical desires. And, besides, it was possible that his blood did *feel* stronger to people who were aware of such things.

In the morning, he would give Amor AND Caldra a half cup of blood. And then, somehow, he must get out of this city, back to Earth if possible, but out in some way. It was already after midnight, and clear, therefore that the end of the twenty-four hour period, which Leear had mentioned, would not automatically return him to the vicinity of his car, near the city of Smailes.

Why, if it meant nothing, had she mentioned a time limit? He dozed, still thinking about that. And wakened to the realization that someone was in the room.

He lay rigid, striving to penetrate the darkness. The fear that pressed on him was the ancient fear of a man in a hostile land being stalked in the blackness. His straining eyes caught a movement against the silhouetting wall, a shadowy figure.

*A woman.* Amor. The identification brought a measure of pity.

Poor girl! What deadly hunger that desire for blood was. In a blurred fashion, he had had in the back of his mind an intention of using a cup to taste his own blood. But her coming under such desperate circumstances ended that intention for the time being. He was only a normal human being. He couldn't afford to be caught in the toils of so potent a drug.

He made an effort to sit up. And couldn't. He was held down by straps.

He lay back, the first annoyance sharpening his temper. It was all very well to feel sorry for her, but this was a pretty raw stunt she was pulling.

He parted his lips to say something scathing. He didn't say it. Memory came that this girl was in a bad way. Let her have her blood.

He wouldn't say a word. In the morning he would pretend that nothing had happened. The determination gave him a temporary satisfaction.

In the darkness, the vague movement continued. The girl seemed to be in no hurry. Just as Slade's impatience reached the vanishing point, a thin needle of light pointed down at his left arm. Almost simultaneously a hand came

36

nto view. It held a syringe, which it inserted deftly into
he largest visible vein. Slade watched, interested, as
he blood drew up darkly into the transparent body of
he instrument.

The seconds slid by, and still the avid needle strained
it him. Slade thought of the eeriness of what was hap-
)ening, an Earthman in a strange world being bled by
i likable vampire girl in the secret dead of the night.

The picture faded with the passing seconds, too many
seconds. Slade said gently:

"Don't you think that's enough?"

For several moments after his words broke the silence,
he syringe held steady; and there was no sound. At
ast, the hand and the syringe jerked slightly in surprise.

It was the time gap between his speech and her re-
iction that brought to Slade his first understanding of
he truth. His gaze fixed for the first time on the hand
•olding the instrument. It was hard to see in the re-
ilections from that narrow band of light. But seeable
t was. And recognizable.

It was a woman's hand. Slade sighed as he stared at
t. Here was one more proof that the mind created its
»wn illusions. He, who had had so much experience with
hat reality, whose very presence in the universe of the
hree-eyed was a living evidence of the importance of
iind over matter, still continued to be fooled.

. His mind had jumped to the conclusion that it was
\mor who had come to his room. When the hand had
rst come into the light minutes ago, he had noticed
othing unusual. Now he did.

It was a woman's hand all right, but rather worn. And
ot young looking at all. How he could have mistaken
: even in the reflected light, was a puzzle.

This was Caldra the mysterious, Caldra the Planner,
'aldra who, apparently, was now breaking her blood
ist. The realization came to Slade that he was partici-
ating in a personal tragedy. A woman whose craving
>r blood had once nearly destroyed her was drinking
lood again.

He was aware of the syringe being withdrawn from
is arm. The light winked out. A pause. The sound of

37

thick liquid squirting heavily into a container came next, and then once more silence.

Slade pictured the hand slowly raising the cup towards the fumbling lips. His timing was perfect. As his mental picture of her hand reached her lips, there came an audible gulping.

The sound made Slade a little sick. But pity came too. The emotion died, as fingers touched the bed. He thought with a scowl: More?

But it was the straps that let go their constricting hold on his chest and arms. Footsteps shuffled towards the door, which closed softly.

Silence settled. After a little, Slade slept. When he wakened, a great paw was pressing down on his mouth and a beast as big as a bear, but with oddly catlike features, was looming over him. Its strong, big, hairy body was illumined by a light held by men in uniform.

Other uniformed men were holding Slade's arms and legs. And he had a dismaying glimpse of still more men in the corridor outside the bedroom.

The animal's great paw withdrew from his face. He was lifted, and carried. There was a light in the living room. He saw Caldra lying face down on the floor, a knife driven to the hilt into her back.

Slade had a horrible, empty sensation. Amor! What about Amor?

It was that thought that must have done it. Under him, the floor dissolved as if it were made of nothingness. He fell about fifteen feet, and struck hard. He lay dizzily for more than a minute before understanding came.

He raised himself slowly, scratching his hands on the frozen stubble of a wheat field. About two miles to the west the lights of the city of Smailes blazoned the night sky. Slade climbed to his feet, and headed for the granary where he had left his car. It was still there silent and lightless.

He waited a few minutes, but there was no sign of Leear. Tired though he was, he drove all the rest of that night, and part of the next morning. It was 11:00 a.m. when he turned up his private drive.

A letter was in the mailbox, in the familiar, masculine

handwriting of Leear. Slade frowned at it, then tore it open. It read:

Dear Michael Slade:
Now you know. You have seen Naze. You must have wondered why nothing happened at the exact end of the twenty-four hours. Nothing could happen until after that time, and then only if you received a sufficiently strong shock.

This shock, of course, was provided when one of the women came in and attempted to obtain some of your blood. It was regrettable that such a situation had to be forced, but there was no alternative.

It was unfortunate, too, that I had to let the group in Naze think that there would be an attack. They have no conception of the kind of man they are fighting. Against the immortal Geean, any plan of theirs would fail automatically. Their inability to understand the nature and strength of the enemy is proved by the fact that they accepted without question that the barrier could be destroyed by an attack with a so-called dissembler on a protuberance at the ninetieth floor of the central tower of Geean.

There is no such instrument as a dissembler, and the protuberance on the tower is a radiator. Geean will never be defeated except by an attack into the heart of his stronghold. Such an attack cannot be made without your help, and this time you must come by yourself, as the device which I used beside the granary has only temporary effects.

Do not wait too long.

Leear.

In the daytime, he read and remained within the limits of his yard. At night, hat pulled low over his third eye, head hunched down into the collar of his overcoat, he walked the frozen streets. Slowly, the fever went out of him, and he became grimly sardonic in his attitude to what had happened.

"I am not," he decided, "the stuff of which heroes are made. And I have no desire to get killed in the war between Naze and the ship."

He had better adjust himself to the idea of remaining on this earth.

The half decision made it possible for him to consider Leear's letter from a less emotional viewpoint than when he had first read it. The rereading after three weeks was even more interesting than he had expected, now that his lips did not tighten with anger at the ruthless way Leear had precipitated him into Naze, and so, callously, caused the death of Amor and Caldra.

The letter was basically far less irritating than he had thought. And it certainly lacked the commanding tone that he somehow expected from her. In addition, her frank admission that his help was necessary mollified Slade tremendously.

He was vaguely pleased, too, that she had underestimated him. Her analysis of the kind of shock that would send him back to Earth had been wrong. Caldra coming for blood had scarcely ruffled his nerves. And it had taken the sight of her dead body and a mental picture of Amor similarly murdered to affect him.

After three weeks, he felt himself immune to shock. Caldra and Amor begin to seem just a little unreal, like figments of a dream. Slade knew that he had come a long way out of a dangerous mental state when he could think of Amor and feel satiric about his impulse to ask her to marry him.

He did not feel contemptuous of the emotions involved. They were human basics, and it struck him that it might be a sound idea to marry again right here on Earth. If he could persuade Miriam to come and live with him again, that would be a decisive act not easily overthrown by any sudden impulse to rush off to that other plane of existence.

He must resume old relationships, return to a normal Earth existence.

It was easier decided than done. One night, while he was still planning the proper approach to make to Miriam, he met two friends of his business days. They nodded and hurried past, and stopped only when he turned and called after them. The conversation that followed was one of those lame, horrible affairs but Slade was persistent. It seemed to him in his dogged

40

frame of mind that if he was going to live on Earth, he had to have friends and a wife. Those were the concomitants of a sane existence, and he knew better than even to attempt to do without them.

Slade did not enjoy the conversation any more than the two men. They were by turns uneasy, jocular, unhappily silent, eager to impart information, and finally, they hurried off with a "Glad to have met you, Mike, but we're late now for an engagement. Be seeing you."

Slade walked home his lips curling ironically, but there was a vague chill in his backbone. He had learned, among other things, that Miriam had had a "new" boy friend for several months, and there was something strangely final about that fact. As if his last escape route was closing inexorably.

He did not give up so easily. He phoned Miriam the next day, and the day after that, and each day for the week following. Each time her maid said, "Who is calling?" Then, "Miss Crenshaw does not care to speak to you."

Slade wrote her a letter, in which he said, "After all I can have the eye covered with grafted skin." He followed up the letter with a personal visit. But Miriam was "out."

It was fairly ultimate. Particularly when a detective called the next day, and asked him to cease his "persecution" of his former wife. The officer was considerably impressed by the beautiful residence, but he was a man who knew his duty. "We have received a complaint, y'understand. We'll have to take action if it continues, y'understand?"

Slade understood. His little dream was over.

## STATEMENT MADE TO
## CORONER'S JURY BY
## WILFRED STANTON

I was first employed by Michael Slade as a houseman about five years ago. I was with him, with only a brief holiday, throughout the past year.

My employer was away from home several times during that period. He always seemed in an upset condition after each such absence, but he did not take me into his confidence. Before his final departure, I noticed a new air of decisiveness about him, as if he had finally made up his mind about something after a long uncertainty. He bought a second automatic, a match to the one he already had, and a great deal of ammunition for both weapons. He also purchased other items, but I did not see what was in the packages that arrived for him. He read almost continuously. I remember one book dealt with metallurgy, another was a volume on physics, and a third about the new rocket ships.

All this time, too, he was sitting out in the yard with his eye charts. These exercises were unusual in that he wore a light durable hunting suit made of waterproof materials, which he had had made. In addition he carried two automatics, a hunting knife and a pouch of ammunition. His pocket's also seemed to be stuffed, but I don't know what was in them.

Mr. Slade was aware of my awareness of the unusualness of this get-up, and he seemed amused at my anxiety. One day, he told me not to be alarmed if he went away without warning.

It was the day after that that I called him for lunch, and he was gone. His disappearance was unusual in that the chair and the charts were just as he had left them, and particularly unusual in that there was snow on the ground, and his tracks should have been visible leading out of the yard. I saw no tracks that would indicate a departure.

I can only say that I was not surprised when Mr. Slade's dead body was discovered last week two hundred miles from here. He was obviously expecting something to happen. And it did.

## CHAPTER VI

THE CHANGE this time was like the click of a camera shutter. He felt his eye working, then his house vanished, and then—

It was raining, a warm but heavy rain. The water came down on the marsh near the caves in a multitude of slanting drops, like millions of tiny knives cutting the surface. Under that blurring curtain of water, the land-scape looked wilder, less civilized. Its very green lusciousness made it primitive, but the green was there, ornamental and gorgeous.

Slade, who had started to mull over the problem of rain in one plane of existence and snow in another, under the same sun, felt a warm, wet trickle of water run down inside the collar of his waterproof suit. It didn't bother him, but it took his mind off of the why of the rain. He stepped automatically under the overhanging branch of a nearby tree, and from its uncertain shelter—the water poured from it—peered up at the ledge.

Some of the excitement died out of him. The hill looked lifeless. All the fires were out, and not a human being was in sight. It was the rain, of course. They'd be inside the caves.

Since he had no intention of climbing to the ledge until he had been discovered—spears and knives might flash just a little too swiftly if he surprised them in their caves—his problem was to find shelter. He constructed himself a crude house of dead branches overlaid with large, fronded leaves. Then he scraped away a heavy layer of dead wet leaves, and was pleasantly surprised to find that the ground underneath was comparatively dry.

He slept fitfully throughout the afternoon and evening. During the night he was awake for a long time. Just before he finally slept, he thought sharply, "I'll have to wake up before they do."

When he opened his eyes, the sun was shining from a blue sky. And several three-eyed men were kneeling around the open end of his shelter. Beyond them were other men, and in the farther background, women and children.

Very slowly, Slade sat up. He pushed the shelter over on its side, and climbed to his feet, but that too, was an automatic movement. The convulsive thought came that the strain inside his head and in his muscles would produce organic tensions strong enough to precipitate him back to the United States.

But nothing happened. The people and the marsh and

43

the cave hill remained in his vision as steady as sanity itself. He was welded to this plane of existence as if he had been born here.

It was not until that thought had come and gone that he noticed none of the men carried arms of any description. The relief that came was almost as tremendous as had been the first shock. Before he could speak, one of the men nearest him said gently:

"Careful. You're not completely stable yet."

The man reached forward and placed his palm over Slade's center eye. The movement was too unexpected for it to be resisted. The delayed reaction, when it finally came, was half-hearted. Slade started to take a step backwards, and then, realizing the meaning of what was happening, he stopped in amazement.

These people knew that he was not of this plane. *And they knew why*. The next thought followed hard on the first:

The cave dwellers were NOT primitives.

It was too big an idea to grasp all in one instant, particularly as the man who had touched his forehead now stepped back with a smile, and said:

"I think you will be all right."

Slade hadn't noticed the fellow's voice before. Now, he did. It was calm and melodic, without harshness, the words so easily spoken that they were like a flow of music produced by a master.

That fact, also, held his mind only a moment. He stood looking around him at the men and at the women, and his relief grew second by second. They were smiling, friendly; they were good-looking and alert, a high physical and mental type. Slade allowed himself a flashing memory of the degenerate blood addicts of the city of Naze, and comprehended with finality that, whatever was the basic reason for the deadly siege of the city by the ship of Leear, these clean and decent-looking cave dwellers were evidence in favor of the ship.

He realized that it was time he said something. He said, "Thank you. I am a friend. My name is Michael Slade."

The tall, eagle-eyed man who had already spoken nodded. "My name," he said, "is Danbar."

44

They shook hands. It was so simply, so generously done that Slade was not sure then or ever afterwards as to whether shaking hands was a common custom among these people. Or whether Danbar had instantaneously and without hesitation responded to the habits of a stranger.

As their hands separated, Slade noted for the first time that the man was inches taller than himself, and marvelously strong-looking. He had a lean, handsome face. Except for his extra eye, he would have been good-looking in any group of two-eyed human beings. He seemed about thirty years old.

He smiled. He took Slade's arm, and led him to another man, a splendid-looking chap who had been watching the proceedings from the background.

Danbar indicated the other, "Malenkens," he said.

The way he said it made it sound a distinctive and important name. And, looking at the man, Slade did not doubt but that he was being introduced to one of the leaders of the tribe. With Malenkens, too, the handshake was warm, but his smile was sterner, more aloof.

Danbar said, "You can meet the others later. Now, let us return to the ledge for breakfast."

Contact was established as easy as that.

The winding path that led up to the caves was made of cement steps flanked by ornamental shrubs. A cement sidewalk ran along the entire length of the ledge, with smaller sidewalks leading into the caves. In between the sidewalks, green, velvety grass grew in neat plots that could only have been planned by skillful gardeners.

Slade, pausing before the first cave, peered into an interior at least as uncavelike as what he had already seen. The floor was of cement, but it was covered with throw rugs. The walls and ceiling were plastered over a base of cement. The chairs, tables and bunks that he could see were of unpainted wood, but they were well-designed and had been sandpapered to a smooth polish. The overall result was astonishingly modern.

Danbar touched Slade's arm, and motioned him to follow Malenkens, who was proceeding along the ledge. As he walked, Slade found himself surreptitiously looking

45

for Leear. He was not greatly surprised when he failed to locate her, but neither did he accept her absence as final. She had been here once. There was no reason why she should not come back. And, besides, she must know that this would be his point of entry into the three-eyed world.

Malenkens stopped, and spoke for the first time. "In here," he said.

The cave was a structural duplicate of the one into which Slade had peered. The three men sat down in chairs, and Malenkens spoke again.

"Slade," he said, "we have been estimating your situation from the time you wakened, and in my judgment it will take about six years to adjust the rhythm of your life to our group. That takes into account your untrained resistance, and the fact that it will probably require several months for you to help Leear destroy the barrier of Naze and Geean. And, of course, it assumes that you will not be killed or dangerously injured."

He added, "I am not trying to alarm you. I am merely stating the facts as I see them. Now, Danbar will take over."

Danbar did not move, but continued to sit in his chair. He looked at Slade speculatively. "You will be wondering," he said, "what Malenkens was talking about. Watch."

He vanished.

For a minute, Slade sat where he was. He had no particular thoughts, though the memory came that, when Leear had hovered above him near the granary, he had not been able to see her against the stars. She, too, must have been invisible.

At the end of the minute, it struck him that perhaps he was expected to do something. He stood up, bent over Danbar's chair, and gingerly moved his arm through the space where Danbar had been sitting. There was no resistance to the movement. He glanced over at Malenkens, but the man did not look up.

Slade sat down again, heavily this time, trembling a little. There was no reason at all why Danbar, having rendered himself invisible, had not climbed to his feet and walked in a leisurely fashion to the cave entrance, or perhaps he was standing beside his chair, watching his guest's reaction. There was no reason why he shouldn't have done one of those things, but Slade had the vaguely sinking conviction that Danbar had done nothing of the kind, and that in fact he was still sitting in the chair.

*Primitives,* Slade thought. *And I believed they were primitives.*

These people had learned the innermost secrets of the human nervous system. They were so far ahead of their two-eyed cousins that comparison seemed almost ridiculous. Or wait a minute—what was it Malenkens had said? ". . . . *It will take you about six years to adjust the rhythm of your life to our group—*"

The first burning excitement stirred Slade. Did he mean that at the end of six years, he, too, might be able to render himself invisible at will? Or did he mean—?

Slade pressed the thought back into his mind. He forced himself to lean back in his chair. He parted his lips to speak to Malenkens, then closed them again. The man was looking the other way. The moments dragged, and there was no sign of Danbar. His absence began to be disturbing. For the second time the possibility occurred to Slade that he was expected to do something.

He stood up uncertainly. On a sudden impulse he seated himself in Danbar's chair. That didn't last long. The thought came that it would be a very humorless situation if the man chose to materialize in the chair.

Slade walked to the entrance of the cave on the doubtful expectation that Danbar would be outside. The ledge was a veritable hive of activity, fires burning brightly, women stirring caldrons, children already becoming nuisances with their games and noise. But of Danbar there was no sign.

Slade stood for a moment peering out over the marsh. The view was gorgeous beyond all imagination. The water gleamed in the sun, and it was alive with colorful growth. Far out, he caught a glimpse of birds fluttering, and he thought with a thrill: Three-eyed birds! In the distance beyond the marsh trees reared to amazing heights, and he could see the haze of mounting hills beyond. Everywhere was the green of perpetual summer.

Slade turned back into the cavern, quivering inside. What a wonderful plane of Earth he was on. Never, surely, would he have the slightest desire to return whence he had come.

There was, of course, the problem of Naze— That brought Slade back to reality with a start. He saw that Danbar had still not rematerialized. He thought, "Invisibility? If I had to figure out some way of making myself invisible, knowing what I do now about the art of seeing, I would try to disturb in some way the vision centers of those who were looking at me. Perfect vision is possible only when the mind is relaxed. Therefore I would try to tense their minds in some way."

The rationalization brought a sudden startled thought. Why, of course. He *was* expected to do something. He drew a deep, slow breath, and let it out with a sighing sound, simultaneously letting all his muscles go lax. The eye specialist, Dr. McIver, had always maintained that the human body could relax with one breath.

In that instant Slade proved it. As he started to draw his second breath, Danbar reappeared in his chair. The man looked up earnestly at Slade.

"Very good, my friend. I was hoping that you would manage to figure that out for yourself." He went on, "You have experienced for yourself one of the basic truths of the human nervous system. During the next few months you will be taught the ultimate secrets of relaxation, relaxation so complete that, even in the final issue, there is no limit to the control that can be exercised over it. But now—"

He stood up, smiling. "Let us," he said, "take our chairs outside and have breakfast."

Slade followed the two men out into the brilliant sun.


CHAPTER VII


On the thirty-second day of his stay with the tribe, Slade lay at ease on a knoll above the marsh. From his position, he could see the caves about a mile away. It was a marvelous day. It had rained a little in the morning, but now the sky was as clear and blue as could be. Before him, in a garden-like vista, the green, green grass and shrubbery still sparkled with raindrops that hung heavy on every blade and sprig and leaf and branch.

The whole world around him was as wonderful as ever, and yet Slade was conscious of dissatisfaction. "I'm an active person," he thought. "My nerves are still afflicted with the neurotic desire to do things."

He even had an impulse pushing at him. That odd metal device that he had found half-buried in the ground near his farm the night he had seen Leear in a shadowed corridor of an old spaceship—it would be interesting to go and get it, and examine it.

He did not move. He had to admit that the previous month had, in its way, been exciting. The world of relaxation was an inward world of unending discovery. His knowledge began with the muscles, lectures about and exercises with. Exercises? It was not exactly the right word for what he was doing, Slade had decided, but he continued to use it for want of a better. Exercise suggested physical activity, but the relaxation exercises were inhalation and exhalation as effortlessly as possible. They were long minutes of lying upon carefully arranged pillows while the mind concentrated gently upon certain muscles, and always the message his brain sent was: "Let go, let go, let go."

Gradually, over the weeks, he learned the basic philosophy behind the relaxation. A correct posture, and good breathing habits. When at fault, those two things alone caused tension repercussions that affected the entire body. Tension made for bad vision and poor hearing. Tension was responsible for quick fatigue, for lack of strength and for narcotic cravings. Tension caused the kidneys to inject a fluid into the blood which caused high blood pressure, melancholy and a negative attitude towards life. Tension subtly changed the acid content of the digestive fluids. Tension was literally, the devil of the nervous system, but getting rid of it was merely the first, preliminary step to the control of the body.

The second phase was normalization of the nerves. Every nerve, individually and collectively, was capable of a positive or negative action. It could pass an impulse to seek another path to the brain. It was doubtful if more than five percent of an ordinary person's nerve impulses followed direct routes. It was true, of course, that many of the detours were used over and over again, but it was no justification for a bad habit to point out that it was repeated endlessly, particularly when the cumulative results were *un*sanity, early old age and a confused mind.

The entire ninety-five percent of misdirected nervous energy had to be re-channeled along direct routes and this was done by concentrating on key nerve paths. In every case, positive training was necessary. As with muscular relaxation, one could not just seek out a lazy environment and take it easy. Definite things had to be done. Muscles consistently relaxed by a system eventually stayed relaxed. Nerves repeatedly told to establish a direct channel, with a picture of that channel clearly visualized, did eventually make the exact channel demanded.

Nerve control led to the third or molecular phase, about which, when Slade had asked him, Danbar merely said, "You will see. You will see."

Lying there on the knoll above the marsh, it seemed to Slade that he knew the muscular relaxation exercises sufficiently well to be able to do them for a short time without an instructor standing by. He should be able to walk to the area where his farm existed on the Earth plane, and get the machine buried in the ground there.

He climbed to his feet with sudden decision. *I'll ask Danbar or Malenkens,* he thought.

Danbar, to whom Slade made the request, after the evening exercises, looked disturbed. Then he glanced questioningly at Malenkens. It was the latter who said:

"Leear told us you would be restless." He paused, frowning. Then he looked at Slade from under lowered lashes. "I've decided to be fairly frank with you, Slade. We are training you to help Leear against Naze. You must not think that we are parties to her plan. We merely exercise certain restraints upon her. You may wonder what that means, so I will explain.

"It is Leear's intention," he went on, "to involve you again in Naze. We have no power to prevent her from doing that, nor actually do we want to. Somehow, Geean

50

must be killed, and the people of Naze freed. According to Leear, only you can do this, how she has never explained.

"What we did was to delay her plans until you could be given at least preliminary training in our marvelous system."

He finished quietly, "I think you will agree that, under these circumstances, you would be wise not to involve yourself in minor side issues."

Slade was shocked. The more he thought about it the greater grew his shock. It was curious but, though he had not for a minute forgotten Leear or Naze—incredible Naze—somehow the long sweet month of pastoral existence had blurred the darker potentialities of that memory.

Now, here it was, plainly stated. On occasion in his past life, he had had a reputation for facing facts with a brutal honesty, and his comparisons had startled his business associates. That was the way he finally looked at his present position. The comparison that occurred to him was that he was like a pig being fatted for the slaughter.

He spent the night, narrow-eyed, sleeping fitfully, and in a fury every time he woke up. By morning his mind was made up.

So Malenkens and the others had only persuaded Leear with difficulty to delay putting him immediately in jeopardy. Well, that was just fine. He owed her nothing anyway but a punch in the nose for being indirectly responsible for the death of Amor and Caldra.

Since her intention was to use him without so much as a by your leave, his purpose could only be to prevent her by every possible means from involving him.

The determination gave him considerable satisfaction until near morning, when it occurred to him that it might not be any too easy to prevent her machinations. The trouble was he knew so little, so desperately little. He had not the faintest idea what methods might be available to these people who knew the innermost secrets of the human nervous system, and in addition had a spaceship loaded with gadgets, one at least of which was capable of transmitting material objects from this plane to the Earth plane and back again.

The new possibilities calmed him. He would have to be very clever indeed, to ensure that she didn't get him into Naze again. And anger would be his poorest asset in carrying out that purpose.

At breakfast time, he emerged from his cave, seated himself beside Malenkens, and said:

"I think it's time that I find out something about the history behind the war between the ship and the city."

Malenkens said, "I see that you have been thinking of, what I told you last night." Slade waited, and Malenkens went on, "I do not regret having said it, but I cannot say more. We promised Leear that we would let her tell you the entire story."

"Then tell me," said Slade savagely, "who is Leear?"

"She is one of the silver belts."

"One of the what?"

Malenkens was grave. "Her personal plans for you would suffer a psychological defeat if I told you more. You must wait. I can say this. If you survive the destruction of Naze, the universe will be yours for the taking."

Temporarily that silenced Slade. Coming from Malenkens, those were momentous words. They brought his first sense of exhilaration at the greatness of the adventure into which his destiny had brought him.

The exhilaration was brief. The tremendousness of the reward implied by Malenkens suggested an enormous compensating sacrifice. Slade stiffened slowly. He disliked the thought of being on an unfriendly basis with these kindly people, but it was time he stated his position without equivocation.

He did so, pretty much as he had already decided. No co-operation with Leear until he was good and ready. It was ridiculous for her to assume that a man could be shoved blindly into a situation, again and again, and told to get out as best he could, each time without having more than a sketchy idea as to what was going on. He for one refused to have anything to do with such a plan. And if he ever went in, it would be on the basis of full information with his eyes wide open.

"You will have to kill a man," said Malenkens in a

strangely drab voice. "You have never killed a human being. It is Leear's unalterable conviction that you could not bring yourself to commit a cold-blooded murder, and that only under the stress of violent danger could you be nerved to kill. Such is her opinion, and, having observed you for an entire moon period, I agree with her."

"Thanks," said Slade dryly. "I'm still not interested."

He finished his meal in silence. He felt uncertain as to just what his position was with the tribe, but he decided in the end that what had happened was not a breakup. He would remain for a while at least, and make his plans on the basis of careful thought. There was no use rushing off, half cocked.

He attended his morning relaxation exercises as usual.

During the second month, the tempo of his life seemed ster to Slade. He realized what it was. He was more alert, more wary, eager to learn things. He kept a watchful eye on the men, and slept with a gun under his pillow.

Towards the end of the month, it struck him that no one in the tribe had ever seen the automatics in action. And that it might be a good idea to fire one of his precious bullets as a sort of a deterrent. He hesitated about that, because even one bullet might be important in a crisis. And yet, it seemed clear that Leear would never get him into Naze against his will unless male members of the tribe trussed him up; and gave him into her power.

It was a month of several discoveries. He had been wondering about the animal life of this plane, "It's there," Malenkens assured him, with an odd smile. "It all depends on whether they decide to find out your reaction to seeing them."

That didn't quite make sense, but over a period of four weeks he had glimpses. And, finally, every time, the glimpse revealed the animal watching *him*. There was a tiny, dark creature too fast for a clear picture to form of its shape. A long, slim, spotted beast, too thin to be well muscled, and resembling a dog, trotted off disdainfully into the brush, after looking Slade over with an aloof eye. There was a horselike beast that peered

at him thoughtfully for several seconds, and then gal-
loped off snorting. And then, finally, there was a really
shocking meeting with an animal.

Slade was walking along in a pathless valley adjoining the valley of the caves when a chance glance to
the rear revealed a beast bigger than himself trotting
along not more than ten yards behind him. It had a
head that had both cat and bear features, and its body
was long, and sleek, and grayish-brown.

*It was the same type of beast that had bent over him
that night in Caldra's and Amor's apartment.*

Slade felt a thrill as sharp as fear, and snatched at
his automatic. The animal's teeth glinted like knives as
it snarled at him. Its great paws came up. It whirled,
and dived into concealing brush.

A nith, Danbar told him, and then was silent when
Slade described what had happened in the apartmen
in Naze. Later, Slade saw him talking earnestly to Malenkens. The two men fell silent as Slade approached,
so he was pretty certain they had been talking about him.

It was startling, that sudden discovery that he was
being discussed. It emphasized the unsatisfactoriness of
his position, and made immediately necessary, it seemed
to Slade, a demonstration of his powerful weapons.

He had been thinking about the best method for
doing that, and finally it seemed to him that he had it.
A bird. For two months he had watched birds with gray
plumage frisking through the foliage over and around
the marsh. Wary were those birds. He could spend an
hour crawling towards a flock. And then, just before he
got close enough for a good look, the birds would take
off towards a remote destination. Gradually, his desire
to have a close look at a winged creature with three eyes
became almost an obsession.

It seemed to him, now that if he could shoot one from
the ledge, he would, figuratively, kill two birds with
one stone.

On the following morning, he brought a chair out of
his cave, laid one of his automatics on his lap, and sat
watching the brush below. Aften ten minutes, he noted
that people were glancing at him from the corner of

their eyes. A few minutes after that, Danbar pulled up a chair and sat down beside him.

"What makes you think," he asked, "that your weapon will fire in this plane of existence?"

"Eh!" said Slade.

After a moment, the possibilities stunned him. He took careful aim at a distant flock of birds. He paused to say, "This gun makes a loud noise, so prepare yourself." Then he squeezed the trigger.

*Click!*

It was an empty sound. It left Slade with the chilled feeling that he was naked and helpless. The sun was as warm as ever, but for two months his two automatics had given him confidence and courage. They buttressed his spirit every time he thought of how easily the several dozen tribesmen could overpower him and give him to Leear.

Now, that buttress was gone.

For a moment, Slade sat quite still, then he ejected the cartridge into his palm, and began to pry out the bullet. He spilled the powder onto the cement sidewalk in a little pile, and then walked over to the nearest fire and picked up a burning faggot. He touched the flame to the powder. It burned with a slow sputter, like thick paper. Beside him Danbar said:

"The chemical combination will have to be slightly different. I have no doubt it could be made to work."

Slade had no intention of waiting to find out. His protection was gone. Without a word, he entered his cave, strapped on his second automatic, stuffed into his pockets the smaller articles he had brought from Earth— and returned to the outside. Danbar fell into step beside him.

"You are leaving us, Slade?"

Slade said, "Where is Malenkens?"

"He's gone."

That was the second great shock. "Gone! Where to?"

He saw that Danbar was looking at him oddly. "Malenkens is not one of us, Slade. He visits us occasionally. He is one of the . . . silver belts."

Slade was silent. He realized what had happened. He had been handed over to one of the Leear's hierarchy.

For the first time it struck him how consistently Malenkens had been in the foreground of his tribal life. Danbar was speaking again:

"Do not blame us too severely, Slade, for anything that happens. None of us here have attained further than the molecular phase of body control. We are helpless in this struggle between the ship and the city, and so long as the city exists we can never attain the final stage of self-control.

"It is a jarring factor. Its existence prevents certain basic rhythms. The *thought* that people like ourselves are caught behind its barrier, forever unable to escape—and that is the main purpose of the barrier—to keep those people there under Geean's control—weighs upon our spirit, and makes it impossible for us to realize our potentialities. And the result of that is that we, too, are at the mercy of Geean."

Slade had the impression that he was listening to an apology. It thawed him. "Thank you," he said, "I have nothing but friendship for your people here."

Danbar said, "Go with luck, my friend."

It took more than an hour before the cave ledge was finally out of sight.

## CHAPTER VIII

THE SCENE grew wilder by the hour. He saw no animals, but birds by the hundreds squawked in the brush and in the trees, on average a very different type of bird than those that had been in the vicinity of the caves. They were less wary. Frequently, he could walk right past them without disturbing them. Towards evening, he picked up a stick and knocked two pigeonlike creatures out of a low shrub, and had his first three-eyed birds.

In that dusk, with his fire sputtering defiance at the gathering darkness, with the cries of night birds all around, he ate fresh fruit and pigeon roasted over a spit.

After eating, Slade pondered the problem of two-eyed and three-eyed creatures, and the worlds they lived in. There must be common ancestry. The human form would not have repeated easily. Way back, various creatures of the two-eyed world had developed a third eye, and had gone automatically, without their even being aware of it, into this special universe.

Actually, like sight and sense itself, the explanation probably went to the very roots of reality. What didn't exist for the mind, the senses ignored. And in some intricate fashion, the object or objects ceased to affect the body as a whole.

It was not a new idea. But the old formulation expressed by the phrase, "Is the cat sleeping under the stove while I'm not around?" failed to take into account the certainties of the human mind. The absolute conviction that the cat was there whether the observer was present or not. Blind folk acquired certainties from hearing and touch.

The mind alone counted.

As the night wore on, Slade began to think, in the uneasy periods between dozes, of guns that wouldn't shoot. It was a thought that was to occur again and again during the days that followed. It almost but not quite altered his plans.

He had intended to get the metal device, then turn sharply southward, and so walk entirely out of the territory of Naze and Leear. It was an unheroic role that he proposed for himself and it made him a little defensive, a little ashamed.

*Here am I, he thought, in the strangest adventure a man ever got into, and I'm playing it cautious.*

There were men, he knew, who would not hesitate a minute about plunging deep into the affair. Such men would now be on their way to Naze with the intention of bearding Geean in his great central tower.

Lying in the darkness, Slade's lips tightened. It was no use kidding himself. Not for him was the bold course. The important thing was that he do not let caution send him southward without the metal object. It might prove without value. But it was a clue, and who could tell, it *might* still be in a workable condition. He couldn't leave it behind him.

The forests were quiet, the valleys long, the hills gradually higher. A great, virgin continent spread before his footsteps, but the amazing realization was the sensational familiarity of the route. There was a slight difference in the depth of the canyons and the height of the hills. The extensive marshes, the trees and the forests of shrubs were absolutely different. But the general contours were the same. And he had made the hundred mile trip to his farm so often that he wasn't lost for a minute. It was a wonderful feeling.

He came finally on the sixth morning to the long, hilly plain at the end of which—on the Earth plane—was his farm. Very cautiously, using every possible cover, he approached the point where the spaceship had been that night. From afar, he saw that it was not there, but his caution did not relax for a minute.

Within ten minutes of reaching the area, he found the machine. He used a sturdy branch he had picked up en route as a crowbar to pry it out of the ground. It was deeply imbedded, and it took considerable perspiration and twenty minutes to loosen it.

It came up finally, and showed its shape. A boxlike affair, with a wheel attached to one end. It was not too small in size, but its lightness was amazing. Pure magnesium, or even lithium, might have matched it, but little else.

He estimated the weight of the box and the wheel together at something less than thirty pounds. It glittered in the sun, untarnished by its long exposure. Slade made no effort to examine it immediately.

All that day, he carried it on first one shoulder, then another. About an hour before dusk he came to a burbling creek, and decided to stay there for the night. It was rather exposed, but he was tired, and the nearest forest looked many miles away.

He ate hurriedly, then, his curiosity as strong as ever, he bent over the machine. Atomic and magnetic power, Malenkens had told him once, were the energy sources of old Naze. "Naturally," the man had pointed out, "they will work a little differently here than where you came from."

After his experience with his automatics, Slade could appreciate that. Nevertheless, he decided that he preferred this one to be magnetic.

He studied the machine intently.

It was the wheel that puzzled him. Only one wheel. And so large, too. The metal box, into which the shaft of the wheel disappeared, was only about a foot cube. The wheel was a little over two feet in diameter, and it curved out from the shaft like a flower with long petals that formed a cup shape. It was big enough to be a small cornucopia. It could have acted easily as a small mixer, so spacious was it.

"Hm-m-m!" said Slade.

Perhaps the angle was not to think of it as a wheel just because it rotated easily on a shaft.

Still, it looked like a wheel.

He spun it. It whirled and finally came to a stop. Nothing else happened.

He fumbled over the box, searching for a control device. In a way he had done that before. Now, however, he was thorough. But there was nothing.

He noticed three brighter spots on one shiny side of the machine. They looked like dents made in the hard substance. But there were no dents. His probing fingers sensed not the slightest depression.

Puzzled, Slade examined the brightnesses. He brought them close to his eyes. Glitter, glitter, glitter, he thought. Wonder what—

Something caught at his eyes.

He jerked back, letting the machine drop.

It didn't drop. It hung a foot from his face, the wheel facing up, the three bright spots like tiny blazing fires poking at his three eyes.

He closed them, then blinked rapidly. The blaze points pierced through his eyelids. In a panic, Slade shoved at the box.

The machine glided a hundred feet through the air, and came to a stop. The three bright spots poured fire towards his eyes, as bright as if he was still a foot away. The extra distance made no difference.

Slade raced towards the machine. Have to turn it away from him, or the thing would destroy his vision. He caught it with trembling hands. And turned it upside down.

It spun around without resistance. And its mind-frightening connection with his eyes broken, it wafted

59

gently, almost balloonlike, to the ground. Slade hid it in the brush beside the creek. Then, still shaking from his experience, lay down on the grassy bank. It was only slowly that he realized that nothing damaging had happened. His vision was as good as ever. His eyes felt cool and rested, and quite untensed.

He slept dreamlessly and without wakening all night. When he opened his eyes, the sun was just coming up. He busied himself gathering fruit from the nearby trees, and he had just finished eating when a thin whistling sound rent the air to one side of him.

Slade jumped a foot as something struck the grass where he had been.


## CHAPTER IX

HE WHIRLED, and stared at the object. A noose made of metal looking rope. It was alive in a mechanical fashion. It shuddered and narrowed, tightening as he watched it. Its two ends withdrew into a little metal box.

Before Slade could examine it further, there was another hissing sound. The second noose struck his shoulder, as he twisted aside. It bounded away like a rubber ball, almost hitting a nearby tree.

"What the—" said Slade. And dived behind a shrub. By the time he reached it, two more nooses were lying on the grass, writhing shut. Slade slid his gaze around the horizon—and saw their source.

Flying things! They were too far away to be clearly visible. They seemed to have legs but no wings. He caught a glint of scarlet, then dazzling silver, then green, and of humanlike arms clinging to something that shimmered above them. It was the shimmering objects that flew. The creatures merely hung on.

And every little while, though the motion that caused it was lost in the distance, one of the creatures would send a noose hissing towards Slade's head.

He felt a horrid thrill. What was this? With an absolutely gruesome fascination, he remembered the girl's letter. Geean and the hunters of the city.

But the hunters were keeping their distance.

A thousand yards, he estimated shakily. Even if they had worked, his automatics would have been useless at that distance. He looked around frantically for a way of escape. But the nearest forest was about ten miles behind him. There was brush, there were shrubs, and by heaven, there was no reason to lose hope until he was actually caught.

Five nooses sprang around him while he observed and had the thought. He began to gather them up frantically. They were probably accustomed to retrieving them, and they couldn't have too many.

He darted behind a shrub. From its shelter he flicked his gaze calculatingly towards every horizon, counting the creatures. One, two . . . seven.

Slade thought jerkily, "If I can keep them off till dark."

A glance towards the sun showed that it hadn't moved a fraction of an inch, seemingly, from its position low above the eastern horizon.

Night was a long, long way off.

His lips tightened. Some of the fever went out of him. His body grew calm with determination. Straight ahead. There was no reason why, with a show of bravado, he shouldn't be able to make it—straight ahead to that distant forest.

As he twisted towards a second shrub, a noose came down from the sky, ringed him, spun a little as it struck his shoulders. And then settled down over his arms, tightening with irresistible strength.

Slade grabbed for his sheathed knife. But his hands were pressed too tightly against his body. He jerked at the snare, and stumbled over a stone, fell hard, rolling over and over.

The noose was like a steel spring. It cut into his flesh with a strength that made Slade gasp. There must be a releasing catch— Have to release it.

He strained to get his fingers up to it, but its hold was too cunning for him. As he struggled, Slade caught a movement in the near sky. It was hard to see through the pain tears that had started into his eyes. But he blinked the tears aside, and, after a moment, he saw the silver-clad hunters clearly. They were about a hundred feet away, and swooping closer.

He ceased his hopeless fight.

The seven hunters of the city dropped from their flying devices twenty feet away. Slade looked them over briefly, wondering if Geean was among them. It seemed unlikely. Swiftly, he forgot the men. It was the reddish flying instruments that snatched all his attention. They clung for a minute to the air above the men. And then, like slowly deflating balloons, they collapsed to the ground. One man carried a spare flyer.

Each instrument was a red-frosted, glasslike extrusion about three inches in diameter and three feet long. There was a sling attached to it, and at the end of the sling some handgrips.

Nothing else. No machinery, no apparent source of energy—Slade had an impulse to make it a closer examination. He repressed it, partly because the noose held him as tightly as ever. And partly because he had his first *close* look at the men.

The day he had seen the soldiers of Geean in Caldra's and Amor's apartment, he hadn't really had time to note character. Now, with these henchmen, he did.

They were intent faces, dissipated looking, very light in color. They bent over him, and two of them were smiling sardonically. One of the men said something, and there was a quick general laughter, that ended, and left the faces intent again. Slade didn't catch the words.

Slade felt the automatics taken from the holsters, and other articles removed from his pockets. Each item was swiftly scanned, then stuffed into a canvaslike bag. Before the search was finished, one of the men fumbled at the noose. It loosened promptly, and came up easily over his head.

And, again, there was speed. Even as Slade climbed to his feet and started to rub the numbness out of his arms, another man shoved the handgrips of the spare flier into his fingers, and pointed at a third, who was just picking one of the fliers off the ground.

"Watch him," he said curtly.

As Slade watched, the third man swung the bar up in front of him with an easy rhythmic swing. And, simultaneously, with dexterity, leaped into the air.

The glasslike bar caught at something. It stiffened,

62

straightened, and pointed like an arrow from a bow. It began to glide forward with the man clinging to the handgrips—as the man beside Slade said curtly, "Now, you."

He expected the thing to come crashing down on his head. And, simultaneously, paradoxically, he expected his arms would be half torn out of their sockets when the device caught "onto" the air.

But it wasn't like that. It wasn't like that at all. It didn't fall. There was no tug, no jerk. Something, a current, a—lightness—saturated his body. And it was that current, and not the machine, that lifted him. Lifted him like thistledown borne on a climbing breeze.

Strong as metal, the flying device rode above him. But it was only a catalytic agent, *affecting* his body not transporting it. His body flew with the machine, was of the machine. The two became one. He remembered how the bars had dropped a few minutes before, after the hunters let go, and it was clear that neither could remain airborn without the other.

A great basic force welded a union between his nervous system and the machine. And the dead weight of gravity let go of him. It was like the wheel machine, he recalled with a start. He glanced back towards where he had hidden the machine, but it was not visible from the air.

The relief that came had mixed in it a great wonder. What incredible secrets of the nervous system had these people discovered, both natural and mechanical? He saw that the other six hunters were swooping up to him. They clustered around him, clinging to their fliers effortlessly. And somehow the sweep of their machines became the direction and speed of his. It was as if his flier was guided by a sympathetic union with the other machines.

They soared low over the land and over a whole series of marshes, in and out along valleys and through forests. Slade noticed that the fliers had a tendency to remain near the ground. Not once was there a real attempt to climb high. They avoided the towering, snow-capped mountains that flanked their course. Like a river, they flowed along the easiest course, and in the end he decided that the motive power was derived from the magnetic currents of Earth. Nothing else, in view of what he knew, could explain the evenness of their course, and the *type* of transportation.

In a surprisingly short time, the clustered group of them came within sight of a city of shining spires. Slade stared at it with glistening eyes because it was one thing to have seen it from inside, quite another to view it like this. It was about four miles wide at the mouth of a widening valley. He couldn't see how long it was. The fliers were too low, and the city stood on a plateau.

Its towers and roofs glinted in the brilliant rising sun. Clearly now, its design was apparent. The whole city sloped up towards the central tower of Geean, that reared like a pylon into the lower heavens. The height of that pylon seemed greater than he remembered it. It rivaled the near mountain peaks, and from its silvery eminence, a hazy, violet glow spread like a mist covering the whole city. The color was remarkably sharp seen from this angle. It was a mist of light that curved like a carefully worn robe onto the grass a mile from every outskirt of the city.

The fliers poised before the barrier. For a moment only. A signal flashed mirror-bright from the distant tower, and the red-frosted devices flowed forward and through the barrier like so many knives cutting through thin gauze.

They almost grazed the rooftops of low built homes. They evaded several spires, and then they began to swoop lower. They were twenty feet, then ten feet from the ground. A man reached over and grasped one handle of Slade's machine.

"Let go," he said curtly. "Drop."

Slade looked at him, amazed and uncomprehending. The surly face, so close to his own was venomous.

*"Drop!"*

Slade glanced down. A cobbled street was below. He hesitated, then let go. The instant return of weight made a thrill in his nervous system. He struck the ground harder than he liked. Twice, he rolled over, and then he was up. The fliers were already disappearing around a nearby spire.

Abruptly, he was alone.

## STATEMENT TO THE CORONER'S JURY
### By John Alden, Farmer,
### Smailes County

It is my custom to arise at 5 a.m. every morning. On the morning of the 19th I got up at my usual hour, and I was doing my chores when I observed what seemed to me a strange spectacle.

A woman and a large bearlike beast were walking in a westerly direction across my stubble field. Since bear are frequently dangerous, the fear came to me that the woman did not know she was being followed by so large and formidable an animal.

I ran and procured my gun, but though I was inside only a minute, and there was no place where anybody could have gone to in such a short time, when I came out of the house, there was no sign of either woman or beast. Almost literally they disappeared into thin air.

It was a little after noon that same day that the smashed body of Michael Slade was discovered in the high valley two miles from my place. According to the doctor, he had died about half an hour before he was found. So it is very likely his death had no connection with the woman and the bear, whom I saw earlier.

But I report the incident for what it is worth in clearing up the mystery of the three-eyed man.

Except for the foregoing, I had never seen Michael Slade until his dead body was brought to my farm by the doctor.

One more thing: When the police from Smailes County and I examined the tracks of the woman and the animal, we discovered that they ended abruptly in the middle of the field.

I am not prepared to offer an explanation for this.


## CHAPTER X

SLADE WALKED slowly along, examining his position. His automatics were gone, but his knife was still in its holster. His handkerchief had been left in his pocket as well as a small case of fishing tackle and a box of morphine tablets, which he had brought along in the event of a violent accident befalling him.

Abruptly, he discovered that the side street he was on was not quite so deserted as it had first appeared. An old woman sidled hurriedly out of an alleyway, and muttered:

"Blood! or I'll murder you tonight." Slade brushed her aside, thinking: *Why had they released him? What did they expect him to do? Do! That was it of course. Geean thought he knew about the plotting that was going on, and somehow the great man of Naze expected him to lead his forces to the plotters.*

Slade laughed grimly. There was a great deal of cunning common sense in Geean's plan, but it had a basic fault. Geean was wrong in his belief that Slade knew anything.

But that didn't matter now. His purpose before the fall of night must be to find the apartment that had once been occupied by Caldra and Amor. And since Geean was aware of its location, he didn't have to be the slightest bit stealthy about it.

He must assume for the moment that he couldn't escape from Naze, and that Geean would arrest him whenever it pleased him.

The sun was high in the heavens when he reached the fifth columnist part of the city. He recognized a street, then another, then he realized that he was near the apartment. As he hurried eagerly forward, a young woman's familiar voice whined:

"Your blood, mister."

Slade was walking on, when a gasp escaped the girl. He whirled, and stared at her. Her face was already stiffening to the encounter.

"Well," she said with a faint sneer, "if it isn't the man who was going to destroy Naze."

Slade said, "Amor!" Then he remembered Geean, and that his movements were probably being observed. "Quick," he said, "meet me at Caldra's apartment. I'll give you some blood then. But now—slap my face as if you're mad at me."

66

She *was* quick. Her hand came up and dealt him a stinging blow on the cheek. She swaggered away, and he walked on, for the first time beginning to realize the implications of what had happened. Amor—on the streets.

He had a sudden sense of personal degradation. Then anger against Leear. She was responsible for this.

He wondered bleakly if the girl would turn up at the apartment.

She was there ahead of him. She opened the door for him, and began to talk even as he crossed the threshold. She chattered with a mad speed. Her face was flushed, her eyes wide and staring. Her hands shook. She looked on the verge of a nervous breakdown.

She had escaped death the night Caldra was killed because she was not in the apartment. She had spent the night with a girl friend.

"I was afraid that I would go to your room if I stayed."

The feverish way in which the words were spoken reminded Slade. He climbed to his feet, and went into her bedroom. The syringe and the cup lay on the table beside her bed.

He thought sickly. *To such depths can the potential Homo Superior sink.*

He took the syringe into the kitchen, boiled some water on one of the curious energy elements, and then sterilized the syringe needle. He inserted the needle into a vein in his left arm. The blood glittered darkly as it flowed into the transparent syringe. When it was full he squirted it into the cup. The liquid hissed a little as it touched the metal, but there was no other reaction. With a steady hand, he set the cup down on the table beside her.

The girl licked her lips, but she did not look at the cup. Her face was stiff, her body rigid. Her eyes were looking fixedly at the floor. She said in a monotone:

"Why have you come back to the city?"

So she was beginning to think things over. It was a good sign. Slade began to talk. He was completely frank, though brief. When he had finished, Amor's eyes were gleaming. She stood up. She was suddenly enormously excited.

"This is it," she said. *"This is it!"* She looked at him, wide-eyed. "Don't you see, it's not an accident your

67

being here. Everybody's being terribly clever but determined. Geean has let himself fall into the trap. Why? Because he feels safe behind his silver belt, but he's desperately anxious to find out how Leear thinks she can use you to destroy him. And in his bold fashion, he'll take risks now so that he'll know in the future."

She had started pacing the floor, as she talked. Now, she stopped, directly in front of Slade. She said in an intense voice:

"Go straight to him. That will baffle him. He's expecting you to do something. He's expecting somebody to tell you to do something. Very well, I'll tell you. Leear has said that only you can kill Geean. That means that nothing can happen until you are present.

"That means that you, under the present circumstances, have to seek him out. You can't escape it in the long run anyway. There is no escape from Naze except through Leear. And you may be sure that she'll keep you here now until you do what she wants. Besides, Geean will have you brought before him sooner or later anyway and—*Here!*"

She had raced off across the room. She came racing back carrying the cup of blood. She held it out to him. She said in feverish tone:

"Take a sip of this. It will give you courage. The effect of a sip won't last longer than an hour."

Slade took the cup curiously. He felt overwhelmed. He had always intended to taste the stuff, though the idea of drinking his own blood was repellent. Nevertheless, he was not going to be rushed so swiftly into putting himself into the clutches of Geean. His impulse was to temporize.

He brought the cup to his lips, hesitated. And then he took a little swallow—

"Get in there," the officer of the tower guard said insolently. "If his excellency Geean decides to speak to you, he'll let you know."

The door shut with a bang.

Slade staggered as he moved farther into the room. The sense of ecstatic, almost unbearable pleasure that had burst along his nervous system within seconds of his swallowing the blood, was gone now. What remained was a blurred memory of mad pleasure-dreams, and a gathering fury.

*That little wretch,* he thought, *that scoundrel, Amor. She knew what would happen.*

A sort of hypnotism it had been, driving him resistlessly through a mist of streets on wings of joyous excitement straight to the central tower of Geean. Blood drinkers must give their brain directional thoughts just before they drank. *His* directions had been to go to Geean, and here he was.

Still dizzy, Slade looked around the room. There was a bed in one corner, and a large window slashed across the opposite wall. Slade peered shakily out of the window, and blinked. He was looking down into a depth of distance. He estimated seventy stories, and he was leaning forward to verify the height when the realization struck into his brain that he was *able* to lean forward. There was no glass in the window.

He retreated back into the room, shocked by his mental condition, that had made it possible, however briefly, for him to be unaware that the window was a hazard. Better lie down, he thought shakily.

He dreamed a miserable afterdrug type dream. In the dream, his body was flung out of an open window, to fall seventy stories to the ground below. He awakened, shivering, and then grew rigid:

A nith was standing beside his bed, its long powerful head projecting above him. Its three eyes staring down at him were pools of unnatural light. It saw that he was awake, but made no effort to move away. It said:

"Who told you to come here?"

It stood there waiting.

Vagueness. Slade's brain had been tensed for almost anything. But not language, not speech. The surprise was too great for ordinary adjustment. Caught completely off guard, his conscious mind temporarily suspended function.

It was not funny. His metabolism was affected. There was a rush of loose nervous energy through his body. Nausea came, followed by an inability to perform certain normal releasing reflexes like swallowing and blinking. The blood seemed to congeal behind his eyes, and his vision blurred sharply.

He had an acute conviction, not a thought but a fear, that he was going to be precipitated back to the other earth. The fear grew so monstrous that his first thought was able to come through. His dream— He would fall seventy stories if he was knocked out of this plane. The picturization of that fall almost petrified his reason.

But the seconds passed, and nothing happened. His confidence returned. The nith's bear-cat head was only a foot away from his face, as it said:

"What is the plan to destroy Geean?"

There were several things about the speech that almost got Slade going again. It was not a speech. There was no sound at all. The creature was thinking at him. This was mental telepathy.

Slade lay stiff, striving to grasp the implications of beast that had a better than human system of commu cation. Memory came of the wild animals that ha watched him, and the wariness of the birds near the caves. Was it possible that they were all mind readers?

The thought ended. The nith was snarling threateningly. A great paw came up.

*What is the plan?*

In a synchronized jerk, Slade flung himself to the far side of the bed, and snatched his knife. Horribly afraid, he tumbled off the bed. Then he was on his feet, knife ready, backing towards the nearest wall.

"Careful," he said, "I'll sink this knife into you six inches at least."

Afterwards, Slade was not clear as to what happened then. He was partly facing the window when a second nith walked in from the empty air of seventy stories above ground. It carried a foot-thick transparent weapon, which cast a pale reddish radiance towards the first nith. The beast must have died instantly, but it took more than a minute for the radiance to dissolve its great body into nothingness. The newcomer looked at Slade. It thought at him urgently:

"A traitor. We've been waiting patiently for Leear to give the word to kill him. But now, there's no time to waste. First, I'd better get rid of this—" Slade didn't get the word it used to describe the weapon.

He watched as the animal dextrously split the instrument in two. Inside was a simple set-up built around a loose strip of metal about an inch by three inches by four. The nith's paw clutched the small object.

"Quick," it said, "put this in your pocket. Like this."

It was not something about which Slade had any say. The animal bounded towards him. Before he could decide whether he was going to resist, it had slipped the metal strip into his left coat pocket. Slade watched as it jammed the two sections of what remained of the weapon under the bed.

It came erect with a jerk. "They're coming for you," it said tensely. "Remember, there's no victory yet. What we have done so far we could have done years ago. *This is the crisis.*"

The door opened, and half a dozen soldiers came in. Without a word they led Slade out into a long, dim corridor and into an elevator. The nith followed. The elevator creaked upward about ten floors. Another corridor, then a door that opened into a spacious apartment.

A tall thin man with a powerful physique was standing looking out of a glassless window. He was dressed in the silver shining clothes of a hunter of Naze, and until he turned Slade had no sense of familiarity. It was that that made terrific the shock of recognition.

Geean was Malenkens.

## CHAPTER XI

IT WAS a morning of devasting shocks for Slade. He was aware of the great man watching him with a faint smile, and it was the contemptuous texture of that smile that finally pulled Slade out of his desperate turmoil.

In a burst of thought, he saw the picture. Danbar's apology. Explained now. Geean's nith that night at Caldra's apartment must have read his mind, and on the basis of the information it secured, Geean had been enabled to lay in wait for him at the cave village. There, without asking any questions, he had learned from Slade the detailed story of what had happened.

Bloodthirsty threats must have been used to silence so completely men like Danbar.

The other's smile was more satiric. "You're quite right," Geean said. "That is what happened."

The words, so accurately reflecting his thoughts, startled Slade. He looked at the nith, and its mind touched his instantly:

"Naturally, I am giving Geean a censored version of your thoughts. That is why he used the traitor nith. He had to have somebody who could read minds, and I was selected as a substitute because of my overall resemblance to the dead-one. But now, you must be on the alert."

It went on with ill-concealed haste: "Geean is not as calm as he appears. He has a tremendous respect for Leear, and something has already happened to make him realize that this *is* the crisis. If he should suddenly become afraid, he will kill you instantly.

"You must accordingly be prepared to act on a flash thought from me."

"But what am I supposed to do?"

There was no answer to that intensely thought question. Slade licked dry lips, as the realization penetrated how completely he was involved in the moment by moment developments. He thought, "I've got to convince Geean, persuade him that I'm no danger." Before he could speak, Geean said:

"Slade, you are alive at this moment because I am undecided. A woman"—his voice grew savage—"named Leear, the only other silver belt immortal, has claimed that she can use you to kill me. I could murder you out of hand, but she would soon be able to produce another person like you with which to threaten me, and the next time perhaps I might not find out about it in advance. This is the time I must take any attendant risks. You are the man who benefits for the moment. Slade, I must find out what her method is. To me, nothing in the world matters as much."

It was impressive. Geean's face had changed as he talked. Earnestness was in every line. The man was

72

fascinated to the core of his soul by the threat to himself. He, who was immortal, was suddenly menaced, and the startling thing must be the vagueness, the lack of detail of that all-embracing menace. Hundreds of years had probably passed since Geean had experienced such an excitement of interest.

Slade's private thoughts ended, for Geean was continuing, his voice harder, his manner more intent:

"Slade, it is clear to me that you are an unwilling pawn in this affair. But I can do nothing about that. Here you are. The issue has been forced despite all my warnings to Leear. At this moment, and there is no question that it is her doing, an atomic fire is raging on the fortieth level of the tower. It will not be long before it reaches us up here."

Briefly, Slade's attention wandered. He stood, startled. An atomic fire. Why, that meant the tower would be destroyed, the barrier would come down forever. Naze was already doomed.

In his mind's eye, he visualized that fire of fires. He began to tremble. The others undoubtedly had methods of escape, but what about him. The implacable voice of Geean went on:

"It has always been possible for Leear to start such an uncontrollable atomic reaction among the machinery of the barrier, but long ago"—his tone grew remote—"*long ago*, I warned her that if she ever did I would murder every human being on the planet."

His eyes, as cold as glass, fixed Slade. The change in the man absolutely astounded Slade. At the beginning, he had had something in him of the stern kindly appearance of Malenkens. All gone now. His face was transformed. It was like a mask, so deadly, so cruel that Slade was taken aback. In the space of a few minutes Dr. Jekyll had become Mr. Hyde. Geean said in an infinitely savage voice:

"At all times Leear has known that if she destroyed the barrier I destroyed the race. She has made her choice. So it shall be."

The words were so ultimately meaningful that they did not immediately make sense. Slade was thinking that the spectacle of Geean changing had been like

73

being in the presence of a man who was drinking himself into a piglike state, like having a sudden glimpse of sewer, like being compelled to watch an obscene picture. Slade shivered with repulsion, and then, abruptly, his absorption with physical things passed. In one jump, the immense meaning of the man's words penetrated.

He felt half paralyzed, and then, stronger than before the realization came that he must convince Geean, must persuade him that Michael Slade would do nothing to injure him. He parted his lips to speak—and closed them again.

A shape was walking into the window behind Geean. It was a woman's shape, momentarily insubstantial. The nith must have warned Geean, for he turned mustering a grimace of a smile. The smile became a broad sneer as Leear came into the room.

Slade looked at her stiffly. He had an idea that his life was hanging in the balance. Now that Leear had arrived, Geean must be tensing to the necessity of dealing swift death to the one man who was supposed to be able to kill him. The nith's tremendously anxious thought impinged upon his mind:

"Relax, man, for your sake and ours. Surely, you have enough experience now with the nature of the nervous system to realize that an unrelaxed man is at a terrible disadvantage. I assure you that I will give you some warning. So be calm, and face this deadly situation."

Relax! Slade clutched at the hope. Relaxation should be easy to him now. The hope went deeper, farther. What a tremendous and terrible joke on Geean was the presence of this nith.

Slade looked at the animal in a great wonder. There it sat on its haunches, a gigantic cat bear, reading everybody's thoughts, passing on to each person a censored version of what it saw. And Geean believed—stood there, cold and confident, and *believed*—that it was his nith.

If he was really unkillable, then that delusion meant nothing. But if Leear had a method of killing him, if there was a weakness in his impregnability, then Geean had made the mistake of his career.

Slade drew a long, deep breath, and let it out——long.

Relaxation was as swift as that. Standing there, he had his first good look at Leear.

It was a different Leear than he remembered from his brief glimpses. She had been nude beside the marsh, and little more than a shadow inside the spaceship. Somehow, he had taken it for granted that she wore the rough and ready clothes of the cave dwellers.

He was mistaken. No cavewoman was here. Her hair was a braided marvel, not a loose fringe, not a straggling curl. And it glowed with a lacquer-like luster. She wore a silkish garment that seemed brand new. And it must have been designed for her. It showed off her figure with an almost demure good taste. Even her dominating attitude was softened, for she sent a quick warm smile at Slade, and then, as she faced Geean squarely, the smile faded. If she intended to speak, she was too slow. Geean it was who broke the silence:

"All decked out in your bridal finery," he sneered. He began to laugh. It was a loud, insulting laughter. He stopped finally, and turned grinning to Slade. "You will be interested to know, my friend, that you are the last hope of this ten thousand year old spinster. It is a little difficult to explain, but the cavemen, by very reason of their type of nerve training, are adversely affected by the aura of a woman who gains her nerve power by mechanical means. Accordingly, she cannot get a husband for herself among them. That leaves my blood drinkers out there"—he waved a hand towards the window—"and you."

The grin was wider. "For reasons of morality, she is not interested in a man who has formed the blood drinking habit, which of course narrows the field down to you. Amusing, isn't it?"

The grin faded. Abruptly savage, the man whirled on Leear. "And you, my dear," he said scathingly, "will be interested to know that Slade is on my side, not yours. The nith has just informed me that he is desperately anxious to convince me that I have nothing to fear from him. Since it will inform me when and if he changes his mind, I find myself in a unique bargaining situation."

He didn't realize. It was amazing, it was almost staggering to see him standing there accepting what the nith was telling him. Not that it had told a lie about Slade's intentions and desires but the fact that it was quite coolly giving him real facts emphasized in a curious fashion how completely at its mercy he was for information.

For his own sake Geean had better be unkillable. Otherwise, he was right behind the eight ball.

"We want to show you," the nith's thought came. "If Geean will let us, we want to show you what is behind this fight of the ship and the city. That is why I told him about your determination not to kill him."

It went on swiftly, "It will be a postponement only. You cannot escape the necessity of choosing between the two worlds at war here, the two people standing before you. I can tell you this much. When the moment comes your choice will be free, but only in the sense that anything in this universe is free.

"But now, we must persuade Geean to let you hear a brief history of Naze."

Geean was quite willing. He looked genuinely amused. "So it's really come down to persuading Slade to do something. I think I ought to warn you that at the moment I am the one who is the most likely to win him over. I've just been remembering some of the things he told me about his country. Only a few years ago they dropped atomic bombs on major cities of some enemies of theirs. The parallel to our own case is most interesting, and augurs so ill for you that I would suggest you simply open your mind to the nith, and so get the whole affair over with as swiftly as possible. All I want to know is, how did you plan to use him to kill me?"

He smiled. "You won't do it? Very well, let's get it over with. It always amuses me to hear biased accounts of events in which I have participated."

He walked over to a couch, and sat down. And waited.

Leear turned towards Slade. "I shall be quick," she said.

It was not a long story that she told them. But it was the picture of the end of a civilization that had attained mechanical perfection. The immortal inhabitants of Naze were indestructible by virtue of their silver belts, which gave them nerve control. There were machines for every purpose, and all worked on the same principle— control of the human nervous system by means of inorganic energies.

As the slow years passed, the very perfection began to pall. It was discovered that individuals were beginning to commit suicide. Boredom settled like a vast doom over that ultimate materialistic civilization, and with each passing day men and women sought surcease in voluntary death.

It became a mass tendency. In the beginning, the planet had been well-populated, almost overcrowded. At the end a handful of millions lived in eighteen cities. It was into this impasse that new discoveries about the human nervous system projected a whole new outlook on the future of man.

Experiments were performed on animals and birds. In an amazingly short time various breeds were able to read minds, something which man, with all his machines, had never been able to accomplish. They reacted marvelously in other ways also, and so a plebiscite was held, and it was decided by an overwhelming vote to put aside artificial immortality and give the new wonderful science a chance.

Leear paused and looked at Slade gravely. "There could be no half measures. It was all or nothing, no volunteer system could be permitted, no exceptions. The new discoveries proved that man, in his primitive simplicity, had followed the wrong road to civilization, and and that he must retrace his steps and make a new beginning. He must go back, and back away from the materialistic gods he had followed so long, away from his cities and his machines. You yourself have seen what men like Danbar can do, and he has attained only a part of the third or molecular phase of control. The final, electronic phase, impossible of attainment so long as the city of Naze exists, goes completely beyond anything that has ever been envisaged by man. With our mechanical belts, our silver belts, we have had tantalizing glimpses, but that is all. Men will be as gods, almost omnipotent, and naturally immortal.

"Do you hear me? *Naturally immortal!* In your world and my own, long ago, thousands of generations of human beings have died unnecessarily. All of them had

77

within their own bodies the power of powers, the innate capacity to realize their every desire."

The picture had been growing on Slade, as she talked. The existence of the cavemen was explained. Odd pieces in the jigsaw puzzle of this world were beginning to fit into place, and he had a sudden dazzling vision of what she was getting at.

Leear was continuing, swiftly: "Think of your own experience," she said in an intense voice. "You came from one plane of existence into another because your mind suddenly accepted a new reality. And then there is a comparison that shows how completely wrong appearances can be. Light. The people of the two-eyed world must have a definition of light as something materialistic, something external,"

She stared at him _____ so andingly that Slade nodded, and gave the wave and corpuscular theories of light.

"Light," said Leear triumphantly, "is a perception of the reactor, not an activity of the actor. Out there in space is a great body we know as the sun. We and every object in this room, whether organic or inorganic, are aware of the presence of that sun. We all react to its presence, just as it reacts to ours. But it sends us no heat, no light, *nothing*. The awareness is inside ourselves, inside the molecules of this table and that chair. To us, that awareness manifests as a perception which we call light. Now, do you see, now do you realize that primitive man, unaided, followed the wrong course. He had no way of understanding the true nature of his world."

Slade hadn't expected to grasp her meaning. But he did. Only a few months before, he had attended a lecture by a disciple of Einstein. And in a distorted fashion, *this* was the famous scientist's latest theory of light. He had forgotten all about it.

He was frowning over the visualization, when he happened to glance at Geean. That brought him back with a start to an entirely different kind of reality. He said:

"Where does Geean fit into all this?"

Geean said dryly, "I was just going to ask that question myself."

Leear was silent for a moment. Then, in a low voice: "There was opposition, of course, to the great plan.

78

All silver belts had been destroyed except those of myself and my companion who had been chosen by lot to man the ship which you saw, to watch over the experiment, to chronicle its progress, and—"

She stopped. "There was opposition," she said, flatly. "A small, selfish minority led by Geean—"

Again, she stopped. This time Geean laughed, but the laughter ended abruptly. He said somberly:

"They had no idea how far I had decided to go."

Something of the remorselessness of the decision he had carried out then came into his face, and into his voice, as he went on:

"My forces struck one night at the seventeen cities, and wiped them out with atomic bombs. By a trick we secured the belt of Leear's companion, and killed him. That is the belt I now wear. We had planned also to destroy the ship, but by pure accident Leear had taken it from its berth."

He breathed heavily with the memory of what must have been the shock of shocks of his long, ruthless life. His eyes were narrowed to slits, his body tense.

"She attacked our storehouse in Naze. By the time we got the barrier up, she had destroyed all chance of our ever making more belts."

Geean gave a final reminiscent shudder, and then straightened slowly. He looked around belligerently. "Enough of this," he said. "I can't quite imagine a stranger to this world getting so heated over something that happened more than a thousand years ago, that he will risk his life to avenge it."

So quickly did the conversation sink to practical verities.


CHAPTER XII

IT WAS TOO LONG, Slade thought gayly. Too many centuries had passed since that colossal crime had been perpetrated. And yet, in spite of the vast time gap, something of the horror of it reached across the years and touched him.

For the problem was still here. *Here,* in this room. The struggle for ascendancy between the ship and the city. That collective entity the ship was going to defeat the entity that was the city. But Geean would survive; and, by that very survival, he would retain the power of death over all the defenseless people of this plane.

But life centered in the individual. A man must save himself.

"You are wrong," thought the nith. "Life is the race. The individual must sacrifice himself."

That was too deep for Slade. He grew aware that Geean was still speaking, at him now:

"My mind reading animal," he said, "has been keeping me in touch with your thoughts. I'm happy to note that you dismiss Leear's arguments as so much impractical metaphysics. It's possible," he went on, "that you and I are closer together mentally than I have suspected. The nith has also told me of the arguments you are marshaling to convince me that I ought to keep you alive. Frankly, I hadn't really thought about your ability to go to your earth as being valuable to me, but I can see how it might be."

Slade, who hadn't even thought of any arguments to save himself, stared at the nith in amazement. It was startling to realize that the beast had been using a skillful psychology to save his life.

"I told you," the nith thought into his mind, "that, when the moment came, your choice would be personally free. He has decided that, if no crisis occurs, he will let you live."

Slade's answering thought was grim. "But how am I going to get down to the ground?"

"That," flashed the nith, "comes under the heading of what I said before. No choice in this universe is absolutely free. You can trust yourself on our side, or you can make arrangements with Geean."

So that was it. They thought they were going to force him to take one risk to avoid another. And when you got right down to it, they pretty well had him. Slade thought savagely:

"What do you want me to do?"

"Geean must die. Only you can kill him."

"I've heard that all before." Impatiently. "What I mean is—"

He stopped. For weeks he had known that this was what would be required of him. The realization had lain there in the back of his mind, to be occasionally brought forward and pondered in an unreal fashion. It was altogether different to think suddenly, *"This* is the moment."

He who had never killed a man must now kill Geean. How?

You have in your left hand pocket an instrument. Turn slowly until your left side is pointing at Geean. Put your hand surreptitiously into your pocket and press the button that you will find right at the top of the device.

That instrument has now had time to integrate itself to your nervous system, a nervous system which, as you know, is not yet completely stabilized in this plane. When you press the button, it will transmit to Geean in a very concentrated form your present instability. He will be instantly projected to the two-eyed plane of existence, and will fall eighty stories to the ground. Just as your bullets would not work when you first came here, so his silver belt will be valueless there.

Slade could feel himself changing color. He was vaguely aware that Leear and Geean were talking sharply to each other, but his mind couldn't begin to focus on them. *Do* that, he was thinking, to anybody.

He remembered his own fear of such a fall. And suddenly a horror came.

Just a minute. If I'm involved in this process of transferring from one plane to another, then I'll fall too.

No, you won't.

He didn't believe it. With a hot terror he saw the whole picture. This was what all that stuff about sacrificing the individual for the race had been leading up to. In his mind, he saw the bodies of Geean and himself hurtling down and down. And it built a curious kinship between himself and the man.

"I swear," said the nith, "that you will not die."

Utter disbelief came.

And utter dismay.

The nith was desperate. "You are forcing us to extremes. Leear has decided that either she or Geean dies here today. If you do not kill Geean, then, unless he wins a complete victory, he will carry out his threat to destroy every man and woman and child on the planet. You can see that Leear cannot permit that to happen. Accordingly, the choice is yours. What you do will determine finally whether the people of this planet shall become slaves of Geean or whether they will have the opportunity to realize their natural potentialities."

Slade thought hesitantly, "You mean Leear is going to kill herself."

The nith was satirical. "Please do not concern yourself about Leear. Concern about her is a moral characteristic, shall we say a racial as distinct from an individual, think-only-of-oneself characteristic. It is purely in your mind, having no external reality. What does it really matter if this woman and all that she stands for dies, provided you live?"

It must have despaired of convincing him in time. It must have projected a thought towards the woman. For she turned even as Geean, narrow-eyed with suspicion, was saying, "Unless you leave here this minute, I shall have to revise my decision about not killing Slade." She turned, and she said to Slade:

"Please, my friend, think of the generations that have been imprisoned in this city. Think of Amor, of—"

She stopped hopelessly. "You force me," she said, "to the final sacrifice."

Her hands moved to her waist, and disappeared under her blouse. They came out again instantly dragging a thin belt. She flung it viciously. It flashed with a silvery metallic fire as it fell to the rug.

*"Your silver belt!"*

It was Geean who shouted the words, piercingly. Never in his life had Slade heard such a yell of mixed triumph and unbelief. The man literally staggered forward and snatched up the belt. His eyes were glassy and, briefly, quite myopic with ultimate pleasure. He began to run towards the wall to Slade's left. There was a coneshaped gadget in the near corner. With trembling fingers Geean stuffed the belt into it. It flared with a vivid fire, and was consumed in one puff.

Slowly, then, the man's sanity came back. He shook himself. He faced the room, and looked from Leear to Slade, and his face showed a mounting consciousness of the extent of his victory.

"Ah," he said ecstatically, "I am at last in a position to decide what I'm really going to—"

Slade never learned what Geean was in a position to decide. He was shocked to the core of his being. Actually, Leear's appeal on Amor's behalf had convinced him. The memory of Amor's degradation had brought a vivid picture of a people held down by a devil-like egotist.

He had turned automatically to follow the man's movements. His hand was in his pocket, and his left side towards Geean. He was thinking that under certain circumstances a man's free choice must include the possibility of personal death.

With a tiny pressure, he pressed the activating button of the gadget in his pocket.

## STATEMENT TO THE CORONER'S JURY
## By DETECTIVE LIEUTENANT JIM MURPHY

When the body of Michael Slade was discovered last week in the foothills near the city of Smailes, I was dispatched to the scene. It was at my request that the inquest hearing was transferred to Mr. Slade's home city, where most of the witnesses lived.

About these witnesses, I wish to say that all of them, without exception, were doubtful about identifying the deceased as Michael Slade when they were first shown the body. Later, on the stand, they were more positive, having apparently resolved their earlier doubts on the basis of "The dead man is three-eyed. Therefore it must be Michael Slade."

One of my reasons for going to Smailes was to make some attempt to find out where Michael Slade had been during the past few months.

I have considerable experience at locating missing persons, but my usual methods produced no results whatever. While the time elapsed since Mr. Slade's death

83

has been very short, I am almost prepared to say that further search will only emphasize the following fact:

Michael Slade walked out of his own back yard in this city several months ago, and his body was discovered last week near the city of Smailes. There is no record of his whereabouts during the interval.

They climbed towards the top of the spire ahead of the ominous hum and crackle of the fire. The direction worried Slade. How were they going to get down, with flames barring the lower levels? And suppose that the fire ate through the main walls, and the upper part of the immense building toppled to the ground far below.

There was a possibility, of course, that she and the nith could get down as easily as they had come in through the windows. But Leear shook her head when Slade asked if that was to be the way.

She had stopped near a window. "We came," she said, "by means of my silver belt. I've been hoping to run into a storeroom of fliers. If we don't find any, then you are our only hope."

"Me?" Slade was startled.

She said, "Tell me, can you visualize in your mind the wheel machine which you hid in the brush near where you were captured by the hunters of Naze?"

Slade gave her an astounded look. So she had known about that. At last, he said, "I think so."

She persisted, "Including the three bright spots?"

This time he merely nodded, for he was beginning to remember what it could do.

"Then be quick," said Leear. "It's top speed is limited, something under two hundred miles an hour. It will take several minutes to get here."

Slade stared at her, and swallowed hard. But he walked with her to the window, closed his eyes, and pictured the wheel machine. The memory was blurred for a moment, then it came sharp and clear.

Standing beside him, Leear said softly, "Blink slowly, and don't strain to hold the picture of it. Let it wax and wane. All this is unimportant in a way, because, during the next six years, both you and I must learn the natural ways."

That pulled him. That caught at his brain. That tore him from his concentration. He pictured himself as he might be six years hence— it was her gentle, almost hypnotic voice that pressed him back.

"Hold it," she said quickly, "*hold* it! It will sink to Earth if you don't, and there is no time to waste. Any minute now the main barrier machinery will be reached, and then the barrier will go down. After that, even the tough materials of the spire will not stand long."

Her words steadied Slade. Away in the back of his mind was a memory of what Geean had said about bridal finery. An edge of worry shadowed his mind. Because, when you came right down to it, a man did not marry a woman ten thousand years older than himself. Amor, yes. Her failings were human, normal, forgivable. He had a feeling the girl would be willing to become his companion. He would certainly ask her.

He was so intent on the wheel machine that he missed entirely a little byplay beside him. The nith informed Leear of what Slade was thinking. The woman hesitated, then her features began to change. Her face was taking on a startling resemblance to the face of Amor when a fierce thought from the nith arrested the process:

"Don't be a fool," it said sharply. "At the moment he will not take kindly to the idea that you were Amor. You assumed that role in order to give him a sympathetic picture of a girl of Naze. He would have been shocked by the character of a real blood-drinking girl. At the moment he might blame you for the death of Caldra, even though you had gone away expecting that Caldra would try to take blood from him, and so precipitate him back to his own plane.

"Another thing," the nith went on, "I have noticed in your mind that you are responsible for his having been born a three-eyed mutation in a two-eyed world. Do not tell him that immediately either. Let him discover later that you have controlled his life from an early embryo stage. Let him find out later that you can be all woman—"

The woman was hesitating. Abruptly, she became Leear again. She saw the wavering of the purple carrier. She let out a very femininelike squeal. "The barrier," she cried, "it's down."

Her words were like a cue. There was a flash of metallic brightness in the distance. The wheel machine came through the open window, and jerked to a stop in front of Slade's eyes.

"The nith first," said Leear urgently. "Then me, then you. And don't worry. It floats swiftly."

It was almost not swift enough. The last time he brought it towards his eyes the roar of the fire was a hideous sound in his ears. He climbed into the flower-shaped wheel, shoved hard—and hung on.

The sun was a bright glory almost directly overhead. There were many people below, but as Slade drew near to the ground, he could still see no sign of either Leear or the nith. A tall, slim young woman put up her arms towards him, and with a start Slade recognized Amor. He shouted at her, and she waved back, frantically.

He came down presently into a city that was already quaveringly conscious of its destiny.


THE VERDICT OF THE CORONER'S JURY

It is the unanimous decision of the jury that there can be no doubt that the dead body is that of Michael Slade. The unusual clothes cannot be regarded as important, and the jury therefore finds that Michael Slade met his death as a result of a fall from a height, very possibly from an airplane. There is no evidence of foul play or murder.

mouth, a gash in the center of his hideous head, slavered a white frost that floated away in little frozen globules.

His brain couldn't hold the flame of that terrific hope. His mind kept dissolving, blurring. Through that blur, he saw a thick vein of light form a circular bulge in the metallic surface of the ship. The bulge became a huge door that rotated open and tilted to one side. A flood of brilliance spilled out the great opening, followed by a dozen two-legged beings in transparent metal armor, dragging great floating machines.

Swiftly, the machines were concentrated around a dark projection on the ship's surface. Intolerable light flared up as what was obviously repair work proceeded at an alarming pace.

He was no longer falling away from the ship. The faint pressure of gravitational pull was drawing him down again ——so slowly. Frantically, he adjusted his atomic structure to the fullest measure of attraction. But even his poorly responding brain could see that he would never make it.

The work was finished. The incandescent glare of atomic welders died to spluttering darkness. Machines were unclamped, floated toward the opening of the ship, down into it and out of sight. The two-legged beings scrambled after them. The vast, curved plain of metal was suddenly as deserted and lifeless as space itself.

Terror struck into Xtl. He'd have to fight, have to get there somehow. He couldn't let them get away now, when the whole universe was in his grasp—twenty-five short yards away. His letching arms reached out stupidly, as if he would hold the ship by sheer fury of need. His brain ached with a slow, rhythmical hurt. His mind spun toward a black, bottomless pit—then poised just before the final plunge.

The great door was slowing in its swift rotation. A solitary being squeezed through the ring of light and ran to the dark projection, just repaired. He picked up an instrument that gleamed weirdly, a tool of some kind forgotten, and started back toward the partly open lock.

He stopped. In the glow from the portholes, Xtl could see the other's face through the transparent armor. The face stared up at him, eyes wide, mouth open. Then the

mouth moved rapidly, opening and shutting, apparently a
form of communication with the others.

A moment later the door was rotating again, opening
wide. A group of the beings came out, two of them
mounted on the top of a large, metal-barred cage, steering
it under power. He was to be captured.

Oddly, his brain felt no sense of lift, no soaring hope,
none of that mind-inflaming ecstasy. It was as if a drug
was dragging him down, down, into a black night of
fatigue. Appalled, he fought off the enveloping stupor. He
must hold to his senses. His race, that had attained the
very threshold of ultimate knowledge, must live again.

THE VOICE, a strained, unrecognizable voice, came to
Commander Morton through the communicators in his
transparent spacesuit: "How in the name of all the hells
can anything live in intergalactic space?"

It seemed to the commander that the question made the
little group of men crowd closer together. The proximity
of the others made them feel easier. Then they suddenly
grew aware of the impalpable yet *alive* weight of the inconceivable night that coiled about them, pressing down
to the very blazing portholes.

For the first time in years, the immensity of that night
squeezed icily into Morton's consciousness. Long familiarity had bred indifference into his very bones—but now,
the incredible vastness of that blackness reaching a billion trillion years beyond the farthest frontiers of man
stabbed into his mind, and brought an almost dismaying
awareness. His deep voice, clattering into the communicators, split that scared silence like some harsh noise,
startled him:

"Gunlie Lester, here's something for your astronomical-
mathematical brain. Will you please give us the ratio of
the *Beagle* at the exact point in space where that thing was
floating? Take a few hours to work it out."

The astronomer replied immediately: "I don't have to
think about it. The chance is unstatable in human arithme-
tic. It can't happen, mathematically speaking. Here we
are, a shipload of human beings, stopping for repairs halfway between two galaxies—the first time we've ever made
a trip outside of our own galaxy. Here we are, I say, a

90

tiny point intersecting without prearrangement exactly the path of another, tinier point. Impossible, unless space is saturated with such—creatures!"

"I hope not," another man shuddered. "We ought to turn a mobile unit on anything that looks like that, on general principles."

The shudder seemed to run along the communicators. Commander Morton shook his great, lean body as if consciously trying to throw off the chill of it. His eyes on the maneuvering cage above, he said:

"A regular blood-red devil spewed out of some fantastic nightmare; ugly as sin—and probably as harmless as our beautiful pussy last year was deadly. Smith, what do you think?"

The cadaverous-faced biologist said in his cold, logical voice: "This thing has arms and legs, a purely planetary evolution. If it is intelligent it will begin to react to environment the moment it is inside the cage. It may be a venerable old sage, meditating in the silence of distractionless space. Or it may be a young murderer, condemned to eternal exile, consumed with desire to sneak back home and resume the life he lived."

"I wish Korita had come out with us," said Pennons, the chief engineer, in his quiet, practical voice. "Korita's historical analysis of pussy last year gave us an advance idea of what we had to face and—"

"KORITA speaking, Mr. Pennons," came the meticulously clear voice of the Japanese archæologist on the communicators. "Like many of the others, I have been listening to what is happening as a welcome break in this, the longest journey the spaceship *Beagle* has ever undertaken. But I am afraid analysis of the creature would be dangerous at this factless stage. In the case of pussy, we had the barren, foodless planet on which we lived, and the architectural realities of his crumbled city.

"Here we have a creature living in space a million years from the nearest planet, apparently without food, and without means of spatial locomotion. I suggest you make certain that you get him into the cage, and then study him—every action, every reaction. Take pictures of his internal organs working in the vacuum of space. Find out every possible thing about him, so that we shall know what we have aboard as soon as possible. Now, when we are fully staffed again and heading for a new galaxy for the first time in the history of man, we cannot afford to have anything go wrong, or anybody killed before we reach there. Thank you."

"And that," said Morton, "is sense. You've got your fluorite camera, Smith?"

"Attached to my suit," Smith acknowledged.

Morton who knew the capabilities of the mournful-looking biologist turned his attention back to the cage fifty feet away. He said in his deep, resonant voice: "Open the door as wide as possible, and drop over him. Don't let his hands grab the bars."

"Just a minute!" a guttural voice broke in. Morton turned questioningly to the big, plump German physicist. Von Grossen continued: "Let us not rush this capture, Commander Morton. It is true that I was not aboard last year when you had your encounter with the creature you persist in calling pussy. But when you returned to the base planet before embarking on the present voyage, the story you told to the world was not reassuring, not to me, anyway."

His hard, gray-dark face stared grimly at the others: "It is true that I can see no real objection to capturing this creature in a cage. But it happens that I am replacing a man who was killed by this—pussy. Therefore I speak for him when I say: Such a thing must never happen again."

Morton frowned, his face lined wtih doubt. "You put me in a spot, von Grossen. As human beings, we must take every possible precaution. As scientists, however, all is grist for our mill; everything must be investigated. There can be no thought of shunning danger before we even know it to be danger. If this voyage is to be ruled by fear, we might as well head for home now."

"Fear is not what I had in mind," said the physicist quietly. "But I believe in counting ten before acting."

Morton asked. "Any other objections?"

He felt oddly annoyed that there were none.

XTL waited. His thoughts kept breaking up into little

pieces of light and lightless—a chain of dazzle and dark —that somehow connected up with all the things he had ever known or thought. Visions of a long-dead planet trickled into his consciousness bringing a vague conceit— and a contempt of these creatures who thought to capture him.

Why, he could remember a time when his race had had spaceships a hundred times the size of this machine that swam below him. That was before they had dispensed completely with space travel, and just lived a quiet homey life building beauty from natural forces.

He watched, as the cage was driven toward him unerringly. There was nothing he could do, even had he wanted to. The gaping mouth of the large, metal-barred construction closed over him and snapped shut the moment he was inside.

Xtl clawed at the nearest bar, caught hold with grim strength. He clung there an instant, sick and dizzy with awful reaction. Safe! His mind expanded with all the violence of an exploding force. Free electrons discharged in dizzying swarms from the chaos of the spinning atom systems inside his brain and body, frantically seeking union with the other systems. He was safe—safe after quadrillions of years of sick despair, and on a material body with unlimited power to take him where he would to go. Safe when there was still time to carry out his sacred purpose. Or was he safe?

The cage was dropping toward the surface of the ship. His eyes became gleaming pools of caution, as they studied the men below. It was only too evident that he was to be examined. With a tremendous effort, stung by fear, he tried to push the clinging dullness from his brain, fought for alertness. An examination of him now would reveal his purpose, expose the precious objects concealed within his breast; and that must not be.

His steely-bright eyes flicked in anxious dismay over the dozen figures in transparent armor. Then his mind calmed. They were inferior creatures, obviously! Puny foes before his own remarkable power. Their very need of spacesuits proved their inability to adapt themselves to environment, proved they existed on a low plane of evolution. Yet he must not underestimate them. Here

93

were keen brains, capable of creating and using mighty machines.

Each of the beings had weapons in holster at the side of his space armor—weapons with sparkling, translucent handles. He had noticed the same weapons in the holsters of the men at the top of the cage. That, then, would be his method if any of these creatures flashed a camera on him.

As the cage dropped into the belt of undiffused blackness between two portholes, Smith stepped forward with his camera—and Xtl jerked himself with effortless ease up the bars to the ceiling of the cage. The gash of his mouth in the center of his round, smooth head was split in a silent snarl of fury at the unutterable bad luck that was forcing this move upon him. His vision snapped full on; and now he could see blurrily through the hard metal of the ceiling.

One arm, with its eight wirelike fingers, lashed out with indescribable swiftness at the ceiling, *through* it, and then he had a gun from the holster of one of the men.

He did not attempt to readjust its atomic structure as he had adjusted his arm. It was important that they should not guess that it was he who fired the gun. Straining in his awkward position, he aimed the weapon straight at Smith and the little group of men behind him—relased the flaming power.

There was a flare of incandescent violence that blotted the men from view. A swirl of dazzling light coruscated virulently across the surface of the ship. And there was another light, too. A blue sparkle that told of automatic defense screens driving out from the armored suits of the men.

In one continuous movement, Xtl released the gun, withdrew his hand; and, by the act, pushed himself to the floor. His immediate fear was gone. No sensitive camera film could have lived through the blaze of penetrating energy. And what was overwhelmingly more important—the gun was no good against himself. Nothing but a simple affair which employed the method of transmutation of one element to another, the process releasing one or two electrons from each atom system. It

94

would require a dozen such guns to do damage to his body.

THE GROUP of men stood quite still; and Morton knew they were fighting, as he was, the blindness that lingered from the spray of violent light. Slowly, his eyes became adjusted; and then he could see again the curved metal on which he stood, and beyond that the brief, barren crest of the ship and the limitless miles of lightless, heatless space—dark, fathomless, unthinkable gulfs. There too, a blur among the blurs of shadows, stood the cage.

"I'm sorry, commander," one of the men on the cage apologized. "The ato-gun must have fallen out of my belt, and discharged."

"Impossible!" Smith's voice came to Morton, low and tense. "In this gravitation, it would take several minutes to fall from the holster, and it wouldn't discharge in any event from such a slight jar of landing."

"Maybe I knocked against it, sir, without noticing."

"Maybe!" Smith seemed to yield grudgingly to the explanation. "But I could almost swear that, just before the flare of light dazzled me, the creature moved. I admit it was too black to see more than the vaguest blur, but—"

"Smith," Morton said sharply, "what are you trying to prove?"

He saw the long-faced biologist hunch his narrow shoulders, as if pulling himself together. The biologist mumbled: "When you put it like that, I don't know. The truth is, I suppose, that I've never gotten over the way I insisted on keeping pussy alive, with such desperately tragic results. I suspect everything now, and—"

Morton stared in surprise. It was hard to realize that it was really Smith speaking—the scientist who, it had seemed sometimes in the past, was ready to sacrifice his own life and everybody else's if it meant adding a new, important fact to the science of biology. Morton found his voice at last:

"You were perfectly right in what you did! Until we realized the truth, you expressed the majority mind of this ship's company. The development of the situation in the case of pussy changed our opinion as well as your

95

own, but it did not change our method of working by evidence alone. I say that we should continue to make such logic the basis of our work."

"Right. And beg your pardon, chief!" Smith was brisk-voiced again. "Crane, turn the cage light on, and let's see what we've got here."

To MORTON, the silence that followed seemed like a sudden, oppressive weight, as the blaze of light showered down on Xtl crouching at the bottom of the cage. The almost metallic sheen of the cylindrical body, the eyes like coals of fire, the wirelike fingers and toes, the scarlet hideousness of it startled even these men who were accustomed to alien forms of life. He broke the spell of horror, half-breathlessly:

"He's probably very handsome—to himself!"

"If life is evolution," said Smith in a stiff voice, "and nothing evolves except for use, how can a creature living in space have highly developed legs and arms? Its insides should be interesting—*but* now—my camera's useless! That flare of energy wo——*S* have the effect of tinting the electrified lens, and of course the film's ruined. Shall I get another?"

"N-n-no-o!" Morton's clean-cut, handsome face grew dark with a frown. "We've wasted a lot of time here; and after all, we can re-create vacuum of space conditions inside the ship's laboratory, and be traveling at top acceleration while we're doing it."

"Just a minute!" Von Grossen, the plump but hard-boiled physicist, spoke: "Let's get this straight. The *Beagle* is going to another galaxy on an exploration voyage—the first trip of the kind. Our business is to study life in this new system, but we're not taking any specimens, only pictures and notes—studies of the creatures in their various environments. If we're all so nervous about this thing, why are we taking it aboard?"

"Because"—Smith beat Morton to the reply—"we're not tied down to pictures and notes. There will, however, be millions of forms of life on every planet, and we shall be forced to the barest kind of record in most cases. This monster is different. In our fears we have almost forgotten that the existence of a creature capable of living in space is the most extraordinary thing we've ever run across. Even pussy, who could live without air, needed warmth of a kind, and would have found the absolute cold of space intolerable. If, as we suspect, this creature's natural habitat is not space, then we must find out why and how he came to be where he is. Speaking as a biologist—"

"I see," interrupted Morton dryly, "that Smith is himself again." He directed a command at the men on the cage. "Take that monster inside, and put a wall of force around the cage. That should satisfy even the most cautious."

Xtl felt the faint throb of the motors of the cage. He saw the bars move, then grew conscious of a sharp, pleasant tingling sensation, brief physical activity within his body that stopped the workings of his mind for a bare second. Before he could think, there was the cage floor rising above him—and he was lying on the hard surface of the spaceship's outer shell.

With a snarl of black dismay that almost cut his face in two, he realized the truth. He had forgotten to re-adjust the atoms in his body after firing the gun. And now he had fallen through!

"Good Heaven!" Morton bellowed.

A scarlet streak of elongated body, a nightmare shadow in that braid of shadow and light, Xtl darted across the impenetrable heavy metal to the air lock. He jerked himself down into its dazzling depths. His adjusted body dissolved through the two other locks. And then he was at one end of a long, gleaming corridor—safe for the moment!

There would be searching for him: and—he knew with a cold, hardening resolve—these creatures would never trust alive a being who could slip through solid metal. Their reason would tell them he was a superbeing, un-utterably dangerous to them.

One advantage only he had—they did not know the deadliness of his purpose.

TEN MINUTES later, Morton's gray eyes flicked questioningly over the stern faces of the men gathered in the great reception room. His huge and powerful body felt oddly

97

rigid, as if his muscles could not quite relax. His voice was mellower, deeper, richer than normal:

"I am going to offer my resignation on the ground that, for the second time under my leadership, an abnormal beast has gotten aboard this craft. I must assume that there is a basic lack in my mental make-up; for results, and not excuses, do count in this universe of ours; even apparently bad luck is rigorously bound up with character. I, therefore, suggest that Korita or von Grossen be named commander in my place. Korita because of the care he advocated, and von Grossen on the strength of his objection to taking any living specimens aboard—both are more fitted to hold the command than I am."

"The honorable commander has forgotten one thing," Korita said softly. "The creature was *not* carried into the ship. I admit it was our collective intention to bring him aboard, but it was he himself who entered. I suggest that, even if we had decided not to bring him into the interior, we could not have prevented his entry in view of his ability to slip through metal. It is absolutely absurd for Commander Morton to feel responsible."

Von Grossen heaved himself out of his chair. Now that he was out of his spacesuit, the physicist looked not so much plump as big and iron-hard. "And that goes for me all the way. I have not been long on this ship, but I have found Commander Morton to be a most able intellect and leader of men. So let us not waste time in useless self-reproach.

"In capturing this being we must first of all straighten our minds about him. He has arms and legs, this creature, yet floats in space, and remains alive. He allows himself to be caught in a cage, but knows all the time that the cage cannot hold him. Then he drops through the bottom of the cage, which is very silly if he doesn't want us to know that he can do it. Which means that he is a very foolish creature indeed, and we don't have to worry very much about him. There is a reason why intelligent living things make mistakes—a fundamental reason that should make it easy for us to analyze him right back to where he came from, and why he is here. Smith, analyze his biological make-up."

Smith stood up, lank and grim. "We've already discussed the obvious planetary origin of his hands and feet. The ability to live in space, however, is an abnormal development, having no connection with natural evolution, but is the product of brain power and science, pure and simple. I suggest that here is a member of a race that has solved the final secrets of biology; and, if I knew how we should even begin to start looking for a creature that can slip through walls, my advice would be: Hunt him down and kill him within an hour."

"ER!" KELLIE, the sociologist, said. He was a bald-headed man with preternaturally intelligent eyes that gleamed owlishly from behind his pince-nez. "Er, any being who could fit himself to vacuum of space condition would be lord of the universe. His kind would dwell on every planet, clutter up every galactic system. Swarms of him would be floating in space, if space floating is what they go in for. Yet, we know for a fact that his race does not rule *our* galactic area. A paradox, which is worthy of investigation."

"I don't quite understand what you mean, Kellie!" Morton frowned.

"Simply, er, that a race which has solved the final secrets of biology must be millions, even billions of years in advance of man; and, as a pure sympodial—capable of adaptation to any environment—would, according to the lay of vital dynamics, expand to the farthest frontier of the universe, just as man is slowly pushing himself to the remotest planets."

"It is a contradiction," Morton agreed, "and would seem to prove that the creature is not a superior being. Korita, what is this thing's history?"

The Japanese scientist shrugged: "I'm afraid I can only be of the slightest assistance on present evidence. You know the prevailing theory: That life proceeds upwards by a series of cycles. Each cycle begins with the peasant, who is rooted to his bit of soil. The peasant comes to market; and slowly the market place transforms to a town, with ever less 'inward' connection to the earth. Then we have cities and nations, finally the soulless world cities and a devastating struggle for power—a series of frightful

99

wars which sweep men back to the peasant stage. The question becomes: Is this creature in the peasant part of this particular cycle, or in the big city 'megalopolitan' era?"

Morton's voice slashed across the silence: "In view of our limited knowledge of this creature, what basic traits should we look for, supposing him to be in the big city stage?"

"He would be a cold, invincible intellect, formidable to the ultimate degree, undefeatable—except through circumstances. I refer to the kind of circumstances that made it impossible for us to prevent this beast entering our ship. Because of his great innate intelligence, he would make no errors of any kind."

"But he has already made an error!" von Grossen said in a silken voice. "He very foolishly fell through the bottom of the cage. It is the kind of blunder a peasant would make—"

"Suppose," Morton asked, "he were in the peasant stage?"

"Then," Korita replied, "his basic impulses would be much simpler. There would be first of all the desire to reproduce, to have a son, to know that his blood was being carried on. Assuming great fundamental intelligence, this impulse might, in the superior being, take the form of a fanatic drive toward race survival—"

He stopped, as half a dozen men came through the doorway.

Morton said: "Finished, Pennons?"

The chief engineer nodded. Then in a warning voice: "It is absolutely essential that every man on the ship get into his rubberite suit, and wear rubberite gloves."

Morton explained grimly. "We've energized the walls around the bedrooms. There may be some delay in catching this creature, and we're taking no chances of being murdered in our beds. We—" Sharply: "What is it, Pennons?"

Pennons was staring at a small instrument in his hand; he said in a queer voice: "Are we all here, Morton?"

"Yes, except for four men guarding the engine room."

"Then . . . then something's caught in the wall of force. Quick—we must surround it."

To Xtl, returning from a brief exploration of the monster ship's interior, the shock was devastating, the surprise unutterable and complete.

One moment he was thinking complacently of the metal sections in the hold of the ship, where he would secrete his *guuls;* the next moment he was caught in the full sparkling fury of an energy screen.

His body writhed with an agony that blackened his brain. Thick clouds of free electrons rose up within him in that hell of pain, and flashed from system to system seeking union, only to be violently repelled by the tortured, madly spinning atom systems. For those long seconds, the wonderfully balanced instability of his structure nearly collapsed into an abyss of disintegration.

But the incredible genius that had created his marvelous body had forethought even this eventuality. Like lightning, his body endured readjustment after automatic readjustment, each new-built structure carrying the intolerable load for a fraction of a fraction of a second. And then, he had jerked back from the wall, and was safe.

In a flare of thought, his mind investigated the immediate possibilities. Obviously, the men had rigged up this defense wall of force. It meant they would have an alarm system—and they would swoop down every corridor in an organized attempt to corner him.

Xtl's eyes were glowing pools of white fire as he realized the opportunity. He must catch one of these men, while they were scattered, investigate his *guul* properties, and use him for his first *guul.*

No time to waste. He darted into the nearest wall, a tall, gaudy, ungraceful streak, and, without pausing, sped through room after room, roughly parallel to a main corridor. His sensitive feet caught the vibrations of the approaching men; and through the wall his full vision followed the blurred figures rushing past. One, two, three, four—five—on this corridor. The fifth man was some distance behind the others.

Like a wraith, Xtl glided into the wall just ahead of the last man—and pounced forth in an irresistible charge. A rearing, frightful shape of glaring eyes and ghastly mouth, blood-red, metal-hard body, and four arms of fire that clutched with bitter strength at the human body.

101

The man tried to fight. His big form twisted, jerked; his lashing fists felt vaguely painful as they pounded desperately against the hard, sheeny crust of Xtl's body. And then, by sheer weight and ferocity, he was overwhelmed; the force of his fall jarring Xtl's sensitive frame.

The man was lying on his back, and Xtl watched curiously as the mouth opened and shut spasmodically. A tingling sensation sped along Xtl's feet, and his mouth opened in a snarl. Incapable though he was of hearing sounds, he realized that he was picking up the vibrations of a call for help.

He pounced forward, one great hand smashing at the man's mouth. Teeth broke, and crushed back into the throat. The body sagged. But the man was still alive, and conscious, as Xtl plunged two hands into the feebly writhing body.

The man ceased suddenly even that shadow of struggle, his widened eyes staring at the arms that vanished under his shirt, stirred around in his chest, stared in petrified terror at the monstrous blood-red cylindrical body that loomed over him, with its round bright eyes glaring at him as if they would see right through him.

It was a blurred picture the frantic Xtl saw. The inside of the man's body seemed solid flesh. He had to find an open space, or one that could be pressed open, so long as the pressing did not kill the man. He must have living flesh.

Hurry, hurry— His feet registered the vibrations of approaching footsteps—from one direction only, but coming swiftly, swiftly.

And then, just like that, it was all over. His searching fingers, briefly hardened to a state of semisolidity, touched the heart. The man heaved convulsively, shuddered, and slumped into death.

The next instant, Xtl discovered the stomach. For a moment, black dismay flooded him. Here was what he was searching for, and he had killed it, rendered it useless! He stared in cold fury at the stilled body, uncertain, alarmed.

Then suddenly his actions became deliberate, weighted with contempt. Never for an instant had he suspected these

102

intelligent beings would die so easily. It changed, simplified everything. There was no need to be anything more than casually careful in dealing with them.

Two men with drawn ato-guns whipped around the nearest corner, and slid to a halt at the sight of the apparition that snarled at them across the dead body. Then, as they came out of their brief paralysis, Xtl stepped into the nearest wall, a blur of scarlet in that brightly lit corridor, gone on the instant. He felt the fury of the energy rays that tore futilely at the metal behind him.

His plan was quite clear now. He would capture half a dozen men, and make *guuls* of them. Then kill all the others, proceed on to the galactic system toward which the ship was heading, and take control of the first inhabited planet. After that, domination of the entire universe would be a matter of a short time only.

COMMANDER MORTON stood very stiffly there in the gleaming corridor, every muscle in his huge body like a taut wire. Only a dozen men were gathered round the dead body, but the audioscopes were on; nearly two hundred tense men throughout the ship were watching that scene. Morton's voice was only a whisper, but it cut across the silence like a whiplash.

"Well, doctor?"

Dr. Eggert rose up from his kneeling position beside the body, frowning.

"Heart failure."

*"Heart failure!"*

"All right, all right!" The doctor put up his hands as if to defend himself against physical attack. "I know his teeth look as if they've been smashed back into his brain, and I know Darjeeling's heart was perfect, but heart failure is what it looks like to me."

"I can believe it," a man said sourly. "When I came around that corner, and saw that thing, I nearly had heart failure myself."

"We're wasting time!" von Grossen's voice stabbed from behind Morton. "We can beat this fellow, but not by talking about him, and feeling sick every time he makes a move. If I'm next on the list of victims, I want to know that the best damned bunch of scientists in the system are

103

not crying over my fate, but putting their best brains to the job of avenging my death."

"You're right," Smith said. "The trouble with us is, we've been permitting ourselves to feel inferior. He's only been on the ship about an hour but I can see now that some of us are going to get killed. Well, I accept my chance! But let's get organized for combat!"

Morton snapped: "Pennons, here's a problem. We've got about two square miles of wall and floor space in our twenty levels. How long will it take to energize every inch of it?"

The chief engineer stared at him, aghast; then answered swiftly: "I could sweep the ship and probably wreck it completely within an hour. I won't go into details. But uncontrolled energization is absolutely out. It would kill every living thing aboard—"

"Not everything!" von Grossen rejected. "Not the creature. Remember, that damn thing ran into a wall of force. Your instrument, Pennons, registered activity for several seconds. Several seconds! Let me show you what that means. The principle underlying his ability to slip through walls is simple enough. The atoms of his body slide through the empty spaces between the atoms of the walls. There is a basic electronic tension that holds a body together, which would have to be overcome, but apparently his race has solved the difficulty. A wall of force would increase those electronic tensions to a point where the atoms themselves would be emitting free electrons; and, theoretically, that should have a deadly effect on any interfering body. I'll wager he didn't like those few seconds he was in the wall—but the point is, he stood them."

Morton's strong face was hard: "You could feed more energy to those walls, couldn't you, Pennons?"

"N-no!" said Pennons reluctantly. "The walls couldn't stand it. They'd melt."

*"The walls couldn't stand it!"* a man gasped. "Man, man, do you know what you're making this creature out to be?"

Morton saw the consternation that leaped along that line of stern faces. Korita's thin, clear voice cut across that pregnant silence:

"Let us not forget, my honorable friends, that he did blunder into the wall of force, and recoiled in dismay, though apparently without damage to his person. I use the word 'blunder' with discretion. His action proves once again that he does make mistakes which, in turn, shows him to be something less than a superbeing—"

"Suppose," Morton barked, "he's a peasant of his cycle. What would be his chief intellectual characteristic?"

Korita replied almost crisply for one who usually spoke so slowly: "The inability to understand the full power of organization. He will think probably that all he has to fight in order to get control of this ship would be the men who are in it. His most instinctive reasoning would tend to discount the fact that we are part of a vast galactic civilization or organization, and that the spirit of that civilization is fighting in us. The mind of the true peasant is very individualistic, almost anarchic. His desire to re-produce is a form of egoism, to have his own blood particularly carried on. There can be no such thing as a peasant co-operative or organization. But this creature may want to have numbers of beings similar to himself beside him to help him with his fight. But, though there would be a loose union, they would fight as individuals, and not as a group."

"A loose union of those fire-eaters ought to be enough!" a crew member commented acidly. "I . . . a-a-a-a—"

His voice sagged. His lower jaw drooped two inches. His eyes, under Morton's gaze, took on a horribly goggled stare. The commander whipped around with an oath.

XTL STOOD HERE, forbidding specter from a scarlet hell, his eyes pools of blazing alertness. He knew with a vast contempt that he could plunge into the nearest wall before any gun could leap out at him in ravening fury. But he felt himself protected by another fact. These were intelligent beings. They would be more anxious to discover why he had deliberately come out of the wall than to kill him immediately. They might even consider it a friendly move; and, when they discovered differently, it would be too late.

His purpose, which was twofold, was simplicity itself. He had come for his first *guul*. By snatching that *guul* from their very midst, he would demoralize them thoroughly.

Morton felt a curious wave of unreality sweep over him, as he stood just behind von Grossen there in that glittering hallway, facing the tall, thick, cylindrical reality of Xtl. Instinctively, his fingers groped downward toward the sparkling, translucent handle of the ato-gun that protruded from his holster. He stopped himself, and said in a steady voice:

"Don't touch your guns. He can move like a flash; and he wouldn't be here if he thought we could draw on him. I'll take his opinion any day on that point. Besides, we can't risk failure. This may be our only chance!"

He continued in a swift, slightly higher, more urgent tone: "Every man listening in on the audioscopes get above and below and around this corridor. Bring up the heaviest portables, even some of the semiportables and burn the walls down. Cut a clear path all around this area, and have your beams sweep that space at narrow focus. Move!"

"Good boy, Morton!" Pennons' face appeared for an instant on the plate of the audioscope. "We'll be there—if you can stall that hellhound three minutes."

Korita's sibilant voice hissed out of the audioscope: "Morton, take this chance, but do not count on success. Notice that he has appeared once again before we have had time for a discussion. He is rushing us, whether intentionally or accidentally matters not, because the result is that we're on the run, scurrying this way and that, futilely. So far we have not clarified our thoughts. I am convinced the vast resources of this ship can defeat any creature—any single creature—that has ever existed, or that ever will exist, but only if we have time to use them—"

His voice blurred briefly in Morton's ears. Von Grossen had taken a notebook from his pocket, and was sketching rapidly. He tore the sheet loose, and stepped forward, handed it to the creature, who examined it curiously.

Von Grossen stepped back, and began to sketch again on the second page, with a swift deftness. This sheet he handed also the creature, who took one glance at it, and stepped back with a snarl that split his face. His

106

eyes widened to blazing pools; one arm half reached forward toward von Grossen, then paused uncertainly.

"What the devil have you done?" Morton demanded, his voice sounding unnaturally shrill even to himself.

VON GROSSEN took several steps backward, until he stood level with Morton. To the commander's amazement, he was grinning:

"I've just shown him," the German physicist said softly, "how we can defeat him—neutronium alloy, of course and he—"

Too late, Morton stepped forward, instinctively trying to interpose his huge form in front of von Grossen. A blur of red swept by him. Something—a hand moving so fast that it was invisible—struck him a stunning blow, and knocked him spinning against the nearest wall. For an instant, his body threatened to collapse from sheer, dazed weakness. The world went black, then white, then black.

With appalling effort, he fought the weakness aside. The immense reservoir of strength in his magnificent body surged irresistibly forward; his knees stopped wavering, but his vision was still a crazy thing. As through a distorted glass, he saw that the thing was holding von Grossen in two fire-colored arms. The two-hundred-and-ten-pound physicist gave one convulsive heave of dismay; and then seemed to accept the overpowering strength of those thin, hard muscles.

With a bellow, Morton clawed for his gun. And it was then that the maddest thing of all happened. The creature took a running dive, and vanished into the wall, still holding von Grossen. For an instant, it seemed to Morton like a crazy trick of vision. But there was only the smooth gleamingness of the wall, and eleven staring, perspiring men, seven of them with drawn weapons, which they fingered helplessly.

"We're lost!" a man whispered. "If he can adjust our atomic structure, and take us through walls, we can't fight him."

Morton chilled his heart to the dismay he read in that rough semicircle of faces. He said coldly:

"Your report, Pennons?"

There was a brief delay, then the engineer's lean leathery face, drawn with strain and effort, stared into the plate: "Nothing!" he replied succinctly. "Clay, one of my assistants, thinks he saw a flash of scarlet disappearing through a floor, going down. That's a clue of course. It means our search will be narrowed to the lower half of the ship. As for the rest, we were just lining up our units when it happened. You gave us only two minutes. We needed three!"

Morton nodded, his thoughtful mood interrupted by the abrupt realization that his fingers were shaking. With a muttered imprecation, he clenched them, and said icily:

"Korita has given us our cue—organization. The implications of that word must be fully thought out, and coordinated to the knowledge we have of the creature. Von Grossen, of course, has given us our defense—neutronium alloy."

"I don't follow the argument," interjected Zeller, the metallurgist.

It was Smith who explained: "The commander means that only two parts of the ship are composed of that incredibly dense metal, the outer shell and the engine room. If you had been with us when we first captured this creature, you would have noticed that, when the damned thing fell through the floor of the cage, it was stopped short by the hard metal of the ship's crust. The conclusion is obviously that it cannot slip through such metal; and the fact that it ran for the air lock is proof. The wonder is that we didn't think of it before."

Morton barked: "Therefore, to the heart of the ship —the engine room. And we won't go out of there till we've got a plan. Any other way, he'll run us ragged."

"What about von Grossen?" a man ventured.

Morton snapped harshly: "Don't make us think of von Grossen. Do you want us all to go crazy?"

IN THAT vast room of vast machines, the men were dwarfs in *gigantica*. It was a world apart; and Morton, for the first time in years, felt the alien, abnormal tremendousness of it. His nerves jumped at each special burst of unholy blue light that sparkled and coruscated upon the great, glistening sweep of the ceiling. Blue light that was alive, pure energy that no eliminators had ever been able to eliminate, no condensers absorb.

And there was something else that sawed on his nerves now. A sound—imprisoned in the very air! A thin hum of terrifying power, a vague rumble, the faintest, quivering reverberation of an inconceivable flow of energy.

Morton glanced at his watch, and stood up with an explosive sigh of relief. He swept up a small sheaf of notes from a metal desk. The silence of unsmiling men became the deeper, tenser silence of men who fixed him with their eyes. The commander began:

"This is the first breathing spell we've had since that creature came aboard less than—incredible as it may seem —less than two hours ago. I've been glancing through these notes you've given me, and I've divided them into two sections: those that can be discussed while we're putting into effect the purely mechanical plans for cornering the thing—these latter must be discussed now. There are two. First, Zeller!"

The metallurgist stepped forward, a brisk, middle-aged, young-looking man. He started: "The creature made no attempt to keep the drawings which von Grossen showed it—proof, incidentally, that von Grossen was not seized because of the drawings. They fell on the floor; and I picked them up. I've been showing them around, so most of you know that the first drawing is a likeness of the creature stepping through a metal wall; and beside the wall is an enlarged atom system of the type of which the wall is composed—two hundred electrons arranged about the nucleus, forming a series of triangles.

"The second picture was a rough, unfinished but unmistakable single atom of neutronium alloy, with only eight hundred of the forty thousand electrons showing, but the design of each eighty electrons with their sixteen sides clearly indicated. That kind of language is intergalactic; and the creature understood the point instantly. He didn't like it, as we all saw by his actions; but apparently he had no intention of being thwarted; and perhaps saw the difficulty we might have in using such knowledge against him. Because, just as we cannot energize the walls of the whole ship—Pennons has said it would take days—so we have no materials to plate the ship throughout with neutronium alloy. The stuff is too rare.

"However, we have enough for me to build a suit of space armor, with which one of us could search for von Grossen, whom the thing is obviously hiding behind some wall. For the search, naturally, we'd use a fluorite camera. My assistant is already working out the suit, but we'd like suggestions—"

There were none; and, after a moment, Zeller disappeared into the machine shops adjoining the engine room. Morton's grim face relaxed slightly.

"For myself, I feel better knowing that, once the suit is built—in about an hour—the creature will have to keep moving von Grossen in order to prevent us from discovering the body. It's good to know that there's a chance of getting back one of the boldest minds aboard the ship."

"How do you know he's alive?" a man asked.

"Because the creature could have taken Darjeeling's dead body, but didn't. He wants us alive—Smith's notes have given us a possible clue to his purpose, but let that go now. Pennons, outline the plan you have—this is our main plan, gentlemen; and we stand or fall by it."

THE chief engineer came forward; and it worried Morton to note that he was frowning blackly. His usually dynamic body lacked briskness and suggested uncertainty. The implications of the lack of confidence were mind-shaking. The mechanical wizard, the man who knew more about energy and its practical application that any other living human being—this man unsure of himself—

His voice added to Morton's dismay. It held a harsh, nasal tone that the commander had never heard from him in all the years he had known the man.

"My news isn't pleasant. To energize this ship under a controlled system would require about a hundred hours. There are approximately two square miles of floors and walls, mostly walls. And of course, as I said before, uncontrolled energization would be suicide.

"My plan is to energize the seventh level and the ninth, only the floors and not the walls. Our hope is this: so far the creature has made no organized attempt to kill us.

110

Korita says that this is because he is a peasant, and does not fully realize the issues at stake. As a peasant he is more concerned with reproduction, though what form that is taking, and why he has captured von Grossen is a matter for our biologist. We know, as apparently he does not, that it's a case of destroy him, or he'll destroy us. Sooner or later, even a peasant will realize that killing us comes first, before anything else, and from that moment we're lost. Our chance is that he'll delay too long—a vague chance, but we must accept it because it is based on the only analysis of the creature that we have—Korita's! If he doesn't interfere with our work, then we'll trap him on the eighth level, between the two energized floors."

Somebody interjected with a swift question: "Why not energize the seventh and eighth levels, so that he'll be in hell the moment he starts down?"

"Because"—Pennons' eyes glittered with a hard, unpleasant light—"when he starts down, he'll have one of us with him. We want that man to have a chance for life. The whole plan is packed with danger. It will take about an hour and a half to prepare the floors for energizing."

His voice became a harsh, grating sound: "And during that ninety minutes we'll be absolutely helpless against him, except for our heavy service guns. It is not beyond the bounds of possibility that he will carry us off at the rate of one every three minutes."

"Thirty out of a hundred and eighty!" Morton cut in with a chill incisiveness. "One out of every six in this room. Do we take the chance? Those in favor raise their hands."

He noted with intense satisfaction that not one man's hand but was raised.

THE REAPPEARANCE of the men brought Xtl up to the seventh level with a rush. A vague anxiety pushed into his consciousness, but there was no real sense of doubt, not even a shadow of the mental sluggishness that had afflicted him at first. For long minutes, he was an abnormal shape that flitted like some evil monster from a forgotten hell through that wilderness of walls and corridors.

111

Twice he was seen; and ugly guns flashed at him—guns as different from the simple action ato-guns as life from death. He analyzed them from their effects, the way they smashed down the walls, and made hard metal run like water. Heavy duty electronic guns these, discharging completely disintegrated atoms, a stream of pure electrons that sought union with stable matter in a coruscating fury of senseless desire.

He could face guns like that, but only for the barest second would the spinning atom system within his body carry that intolerable load. Even the biologists, who had perfected the Xtl race, had found their limitations in the hot, ravening energy of smashed atoms.

The important thing was: "What were the men doing with such determination? Obviously, when they shut themselves up in the impregnable engine room, they had conceived a plan—" With glittering, unwinking eyes, Xtl watched that plan take form.

In every corridor, men slaved over atomic furnaces, squat things of dead-black metal. From a hole in the top of each furnace, a while glare spewed up, blazing forth in uncontrollable ferocity at the ceilings; intolerable flares of living fire, dazzling almost beyond endurance to Xtl protected by a solid metal wall as well as by his superlatively conditioned body.

He could see that the men were half dazed by the devastating whiteness that beat against their vision. They wore their space armor with the ordinary transparent glassite electrically darkened. But no light metal armor could ward off the full effect of the deadly rays that sprayed, violent and untamed, in every direction.

Out of the furnaces rolled long dully glowing strips of some material, which were instantly snatched into the maw of machine tools, skillfully hacked into exactly measured sections, and slapped onto the floors. Not an inch of floor, Xtl noticed, escaped being inclosed in some way or another by these strips. And the moment the strips were laid, massive refrigerators hugged close to them, and froze the heat out of them.

His mind refused at first to accept the result of his observations. His brain persisted in searching for deeper purposes, for a cunning of vast and not easily discernible scope. Somewhere there must be a scheme that would explain the appalling effort the men were making. Slowly, he realized the truth.

There was nothing more. These beings were actually intending to attempt the building of walls of force throughout the entire ship under a strict system of controls—anything less, of course, was out of the question. They could not be so foolish as to think that a partial energization could have the faintest hope of success. If such hope smoldered, it was doomed to be snuffed out.

And total energization was equally impossible. Could they not realize that he would not permit such a thing; and that it would be a simple matter to follow them about, and tear loose their energization connections?

IN COLD CONTEMPT, Xtl dismissed the machinations of the men from his mind. They were only playing into his hands, making it easier for him to get the *guuls* he still needed.

He selected his next victim as carefully as he had selected von Grossen. He had discovered in the dead man—Darjeeling—that the stomach was the place he wanted; and the men with the largest stomachs were automatically on his list.

The action was simplicity itself. A cold, merciless survey of the situation from the safety of a wall, a deadly swift rush and—before a single beam could blaze out in sullen rage—he was gone with the writhing, struggling body.

It was simple to adjust his atomic structure the instant he was through a ceiling, and so break his fall on the floor beneath; then dissolve through the floor onto the level below in the same fashion. Into the vast hold of the ship, he half fell, half lowered himself.

The hold was familiar territory now to the sure-footed tread of his long-toed feet. He had explored the place briefly but thoroughly after he first boarded the ship. And the handling of von Grossen had given him the exact experience he needed for this man.

Unerringly, he headed across the dimly lit interior toward the far wall. Great packing cases piled up to the ceiling. Without pause, he leaped into them; and, by dexterous adjustment of his structure, found himself after

113

a moment in a great pipe, big enough for him to stand upright—part of the miles of air-conditioning pipes in the vast ship.

It was dark by ordinary light, but to his full vision a vague twilight glow suffused the place. He saw the body of von Grossen, and deposited his new victim beside the physicist. Carefully now, he inserted one of his slender hands into his own breast; and removed one precious egg —deposited it into the stomach of the human being.

The man had ceased struggling, but Xtl waited for what he knew must happen. Slowly, the body began to stiffen, the muscles growing rigid. The man stirred; then, in evident panic, began to fight as he realized the paralysis that was stealing over him. But remorselessly Xtl held him down.

Abruptly, the chemical action was completed. The man lay motionless, every muscle stiff as a rock, a horrible thing of taut flesh.

There were no doubts now in Xtl's mind. Within a few hours, the eggs would be hatching inside each man's stomach; and in a few hours more the tiny replicas of himself would have eaten themselves to full size.

Grimly complacent, he darted up out of the hold. He needed more hatching places for his eggs, more *guuls*.

ON THE ninth level now, the men slaved. Waves of heat rolled along the corridor, a veritable inferno wind; even the refrigeration unit in each spacesuit was hard put to handle that furious, that deadly blast of superheated air. Men sweated in their suits, sick from the heat, dazed by the glare, laboring almost by instinct.

At last, Morton shut off his own furnace. "Thank Heaven, that's finished!" he exclaimed; then urgently: "Pennons, are you ready to put your plan into effect?"

"Ready, aye, ready!" came the engineer's dry rasp of a voice on the communicators. He finished even more harshly: "Four men gone and one to go. We've been lucky—but there is one to go!"

"Do you hear that, you spacehounds!" Morton barked. "One to go. One of us will be bait—and don't hold your guns in your hands. He must have the chance at that bait. Kellie, elaborate on those notes you gave me before.

114

It will clear up something very important, and keep our minds off that damned thing."

"Er!" The cracked voice of the sociologist jarred the communicators. "Er, here is my reasoning. When we discovered the thing it was floating a million light-years from the nearest system, apparently without means of spatial locomotion. Picture that appalling distance, and then ask yourself how long it would require for an object to float by it by pure chance. Gunlie Lester gave me my figures, so I wish he would tell you what he told me."

"Gunlie Lester speaking!" The voice of the astronomer sounded surprisingly brisk. "Most of you know the prevailing theory of the beginnings of the present universe: that it was formed by the disintegration of a *previous* universe several million million years ago, and that a few million million years hence our universe will complete its cycle in a torrent of explosions, and be replaced by another, which will develop from the maelstrom. As for Kellie's question, it is not at all impossible; in fact, it would require several million million years for a creature floating by pure chance to reach a point a million light-years from a planet. That is what you wanted, Kellie?"

"Er, yes. Most of you will recall my mentioning before that it was a paradox that a pure sympodial development, such as this creature, did not populate the entire universe. The answer is that, logically, if his race *should* have controlled the universe, then they *did* control it. We human beings have discovered that logic is the sole stable factor in the all; and we cannot shrink even from the most far-reaching conclusions that the mind may arrive at. This race did control the universe, but it was the previous universe they ruled, not our present one. Now, naturally, the creature intends that his race shall also dominate this universe."

"In short," Morton snapped, "we are faced with the survivor of the supreme race of a universe. There is no reason to assume that they did not arrive at our present level of progress any later than we did; and we've still got several million million years to go before our universe crashes into flaming death. Therefore, they are not only billions of years ahead of us, but millions of millions of years." His voice took on a strained note: "Frankly, it scares me. We're not doing enough. Our plans are too sketchy. We must have more information before we can hope to win against such a super-human monster. I'm very much afraid that—"

The shrill scream of a man protruded horribly into his words, and there came a gurgling "——got me . . . quick . . . ripping me out of my suit—"

The voice collapsed; and somebody shouted in frank dismay: "Good Heaven! That was Dack, my assistant!"

THE WORLD of ship became, for Morton, a long, shining corridor that persisted in blurring before his eyes. And it was suddenly as if he were looking, not out at it, but down into its depths—fearsome depths that made his brain reel.

Ages seemed to pass. But Morton, schooled now to abnormal calm, knew that only fractions of seconds were dragging by. Just as his nerves threatened to break, he heard a voice, Pennons' voice, cool, steady, yet almost unrecognizable:

"One!" said Pennons; and it sounded absolute mumbo-jumbo in that moment when out there another man was going through a hell of fear and torment.

"Two!" said Pennons, cold as ice.

Morton found himself staring curiously at his feet. Sparkling, brilliant, beautiful blue fire throbbed there. Little tendrils of that gorgeous flame reared up hungrily a few inches from his suit, as if baffled by some invisible force protecting the suit.

There was a distinct click in Morton's mind. Instantly, his brain jumped to full fear. In a flash of thought, he realized that Pennons had energized floors seven and nine. And that it was blue ferocity of the energization that was struggling to break through the full-driven screens of his space armor.

Through his communicators came the engineer's hiss of indrawn breath: "If I'm right," Pennons almost whispered, all the strength gone from his voice, "we've now got that —devil—cornered on the eighth floor."

"Then," barked Morton efficiently, "we'll carry on according to plan. Group one, follow me to the seventh floor."

116

The men behind Morton stopped short as he halted abruptly at the second corner. Sickly, he went forward, and stood staring at the human body that sagged against the floor, pasted to the metal by almost unbearably brilliant fingers of blue fire. His voice, when he spoke, was only a whisper, but it cut across the strain of silence like a whiplash:

"Pull him loose!"

Two men stepped gingerly forward, and touched the body. The blue fire leaped ravenously at them, straining with futile ferocity to break through the full-driven defense screens of their suits. The men jerked, and the unholy bonds snapped. They carried the body up the nearest stairs to the unenergized eighth level. The other men followed silently, and watched as the body was laid on the floor.

The lifeless thing continued to kick for several minutes, discharging torrents of energy, then gradually took on the quietness of natural death.

"I'm waiting for reports!" Morton said stiffly into his communicators.

Pennons' voice came. "The men are spread out over the eighth floor according to plan, taking continuous pictures with fluorite cameras. If he's anywhere on the floor, we'll get a picture of his swift-moving body; and then it will be a matter of energizing the floor piecemeal. It'll take about thirty minutes yet—"

And finally the report came: "Nothing!" Pennons' voice held an incredulous note tinged with dismay. "Morton, he's not here. It can only mean that he passed through the energized floor as easily as through ordinary metal. We know he must have gone through it because Dack's dead body was on *this* side."

Somebody said hopelessly: "And now what are we going to do?"

Morton didn't answer. It struck him abruptly, with a shock that tore away his breath, that he had no answer.

THE SILENCE in that shining corridor was a form of death. It pressed against Morton, a queer, murky, lightless thing. Death was written too in the faces that blurred

117

around him, the cold, logical death expectancy of men who could see no way out.

Morton broke the silence: "I am willing to accept von-Grossen's analysis of how the thing passes through metal. But he intimated the creature recoiled from the energized wall. Can anyone explain then—how?"

"Zeller speaking!" The brisk voice of the metallurgist came through the communicators. "I've finished the neutronium-alloy suit, and I've started my search at the bottom of the ship—I heard your question, Morton. To my mind, we missed one point the first time the creature struck the wall of force: The point is that he *was* in it. And what basic difference is there between being partially inside the wall, and actually passing through? He could pass through in less than a second. The first time, he touched the wall for several seconds, which probably means that, in his surprise, he recoiled and lost his balance. That must have made his position very unpleasant. The second time, however, he simply released poor Dack and passed on through with a minimum of discomfort."

"Hm-m-m!" Morton pondered. "That means he's still vulnerable to walls of force, provided we could keep him inside one for a long enough time. And that would mean complete energization of the ship which, in turn, would depend on his allowing us to make the connections without interference. I think he would interfere. He let us get away with energizing the two floors because he knew it didn't mean anything—and it gave him a good opportunity to kidnap some more men. Fortunately, he didn't grab off as many as we expected, though Heaven help those four."

Smith said grimly, his first words in a long time: "My firm opinion is that anything that would require more than two hours to complete will be fatal. We are dealing with a creature who has everything to gain by killing us, and obtaining control of the ship. Zeller, how long would it take to build neutronium-alloy suits for every man on this ship?"

"About two hundred hours," the metallurgist replied coolly, "mainly because I used up nearly all the available alloy for this one suit. We'd have to break down the

118

walls of the ship, and build the alloy from an electronic base. We're not in the habit of carrying a lot of metal on this ship, as you know, because there's usually a planet a few minutes from anywhere. Now, we've still got a two week's trip either way."

"Then that's out!" frowned Smith blackly. He looked stunned. "And since the complete energization is out—we've got nothing else."

The usually lazy voice of Gourlay, the communications chief, snapped: "I don't see why those ways are out. We're still alive; and I suggest we get to work, and do as much as we can as soon as we can—everybody working first at making suits for the men who go out to prepare the walls for energizing. At least, that will protect them from being kidnaped."

"What makes you think," Smith asked coldly, "that the creature is not capable of smashing down neutronium alloy? As a superior being, his knowledge of physics should make it a simple matter for him to construct a beam that could destroy anything we have. Heaven knows there's plenty of tools lying in the various laboratories."

THE TWO MEN glared at each other with the flashing, angry eyes of men whose nerves have been strained to the utmost limit. Before Morton could speak, Korita's sibilant voice cut across the tense silence: "I am inclined to agree with Smith. We are dealing with a being who must now know that he cannot allow us time for anything important. I agree with the commander when he says that the creature will interfere if we attempt to prepare the ship for complete controlled energization. The honorable gentlemen must not forget, however, that we are dealing with a creature whom we have decided is in the peasant stage of his particular cycle.

"Let me enlarge on that. Life is an ebb and flow. There is a full tide of glorious accomplishment, and a low tide of recuperation. For generations, centuries, the blood flows in the peasant, turgid, impure, gathering strength from the soil; and then it begins to grow, to expand, reaching finally for the remotest stars. At this point, amazingly enough, the blood grows weary; and, in this late megapolitan era, men no longer desire to prolong their race. Highly cultivated people regard having children as a question of pros and cons, and their general outlook on life is tinged with a noble skepticism.

"Nature, on the other hand, knows nothing of pro and con. You cannot reason with a peasant—and he cannot reason except as a peasant. His land and his son, or—to put a higher term to it—his property and his blood are sacred. If a bourgeoisie court orders him off his land, he fights blindly, ignorantly, for his own. It matters not to him that he may have accepted money for a mortgage. He only knows they're trying to take his property, to draw his roots from the soil where his blood has been nourished.

"Honorable sirs, here is my point: This creature cannot begin to imagine anyone else not feeling about his patch of home—his own property the way he does.

"But we . . . we can make such a sacrifice without suffering a spiritual collapse."

Every muscle in Morton's body grew taut, as he realized the implications. His exclamation was almost a whisper: "Korita, you've got it! It means sacrificing von Grossen and the others. It means sacrifice that makes my brain reel, but property is not sacred to us. And as for von Grossen and the other three"—his voice grew stern and hard, his eyes wide with a chill horror—"I didn't tell you about the notes that Smith gave me. I didn't tell you because he suggested a possible parallel with a certain species of wasp back home on the earth. The thought is so horrible that I think instantaneous death will come as a release to these bold men."

"The wasp!" A man gasped. "You're right, Morton. The sooner they're dead the better!"

"Then," Morton cried, "to the engine room. We—"

A swift, excited voice clamored into his communicators; it was a long second before he recognized it as belonging to Zeller, the metallurgist:

"Morton—quick! Down to the hold! I've found them—in the air-conditioning pipe. The creature's here, and I'm holding him off as best I can. He's trying to sneak upon me through the walls. Hurry!"

Morton snapped orders with machine-gun precision,

120

as the men swarmed toward the elevators: "Smith, take a dozen men and get Kent down from the bedrooms to the engine room. I'd almost forgotten about him and his broken leg! Pennons, take a hundred men to the engine room and make the preparations to carry out Korita's plan. The rest take the four heavy freight elevators and follow me!"

He finished in a ringing voice: "We won't kill him in the hold of course, unless he's gone stark mad. But the crisis has come! Things are breaking our way at last. And we've got him! We've got him!"

XTL retreated reluctantly, sullenly, as the men carried off his four *guuls*. The first shrinking fear of defeat closed over his mind like the night that brooded beyond the inclosing walls of the ship. His impulse was to dash into their midst, a whirlwind of ferocity, and smash them. But those ugly, glittering weapons congealed that wild rage.

He retreated with a dismaying sense of disaster, conscious that he had lost the initiative. The men would discover his eggs now; and, in destroying them, would destroy his immediate chances of being reinforced by other Xtls. And, what was more, they were temporarily safe in the engine room.

His brain spun into a cold web of purpose. From this moment, he must kill, and kill only. It seemed suddenly incredible that he had thought first of reproduction, with everything else coming secondary, even his every other thought blurred by that subordination to his one flaming desire.

His proper action was preternaturally clear now. Not to get his *guuls* first, but to kill these dangerous enemies, to control the ship, then head for the nearest inhabited planet, where it would be a simple matter to find other, more stupid *guuls*.

To kill he must have an irresistible weapon, one that could smash—anything! And valuable time had already been wasted. After a moment's thought, he headed for the nearest laboratory, conscious of a burning urgency, unlike anything he had ever known.

As he worked—tall, nightmare body and hideous face bent intently over the gleaming metal of the queer-shaped mechanism—his sensitive feet grew aware of a difference in the symphony of vibrations that throbbed in discordant melody through the ship.

He paused, straightened, alert and tense; and realized what it was. The drive engines were silent. The monster ship of space had halted in its head-long flight, and was lying quiescent in the black deeps.

An abrupt, indefinable sense of urgency came to Xtl —an icy alarm. His long, black, wirelike fingers became flashing things as he made delicate connections, deftly and frantically.

Suddenly, he paused again. Through his brain pulsed a distinct sensation of something wrong, dangerously, desperately, terribly wrong. The muscles of his feet grew taut with straining. Abruptly, he knew what it was.

He could no longer feel the vibrations of the men. *They had left the ship!*

Xtl whirled from his nearly finished weapon, and plunged through the nearest wall. He knew his doom with a burning certainty that found hope only in the blackness of space.

Through deserted corridors he fled, slavering slit-faced hate, scarlet monster from ancient, incredibly ancient Glor. The gleaming walls seemed to mock him. The whole world of the great ship, which had promised so much, was now only the place where sudden intolerable hell would break loose in a devastating, irresistible torrent of energy.

He saw the air lock ahead—and flashed through the first section, then the second, the third—then he was out in space. There was a sense of increasing lightness as his body flung by momentum darted from the side of the ship, out into that blackest of black nights.

For a brief instant, his body glinted and flashed a startling scarlet, reflecting the dazzling light from the row on row of brilliant portholes.

The queerest thing happened then. The porthole lights snuffed out, and were replaced by a strange, unearthly blue glow, that flashed out from every square inch of that dark, sweeping plain of metal.

The blue glow faded, died. Some of the porthole lights came on again, flickering weakly, uncertainly; and then, as mighty engines recovered from that devastating flare of blue power, the lights already shining grew stronger. Others began to flash on.

Xtl was a hundred yards from the ship when he saw the first of the torpedolike craft dart out of the surrounding night, into an opening that yawned in the side of the mighty vessel. Four other dark craft followed, whipping down in swift arcs, their shapes blurred against the background of immensity, vaguely visible in the light that glowed now, strong and steady from the lighted portholes.

The opening shut; and—just like that—the ship vanished. One instant, it was there, a vast sphere of dark metal; the next he was staring through the space where it had been at a vague swirl of light, an enormous galaxy that swam beyond a gulf of a billion years.

Time dragged drearily toward infinity. Xtl sprawled moveless and unutterably hopeless on the bosom of endless night. He couldn't help thinking of the sturdy sons he might have had, and of the universe that was lost because of his mistakes. But it was the thought of the sons, of companionship, that really brought despair.

MORTON watched the skillful fingers of the surgeon, as the electrified knife cut into the fourth man's stomach. The last egg was deposited in the bottom of the tall neutronium alloy vat.

The eggs were round, grayish objects, one of them slightly cracked.

As they watched, the crack widened; an ugly, round, scarlet head with tiny, beady eyes and a tiny slit of a mouth poked out. The head twisted on its short neck, and the eyes glittered up at them with a hard ferocity.

And then, with a swiftness that almost took them by surprise, it reared up and tried to run out of the vat, slid back—and dissolved into the flame that Morton poured down upon it.

Smith, licking his dry lips, said: "Suppose he'd got away, and dissolved into the nearest wall!"

Nobody said anything. They stood with intent eyes, staring into the vat. The eggs melted reluctantly, under the merciless fire of Morton's gun, and then burned with a queer, golden light.

"Ah," said Dr. Eggert; and attention turned to him, and the body of von Grossen, over which he was bending- "His muscles are beginning to relax, and his eyes are open and alive. I imagine he knows what's going on. It was a form of paralysis induced by the egg, and fading now that the egg is no longer present. Nothing fundamentally wrong. They'll all be O. K. shortly. What about the big fellow?"

Morton replied: "Zeller swears he saw a flash of red emerge from the main lock just as we swept the ship with uncontrolled energization. It must have been, because we haven't found his body. However, Pennons is out with half the men, taking pictures with fluorite cameras; and we'll know for certain in a few hours. Here he is now. Well, Pennons?"

The engineer strode in briskly, and placed a misshapen thing of metal on one of the tables. "Nothing definite to report yet—but I found this in the main physics laboratory. What do you make of it?"

Morton frowned down at the fragile-looking object with its intricate network of wires. There were three distinct tubes that might have been muzzles running into and through three small, round balls, that shone with a queer, silvery light. The light penetrated the table, making it as transparent as glassite. And, strangest of all, the balls irradiated, not heat, but cold.

Morton put his hand near, but the cold was of a mild, water-freezing variety, apparently harmless. He touched the metal ball. It felt as chilled metal might feel.

"I think we'd better leave this for our chief physicist to examine. Von Grossen ought to be up and around soon. You say you found it in the laboratory?"

Pennons nodded; and Morton carried on his thought: "Obviously, the creature was working on it, when he suspected that something was amiss—he must have suspected the truth, for he left the ship. That seems to discount your theory, Korita. You said that, as a true

124

peasant, he couldn't even imagine what we were going to do."

The Japanese historian smiled faintly through the fatigue that paled his face. "Honorable commander," he said politely, "a peasant can realize destructive intentions as easily as you or I. What he cannot do is bring himself to destroy his own property, or imagine others destroying theirs. We have no such limitations."

Pennons groaned: "I wish we had. Do you know that it will take us three months at least to get this ship properly repaired after thirty seconds of uncontrolled energization. For those thirty seconds, the ship created a field in space millions of times more intense than the energization output. I was afraid that—"

He stopped with a guilty look. Morton grinned: "Go ahead and finish what you were going to say. You were afraid the ship would be completely destroyed. Don't worry, Pennons, your previous statements as to the danger involved made us realize the risks we were taking; and we knew that our lifeboats could only be given partial antiacceleration; so we'd have been stranded here a million years from home."

A man said, thoughtfully: "Well, personally, I think there was nothing actually to fear. After all, he did belong to another universe, and there is a special rhythm to our present state of existence to which man is probably attuned. We have the advantage in this universe of momentum, which, I doubt, a creature from any other universe could hope to overcome. And in the world of man there is no just place for a creature that can even consider laying its eggs in the living flesh of other sensitive beings. All other intelligent life would unite against such a distinctly personal menace."

Smith shook his head. "There is no biological basis for your opinion, and therefore it falls in the category of 'things darkly spoken are darkly seen.' It dominated once, and it could dominate again. You assume far too readily that man is a paragon of justice, forgetting apparently that he lives on meat, enslaves his neighbors, murders his opponents, and obtains the most unholy sadistical joy from the agony of others. It is not impossible that we shall, in

125

the course of our travels, meet other intelligent creatures far more worthy than man to rule the universe."

"By Heaven!" replied the other, "no creature is ever getting on board this ship again, no matter how harmless he looks. My nerves are all shot; and I'm not so good a man as I was when I first came aboard the *Beagle* two long years ago."

"You speak for us all!" said Morton.

# M 33 IN ANDROMEDA

The night whispered, the immense night of space that pressed against the hurtling ship. Voiceless susurration it was, yet somehow coherent, alive, deadly.

For it called, it beckoned and it warned. It trilled with a nameless happiness, then hissed with savage, unthinkable frustration.

It feared and it hungered. How it hungered! It died— and reveled in its death. And died again. It whispered of inconceivable things, wordless, all-enveloping, muttering flow, tremendous articulate, threatening night.

"This is an opinion," said somebody behind Morton. "The ship ought to go back home."

Commander Morton did not turn from the eyepiece of the telescope through which he was peering. But he found himself waiting for others of the score of men in the control room, to echo the empirical statement of him who had already spoken.

There was only silence. Very slowly, then, Morton forgot the spectators, and concentrated on the night ahead, from which the disturbing sibilation was coming, stronger with each passing minute.

Lights were out there, a great swirl of them, an entire galactic system. Lights still so far away that the electronic telescope could only brighten, could not begin

127

to enlarge the needle-sharp points of brilliance that made up the myriad units of the wheel-shaped universe.

Morton grew conscious of Gunlie Lester turning away from the other eyepiece; the astronomer said in a blank tone:

"Nothing, absolutely nothing. Basically, that system of stars looks no different from our own great galaxy. The thing is incredible. Vibrations almost palpably strong, overflowing the entire space-time continuum of a galaxy with two billion suns."

He stopped, finished more quietly: "Commander, it seems to me this is not a problem for an astronomer."

Morton released his own eyepiece, said grimly: "Anything that embraces an entire galaxy comes under the category of astronomical phenomena. Or would you care to name the science that is involved?"

Gunlie Lester said nothing; and Morton turned toward the men who sat in the cluster of seats alongside the chromatic splendor that was the control board. He said:

"Someone suggested a few seconds ago that we turn around and go home. I would like whoever did so to give their reasons."

There was no reply; and, after a little, that was astounding. Morton frowned at the very idea that there was anyone aboard unwilling to acknowledge an opinion however briefly held, however quickly discarded.

He saw that the others were looking at him; and several of the faces had startled expressions on them. It was the long, thin, bony Smith who said finally, diffidently:

"When was this statement uttered, chief? I don't recall hearing it."

"Nor I!" echoed half a dozen voices.

"Eh!" said Morton sharply. Abruptly, he was tense, alert; his great shoulders squared; his eyes narrowed to steel-gray pin points. His voice rapped across the silence:

"Let me get this straight. There was such a statement, or there wasn't. Who else heard it? Raise hands."

Not a hand came up; and Morton held himself stiff as a board, said tautly:

"The words spoken were, as I remember them: 'This is an opinion. The ship should go home.' Notice the unusual, the almost formal phrasing. There is suggestion

128

YEAR'S MOST EXCITING SC

# YOURS FOR ONLY 10¢

with trial membership

1,000
• HE
AND
CLA
WYN

A TREASURY OF GREAT SCIENCE FICTION

EDITED BY ANTHONY BOUCHER

John Wyndham
Richard Deming
Ray Bradbury
Robert A. Heinlein
Philip K. Dick
Henry Kuttner
C. L. Moore
C. M. Kornbluth
Theodore Sturgeon
George P. Elliott
Joel Townsley Rogers
Poul Anderson
A. E. van Vogt

VOLUME 1

DOUBLEDAY

VOLUME 2

WORTH
$5.95
IN ORIGINAL
PUBLISHER'S
EDITION.

•

2 GIANT VOLUMES

•

OVER 1,000
FULL-SIZE
5½ x 8½ PAGES

•

HARD-COVER
BINDING
WITH JACKET

*CIENCE FICTION FIND*

# A TREASURY OF GREAT SCIENCE FICTION

PAGES OF VAN VOGT
INLEIN · BRADBURY ·
ERSON · STURGEON ·
RKE · KORNBLUTH ·
NDHAM...and others

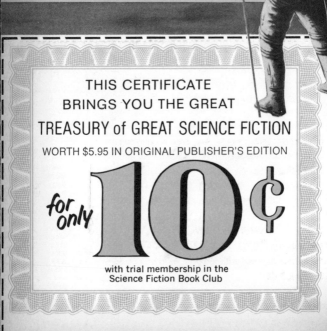

THIS CERTIFICATE
BRINGS YOU THE GREAT
TREASURY of GREAT SCIENCE FICTION

WORTH $5.95 IN ORIGINAL PUBLISHER'S EDITION

for only **10¢**

with trial membership in the
Science Fiction Book Club

in that wording of something alien striving to be casually human.

"I admit," he went on, "that is a great deal to educe from such small evidence, but in moments of crisis quick opinions are better than none at all."

His gaze, steady and cold, swept the thoughtful faces before him. He finished quietly:

"I think, gentlemen, we had better face the fact that we have entered somebody else's stamping ground. And it's SOME somebody."

There was silence in the control room. But Morton noted with satisfaction that it was a silence of tight-lipped tensing against danger. He said softly:

"I am glad to see that no one is even looking as if we ought to turn back. That is all to the good. As servants of our government and our race, it is our duty to investigate the potentialities of a new galaxy, particularly now that the dominating power in the new system knows *we* exist. Its ability to project a thought into my mind indicates that it has already observed us, and, therefore, knows a great deal about us. We cannot permit that type of knowledge to be one-sided."

He finished on a harder tone: "I should say we were very wise indeed to spend seven months in the space between our galaxy and this one repairing the damage caused by that scarlet beast. There was some suggestion, I believe, of heading for a planet, and doing our fixing up in more congenial surroundings. In our wisdom, we played safe—But now, Kellie, as our sociologist, what do you think of the environment we're heading into?"

His gray gaze fixed on the bald-headed man, who adjusted his pince-nez, and said:

"That's a large order, commander. But I would say we are merely entering a civilized galaxy, and these whispers are simply the outward signs like coming out of a wilderness into an area under cultivation."

"*Some* cultivation," said Smith in a mournful tone. He hunched his long, bony body back into his seat. "Beg your pardon. As a biologist, I haven't any business in this conversation."

"You have every business," said Morton. "This is life with a capital L. But go on, Kellie."

Kellie said: "Remember, man, too, has left his imperishable imprint on his own galaxy. If he desires he can light fires that will be seen a hundred galaxies away; at his touch suns flash into Nova brilliance; planets leave their orbits, dead worlds come alive with green and wonderful verdure; oceans swirl and rage where deserts lay lifeless under blazing suns.

"And even our presence here in this great ship is an emanation of man's power, reaching our farther than these vibrations around us have ever dared to go."

The long-faced Smith gave a dry laugh, said: "Man's imprints are almost always linear. When he acts in three dimensions, he is restricted to planets, and even there, he is, for all practical purposes, confined to the flat bosom of the land. His ships that cross the sea leave a gentle swell, which merges with the tide and, after an hour, cannot be traced by the finest instruments in the universe.

"His ships that fly the air likewise leave no trail in the wind. When they have passed, they might as well not have been for all the record they make.

"How can you, therefore, speak of such things in the same breath with *this*? Man, these pulsations are alive. We can feel them; and they mean something; they're thought forms so strong, so all-pervading that the whole of space whispers at us.

"This is no tentacled pussy, no scarlet monstrosity, no single entity, but an inconceivable totality of minds speaking to each other across the miles and the years of their space. This is the civilization of the second galaxy; and if a spokesman for that galaxy has now warned us to go away, all I can say is we'd better watch out."

Kellie said: "Merely a different form of imprint. Man— ugh!"

The exclamation had in it a terrible quality of dismay. As Morton stared at the sociologist in amazement, Kellie snatched his atomic gun. He was not a young man, but the speed of that draw showed reflexes of spring steel.

Almost straight at Morton, the intolerable energy from that gun belched. There was a thunder howl of agony behind Morton, then a crash that shook the floor.

130

The commander whirled, and stared with a sense of insanity at a thirty-foot armored beast that lay half a dozen feet to one side of him. As he stood there, half-paralyzed, a red-eyed replica of the first beast materialized in midair, and landed with a thud ten feet away. A third, devil-faced monster appeared, and half slid off the second, rolled over and over—and got up, roaring.

A second later, there were a dozen of the things.

As the first attack came, Morton drew his own gun, and, desperate, leaped toward the others, who were backed against the towering control board.

Guns raged even as he reached them. The beast roaring redoubled in intensity; metallike scales scraped metal walls and metal floors; claws rattled and paws thudded.

Morton paid no attention to the firing, or the frightful bellowing. Ignoring any possible danger from the side, he ran along the lowest tiered walk; and, in a moment had thrown the switch that activated the multiple energy screen around the outer walls of the ship.

As he turned to help his friends, a hideous shadow loomed beside him. Too late he brought up his gun. A three-foot mouthful of eight-inch teeth lashed forth to embrace him—and dissolved in a spray of violet fire from a gun somewhere to Morton's left.

A minute after that, the fight was over; and Morton turned to the young man who had saved his life.

"Thanks, Grosvenor," he said quietly. "That was fast, efficient work. If that is what Nexial training does for a man, I'll have to see to it that more of it is put into use around this ship."

The young Nexialist flushed. "I'm afraid my training had nothing to do with the fact that I happened to turn and see your danger. Besides—

"Besides, you were the efficient one, sir. By throwing the multiple energy screen around the ship, you prevented more of the beasts from getting through. And, after that, naturally, it was simple for us to kill those already inside."

Morton smiled, and put his great arm across the young man's slighter shoulders. Here was, he realized now that

131

the immediate danger was over, an opportunity not to be missed.

Grosvenor was a problem. He was the first of the new, young supermen——so the radiopress called the graduates of Nexial training—but just what to do with him, how to use his all-around qualifications had been a puzzle from the day he was posted aboard the ship.

The *Space Beagle* swarmed with experts, who knew so much about their special subjects that they could not but regard a Jack-of-all-trades as an incomplete development.

For the first part of the trip, Grosvenor had absolutely nothing to do. Morton had noticed him occasionally, a lonely, aloof young man who existed on the outermost fringes of the ship's violent intellectual life. When the assistant of the astrogeologist was killed by a scarlet monster that boarded the ship, Grosvenor agreed to be substitute. But he did so without comment, seemed instead to withdraw further into his shell of reserve. He—

Morton forced the brief reverie out of his mind. "O. K.," he said, "we were all heroes. But now let's see what we've got here."

He did not let go of the young man, but drew him along, diffidence and all. They treaded their way gingerly among squirming remnants of monster bodies, Morton issuing orders in his quietest voice.

He fell silent finally, as a quaver of reaction set in. He thought: This must be a dream; it couldn't be real. These things transported alive across light centuries!

But a sick odor thickened the air. He kept slipping on the bluish-gray slime that was beast blood. The shiningness of disintegrated matter mingled with the air he breathed, bringing a sense of suffocation.

It was real, all right.

As Morton's commands bore fruit, cranes floated in, and began to remove carcasses, communicators buzzed with a crisscross of messages; and finally the picture was complete.

The reptilian creatures had been precipitated only into the control room. The Sensitives registered no material object such as enemy ship, or anything similar. The distance to the nearest star on the outer fringe of the second galaxy was a thousand light years, two hours journey at top speed.

Around Morton, men cursed as those scanty facts penetrated.

"A thousand light years!" Selenski, the chief pilot, ejaculated. "Why, we can't even send astroradio vibrations that far."

Another man said sharply: "Really, Commander Morton, is it wise to spend time and energy clearing up this mess, and generally concentrating on the inside of the ship, when it is the outside that matters? Come to think of it, you seemed to lose all interest in the outside the moment you had thrown the switch activating the multiscreen. Extremely dangerous, in my opinion."

Morton half turned, wearily. He was startled to realize that the criticism jarred him. He thought: "I'm upset, and if I am, so are the others."

Consciously squaring his great shoulders, he faced his critic, a construction technician, named Delber, a tall man with glasses. Morton said strongly:

"Are you serious?"

The other frowned. "Why, y-yes. A detailed study of space segments for trivia effects would seem simple precaution. This thing is BIG."

Morton said: "Do you realize that the multiscreen is the greatest defense ever devised by man? Either we can move behind its protecting vault calmly oblivious of all extrania, or else nothing can protect us."

Beside Morton, Grosvenor said fiercely to Delber:

"That screen, sir, is flawless not only mechanically but mathematically. It provides an infinite overlapping series; and that's a literal statement of its action."

The objector bowed sardonically first to Grosvenor, then to Morton. "In the face of such an ardent argument from one who knows all about every subject, I yield my opposition."

Grosvenor flushed, then turned pale before the satire. He walked off rapidly to one side. Morton half started after him, then stopped himself.

This was no time to nurse the sensitive ego of a bright

133

young Nexialist. A council of war was the imperative necessity of the moment.

When the men were assembled, Morton pushed his bulk along one of the control board tiers overlooking the room. He began:

"We've gotten ourselves into quite a mess; and we're going deeper. I need hardly point out that for one ship to confront a galactic civilization of any real proportions has no relation whatever to our past dangers from individual super beasts.

"For the moment, we're safe behind our superb defenses, but the nature of the menace requires us to set ourselves limited objectives. Not too limited. We must find out why we are being warned away. We must discover the nature of the danger and of the intelligence behind it, and it is just possible we can interpret up to a point what has happened. The facts are as follows:

He enumerated them briefly: The mind whisperings, the mental warning, the attack on the control room only— He finished:

"I see our chief biologist is still examining our late adversaries. Smith, what kind of beasts are they?"

Smith turned from one of the monsters. "Purest primeval reptile," he said briskly. "Earth could have produced their type during the dinosaur age. Judging by the two brains I've cut out, intelligence is about point oh four."

Morton frowned. He said finally, slowly: "Gourlay tell me, the beasts must have been precipitated through hyperspace. I'm sure he can tell us how this will affect our entire offensive and defensive position. Go ahead, Gourlay."

Morton waited, quietly, his gaze expectantly on the slouched figure of the communications expert. Abruptly, he was startled. Gourlay, the great man of the ship next to Kent—that Gourlay slow in responding. Perhaps better than anyone on the ship, Morton knew the extraordinary man, whose drawl and surface laziness concealed a mind that was chain lightning. If the information, the capacity for counteraction existed, Gourlay would know about it and it would be there on the tip of his tongue, slow, concise, immensely coherent. He—

Gourlay was straightening; and Morton breathed again. "Hyperspace," came the familiar drawl, "is not strictly

134

an energy field, though there is a relation. You all know what space is: a tension in time; the function involved is roughly time plus an enviroment of the basic energy *deka*."

He stopped there; and it was several seconds before it struck Morton that he was finished.

"Just a moment," the commander said hastily, "we all know that man uses hyperspace in planet to planet transmission of material objects. Why shouldn't he, therefore, be able to transmit from a planet to this ship? After all, we've got an atmosphere inside here."

Gourlay said. "The problem of focusing a hyperspace transmitter on a ship whose speed is measured in light-year units involves about nine hundred thousand dimensions, mathematically speaking. Accordingly, it's impossible even theoretically. I think that should answer all your questions."

Having spoken, Gourlay leaned back and closed his eyes. Morton waited, but there was no further sign from the man.

The whole effect was unpleasantly unsatisfactory; and Morton, who had a very sharp sense of human reaction to bad news, said coolly:

"Obviously, there's no one in the world *that* much smarter than we are. There must be simple solutions to the problem of hyperspace which our scientists missed out on.

"No doubt, of course, that these beings have got a lot on the ball, but they haven't penetrated the multiple energy screen around the *Space Beagle*. On top of that they pulled the damnedest, dumbest trick in attacking us with a bunch of mindless monsters, when they could have taken the ship by using a more intelligent and organized attacking force, and exploiting their initial surprise to the full. And, finally, they must be scared stiff of our finding out something dangerous if they don't even want to let us into their galaxy."

"Look, Morton," said a bass-voiced man, "if that little pep talk is designed to brace up our morale, you'd better think again. The fact is we're up against something so big we can't even imagine it. Let's start from there."

It was, Morton reflected grimly, a damned low starting point.

He stood for a moment, then, a brooding giant of a man. His heavy face was dark with the determination that was growing into it. He said finally:

"I don't accept that pessimism so completely. We're alive. That's proof that we're not pushovers to whatever is out there."

Slowly, he relaxed. He waved one great hand toward a group of men who sat at his left. He said:

"I see our military expert sitting well to the forefront over there. He's had about point oh four work to do since this voyage started, but I think we can use his knowledge at last. What do you make of the attack, Dysart?"

Dysart was a medium-sized, oldish man with a lined faced and a bushy beard. He had a sour voice. He said:

"If the objective was our destruction, it failed one hundred percent. If the intention was to scare us, the assault was a smashing success."

There was a little flurry of laughter, and Morton smiled with a grim satisfaction at the relaxing of tension in the enormous, domed room. He waited a moment, then said:

"Supposing the intention was not destruction."

Dysart looked abruptly more serious. "I see this affair as a progression of warnings. First, there was a mental warning, now has come a concrete warning."

His expression grew darker, and the sour rasp in his tone took on a more resonant quality:

"I will not speculate on the purpose behind the warnings. But I think we can safely draw the conclusion that the beasts were symbols of a remorseless and murderous determination, and that the purpose behind them was no mere friendly advice to get out."

"There is no doubt," said a small man at the back of the room, "that a great effort is being made to get us to turn around and go back home—*alive!*"

Morton called: "Come on out here, Kent, and explain that."

He frowned in puzzlement as the little chemist pushed forward from his seat. Morton regarded Kent as the smart-

136

est man on the ship, but the significance of the scientist's words completely escaped him.

In a ringing voice, Kent began: "It's possible I have the wrong slant on things, but I always look for ulterior motives. You people see an effort to keep us away from the galaxy we are approaching. My mind instantly jumped to the possibility that our friend out there would like to know where we came from."

Morton said slowly: "Maybe you've got something there, Kent."

Kent continued: "Just look at it from—his—point of view. Here is a ship approaching from a certain general direction. In that direction, within ten million light years, are a large number of nebulae, star clusters, star clouds. Which is us?"

There was a dead silence in the room. Morton had the queer feeling that men were shuddering, each from his own mental picture of the hell that could be here. It was Smith who said finally in a gloomy voice:

"What would you suggest, Kent?"

The little chemist replied promptly: "Destruction or scrambling of all identification star charts or pools. Gunlie Lester, his assistant and all the people aboard who have too much astronomical knowledge in their heads to wear spacesuits with energy guards whenever and wherever we land.

"It is possibly already too late. We know that the creature has been poking around in Morton's brain, and God only knows how many other minds he's ransacked. We'd better start exploring this galaxy at top speed, and we'll be wise to see to it that nowhere along the line does our enemy have even an edgewise chance to study us again."

He broke off. "Morton, when do we get to the nearest star of this galaxy?

"Approximately three hours," said the commander.

The meeting broke up in silence.

The first sun grew big out of space, a ball of light and heat, burning furiously into the great night, and supporting seven planets.

One was habitable, a world of mists and jungles and nightmare beasts. They left it, unexplored, after flashing

137

low over an inland sea, across a great continent of marsh and fungi growth.

Left it because, as Morton said: "We have set ourselves an objective: to find the nature of the intelligence that dominates this galaxy. Conceivably the clues may exist in the vastness of the jungles below—I wouldn't be surprised if the beasts that were precipitated into the control room came from there—but I think we should search for a more civilized source of evidence."

Lonely and remote were the suns at this distant rim of the galaxy. They spun on their courses, aloof, like glowworms on a clouded night, in their relation one to the other. Three hundred light years, the *Space Beagle* sped, and came to a small red sun with two planets crowding up close to its cherry-red warmth.

One of the two planets was habitable, a world of mists and jungles and nightmare beasts. They left it, unexplored, after darting down low over a marshy sea and a land choked with fungoid growth.

There were more stars now; a sprinkle of them daubed the near distance of the next hundred light years. A large, blue-white sun sporting thirty-seven planets attracted the superbly swift Earth ship.

The great machine spat out of space, raged past seven planets that were burning hells, spiraled toward the three close-together planets that were habitable—and flicked off into the night with its startled crew.

Behind, three steamy jungle planets swirled in their separate, eccentric orbits around the hot sun that had spawned them. "Identical triplets, by God!" Gunlie Lester exploded on the general communicator. "Morton, the axial tilt of those planets was a design to regulate their heat to the requirements of a jungle world. Somebody's deliberately creating primeval planets. If the next sun has a jungle world also, I think we'd better investigate."

The fourth star was Sol-size, Sol-type. Of its three planets, one made a neat orbit at eighty million miles, a steaming world of jungle and primeval seas.

The *Space Beagle* settled through that gaseous envelope and began to fly along at a low level, a great, alien ball of metal in a fantastic land.

In the geology lab, Grosvenor watched the bank of instruments that registered the nature of the terrain below. Particularly, he stared with strained attention at the density recorder needle as it shifted along its thin range of mud, stone, clay, mud, water, fungi—

The needle jumped like flame in high wind—steel, clay, concrete, steel.

*Steel!*

Grosvenor reacted. His hand snatched up at the geared alarm, and tugged wth the frantic sense that it was his strength that must stop the mighty ship. He let go only when the voice of Jarvis, his superior, rasped beside him, reporting to the control room:

". . . Yes, Commander Morton, steel not just iron ore. Our instruments are registering developed metal, not nature in the raw. Depth? . . . What's the depth there, Grove?"

"T-ten, twenty, f-fifty feet!" Grosvenor stammered. Inwardly, he cursed the way his heart was pounding, caught his voice into a stiff bar of sound. "It varies, and it's spread over a wide area."

Jarvis was saying into the communicator: "As you know, commander, we set our instruments at fifty feet maximum. This could be a city buried in the jungle mud."

It was in a way. It was an incredible rubble of what had been a city. The scenes uncovered by the drillers were shambles. Everywhere was shattered steel and concrete and stone. And bodies!

The bodies were at the street line about fifty feet below the surface; a whole pack of them turned up where Grosvenor was directing a drilling crew. Everything stopped as the great men of the ship came over to examine the find.

"Rather badly smashed," said Smith, "but I think I can piece together a coherent picture."

His skillful fingers arranged an assembly of scattered bones into a rough design. "Four-legged," he said. He turned a curious hazy light on the fragile structure. "This one has been dead about twenty-five years."

He frowned, and picked up a bone, and brought the hazy, whitish light nearer to it. "Funny," he said, "there's

139

a resinous substance on this end of the bone that's impervious to ultra-light. It reflects it. In all my experience, nothing concrete, nothing except energy itself has ever stopped ultra-light. Kent, what do you make of that?"

He handed the bone over; and Grosvenor stood, watching and waiting. He felt fascinated, not by the mystery of the bone, but because time and again, since he had joined the ship's company, he had tried to picture the difference between himself and these men.

Perhaps, he thought now, with intense absorption, it was this ability of theirs to concentrate utterly on some detail of their special science.

Whereas he, Grosvenor, had already rejected as irrelevant everything directly connected with the bones of these long-dead creature. These were the pitiful victims, not the arrogant and deadly destroyers.

The shattered relics that lay around in such abundance might hold the secret of the fundamental physical character of a vanished race, but no clue could there be *in* them of the unimaginably merciless beings who had murdered them.

The incredible beings who went around deliberately jungle-izing habitable planets.

In spite of his conviction of irrelevancy, Grosvenor had a brief, vivid, mental picture of a civilization of four-legged, two-armed, small-headed creatures whose bodies could reflect every wave of light. And then, Morton's voice was resonating quietly on the general communicator:

"The . . . curious . . . reflecting feature of the bone . . . undoubtedly deserves study, but in more leisurely moments, not now when our whole will and effort must be concentrated on our search to locate the great forces that rule this galaxy."

It was vindication for his own opinion. But Grosvenor said nothing. A dark thought came that the vanished race had not been able to reflect the millions of tons of earth that buried them and all their works. But he had no sense of tragedy.

There was excitement in him, and an intense pleasure in the scene of men working with machines that were almost human in their sensitivity, abnormal and terrible in their irresistible power.

For the moment, he felt a part of the scene. Up to a point, it was a geology show. As the geologists were Jarvis and himself, and Jarvis was too busy to bother him, for the first time Grosvenor was on his own.

He flew from drill crew to drill crew, setting up his instruments, registering for five hundred feet now, testing the earth the drills removed.

His communicator buzzed with voices, but only occasionally did he tune them in. Once when he heard Jarvis talking, he listened as his superior said:

"Commander Morton, I'm willing to commit myself. The jungle is a superimposed layer. It was *brought* here in some sort of a cataclysm. The strata below resembles that of an older, less primitive planet. It could have been Earth, with certain variations. I would suggest that an astronomical study be made of nearby planets to determine if they show any of the effects that must have resulted when this planet was violently moved out of its original orbit, and violently put into its present one."

It was about half an hour later that Zeller, the metallurgist, added his words to the developing picture of a cosmic catastrophe. Zeller's voice blurred on the communicator:

"This broken steel girder was rolled less than seventy-five years ago. Its electronic fatigue gap is only $23 \times 10^{-14}$."

"Thanks!" Morton's voice was quiet. "I think we can be pretty safe now in assuming that the catastrophe was of comparatively recent origin. Accordingly, our work on this planet may be considered finished. I'm going back to the ship now, and I'll issue a general recall from there."

Grosvenor was thinking unsteadily: "If I could solve this mystery! If I could even get the first clue— The next planet, of course, will be jungle, too, and I'll concentrate on—"

His thought drained like water running down a sink-hole. His brain twirled. He whispered finally, shakily:

*"The next planet will be jungle, too*—Good God, that's it! That's the angle—and I'm the only one on all the ship who can handle it."

With an effort, he caught that egotistical twist of his

141

mind. He thought with wry grimness: It was the solution of the problem that counted, not who solved it. But the thought that had come wouldn't go away.

For beyond all doubt, the hour of hope had struck for the lone, despised Nexialist of the battleship *Space Beagle*.

Now that the moment was here, Grosvenor felt a spasm of doubt. He stood near Morton looking at the seated scientists and there was no sense of satisfaction in the victory that was going to be his. He grew aware of Morton pushing forward, and raising his hand for silence. The commander said:

"You have probably been wondering, all of you, the purpose of our careening around during the past two days. As you know, we have visited three widely separated star systems, and it is interesting to note in that connection that no interference has been offered to our flight. Where we willed to go we went.

"What you do not know is that the stars we visited were selected for investigation by Nexial mathematics under a theory conceived and executed by Elliott Grosvenor. Grosvenor, tell your colleagues what you discovered."

Astoundingly, it was a bad moment for Grosvenor. He stood, shaking inwardly, in abrupt funk. He stood in the grip of a hell of unexpected thoughts that included the devastating realization that you couldn't just face men whose attitude had denied your intelligence and training. All the months that he had been treated like a grown-up child reached at his tongue and twisted at it, striving to stop him from speaking.

The curious thought came finally that there was only one way to begin a speech; and that was to begin it. He said:

"What I did was to obtain from Gunlie Lester his most developed photographic map of this galaxy. The important thing there was that he had already marked the galactic longitude and latitude planes, and the course we had taken.

"I must now call your attention briefly to a branch of science which has not, I know from experience"—Grosvenor smiled bleakly—"commended itself very highly to the science specialists of this great ship with which we are to explore the entire attainable universe. I refer to the science of Nexialism, which has its own mathematics, and is a method of training designed to bridge the gap between facts that are related but separated, for instance, by being contained in the brainpans of two individuals. Nexialism joins. It seeks to unify apparent irrelations; and its scope is so great that the data of an entire galaxy is not too complicated for it to cast into a recognizable design."

Grosvenor paused. Because he was doing well. His voice was cool and steady. His brain was working with hair-trigger, split-second alertness. He went on; and his voice sounded thrillingly clear in his own ears:

"As I saw it, what we were primarily interested in was this: Are all the planets of this galaxy jungle-ized, or aren't they? The mathematics involved—"

He saw that the men were staring at him. "Good heavens," somebody said, "if you can prove that—"

Triumph was sweet, but it had a strong drink quality, too. It put a tremor into Grosvenor's voice, as he interrupted:

"It is proved, sir. The three-star systems we have just visited were selected by Nexial mathematics. When examination verified that their habitable planets were jungle worlds, it followed automatically that every habitable globe in this entire vast galaxy was a land of jungle and beasts."

He had them now; there was no doubt of that. Men stirred, and looked at each other. Finally, the great Smith said:

"But, Grosvenor, what about the intelligences that rule this galaxy? We've opened the multiscreen several times; and the roar of myriad thoughts remains. There are colossal minds out there. They can't possibly be living on monster-inhabited jungle planets."

Grosvenor said quietly: "Mr. Smith, this whole problem is solved. The intelligence out there is a single entity. We *know* what it is. If you will have a moment of patience—"

"Gentlemen"—it was Morton, smiling but grim—"what you are hearing is no fantastic theory. These are the facts. You are listening to the recount of the most brilliant one-man show that has ever been staged. Go on, Grosvenor."

There was dead silence, then, except for the pattern that Grosvenor's voice made against the quiet vastness of the control room.

He told them the thoughts that had led up to the finale, his attempts to fit in what Gourlay had said about hyperspace, the need for a gas environment, and possibly for some nearby directive to control the aim of the transmitter.

"I went down finally to the engine room to check the graph of power discharge of automatic C-9." Grosvenor smiled almost apologetically. "We have *so* many automatic devices aboard this ship, that some of them never receive any attention except mechanical checkups. This is particularly true of our automatic screens against the presence of tenuous matter in space.

"Suffice to say that C-9 had been on from the moment we heard the space whisperings until we slapped on the multiple screen, the complicated energy structure of which, of course, assumed C-9's duties."

Grosvenor went on: "With Commander Morton's permission I then had the multiple screen briefly cut off, sent out a G-ship and obtained a representative sample of the space around us. I tested this myself, then for verification took it to Mr. Kent who—"

"What's that?" Kent was on his feet; there was a wild look in his eyes. "Was that gas you brought me a sample of surrounding space? Why, it's a hydrogen carbon compound, stabilized by a three-tie juncture with the brain cell element that—"

He broke off: "Good heavens, man, it's life. It's—"

"But why does it jungle-ize planets?" a man cried.

Grosvenor silenced the gathering clamor by raising his hand. "I can answer that, too. The problem actually was, what did it feed on? I tried various methods of stimulation and—"

The *Anabis* lay in an immense, suffused, formless form, spread through all the space of the second galaxy. It writhed a little, feebly, in a billion portions of its body, shrinking with automatic adjustment away from the destroying fury of two billion blazing suns, but pressing down tight against the myriad planets, sucking with a feverish, insatiable hunger around the quadrillion tingling points where were dying the creatures that gave it life.

It wasn't enough. Through all the countless, tenuous cells of its titanic structure, that dread knowledge of an imminent starvation seeped to the farthest reaches of its weakened body-gigantic.

Not enough food, the dreary message pulsed on and on through its imponderable elements, not enough, not enough —its mass was too big. It had made a fatal mistake in growing with such vast abandon during the early days.

In those years the future had seemed limitless, the Galactic space where its form could wax ever huger had seemed of endless extent; and it had expanded with all the vaunting, joyous egoism of a lowborn grown conscious of stupendous destiny.

It *was* lowborn. In the dim beginning was only gas oozing from a mistcovered swamp. Odorless, tasteless, colorless gas, yet somehow, someway, a dynamic combination was struck; and there was life.

At first it was nothing but a puff of invisible mist ardently darting hither and thither over the muggy, muddy waters that had spawned it, darting, twisting, diving, pursuing, incessantly and with a gathering alertness, a gathering need, striving to be present while something— anything—was being killed.

For the death of others was its life.

What a terrible joy it was to swoop over two insects buzzing in a furious death struggle, envelope them, and wait, trembling in every gassy atom, for the life force of the defeated to spray with tingling effect against its own insubstantial elements.

There was a timeless period then when its life was only that aimless search for food; and its world was a narrow swamp, a gray, nubiferous environment where it lived its contented, active, idyllic, almost mindless existence.

But even in that world of suffused sunlight it grew bigger imperceptibly. It needed more food, more than any haphazard search for dying insects could bring it.

And so it developed cunnings, special little knowledges that fitted the dank swamp. It learned which were the

145

insects that preyed and which the prey. It learned the hunting hours of every species, and where the tiny non-flying monsters lay in wait—the flying ones were harder to keep track of. It learned to use its eviscerated shape like a breeze to sweep unsuspecting victims to their fate.

Its food supply became adequate, then more than adequate. It grew and once more it hungered.

By purest necessity it became aware of a world beyond the swamp. And, oh, what a day it was when it ventured forth, and came upon two gigantic armored beasts at the bloody climax of a death struggle. The sustained thrill of the defeated monster's life force streaming through its vitals, the stupendous quantity of force provided ecstasy greater than that experienced during all its previous life put together.

In one brief hour, while the victor devoured the writhing vanquished, the *Anabis* grew by ten thousand times ten thousand.

During the single day and night period that followed, the steaming jungle world was enveloped. The *Anabis* over-flowed every ocean, every continent, and spread up into the brighter reaches of the atmosphere, where the sun shone on it directly for the first time.

Explosive result! Later, in the days of its intelligence, it learned that sunlight provided a necessary reaction on its elements, provided mass and weight.

But in that first minute there was only the effect, the dynamic expansion. On the second day it reached the first, adjoining planet. It reached the limits of the galaxy in a measurable time, stretched out instinctively for the shining stuff of other star systems and met defeat in distances that seemed to yield nothing to its groping, tenuous matter.

The days of its power seemed but a moment. Jungle worlds, with their prolific life-and-death cycles chilled; the supply of life force diminished notably. It hungered and once more grew in cunning.

It discovered that by concentrating its elements it could make holes in space, go through, and come out at a distant point. It learned to transport matter in this fashion. It began to jungle-ize planets long before it discovered that some of them were inhabited by curious, intelligent things.

It believed—and there was no one to dispute—that primeval worlds provided the most life force. It transported great slices of other jungle worlds through hyperspace. It knocked cold planets nearer their suns.

And it wasn't enough.

The coming of the ship brought hope. It would follow the ship to wherever it had come from; and, after that, no more wild, mindless, greedy growth—

Pain! The ship after darting aimlessly about, landed on a barren planet, and was sending forth incredible agony.

Darkness made no difference. The *Space Beagle* crouched on a vast plain of jagged metal, every porthole shedding light, great searchlights pouring down their flood of illumination on the row on row of engines that were tearing enormous holes into the hard, all-iron world.

There was no attempt to make steel, simply the creating of unstable iron torpedoes that were launched into space at the rate of one a second. That was the beginning.

By midnight the manufacturing machine itself began to be manufactured; and each one in turn created those slim, dark torpedoes that soared into the surrounding night scattering their substance a quarter of a light year to every side. Thirty thousand years those torpedoes would shed their destroying atoms; and they were designed to remain within the gravitational field of their galaxy, but never to fall on a planet or into a sun.

As the slow, red-dawn crept toward fruition, Engineer Pennons reported hoarsely to Morton:

"We're now turning out nine thousand a second; and I think we can safely leave the machines to finish the job. I've put a partial screen around the planet to prevent interference. Three more iron worlds properly located; and I think our bulky friend will begin to have a hollow feeling in his vital parts. But what comes after that?"

Morton smiled grimly: "N. G. C. fifty thousand three hundred fortyseven."

Pennons whistled. "Nine hundred million light years! Do you think it will follow?"

"It's got to. The alternative is to be destroyed by our

torpedoes, or a blind stab at another galaxy of its own choosing. But we'll see—"

Through telescopes they watched the faint fuzz of a gas stream out behind them and follow.

Morton turned finally from the eye-piece. "We'll go on for about a year," he said, "then go invisible and turn aside."

As he was going out of the door a few minutes later, he came upon Zeller and Grosvenor. The metallurgist was saying:

"Er, Grosvenor, I have a little problem in metal chemistry that I think needs tying up with an energy function. Do you think Nexialism could—"

Grosvenor said: "Why, I think so, Mr. Zeller. What—"

Morton passed on, smiling.

THE END

# THE EXPENDABLES

## I

One hundred and nine years after leaving Earth, the spaceship, *Hope of Man,* went into orbit around Alta III.

The following "morning" Captain Browne informed the shipload of fourth and fifth generation colonists that a manned lifeboat would be dropped to the planet's surface.

"Every member of the crew must consider himself expendable," he said earnestly. "This is the day that our great grandparents, our forefathers, who boldly set out for the new space frontier so long ago, looked forward to with unfaltering courage. We must not fail them."

He concluded his announcement over the intercom system of the big ship by saying that the names of the crew members of the lifeboat would be given out within the hour. "And I know that every real man aboard will want to see his name there."

John Lesbee, the fifth of his line aboard, had a sinking sensation as he heard those words — and he was not mistaken.

Even as he tried to decide if he should give the signal for a desperate act of rebellion, Captain Browne made the expected announcement.

The commander said, "And I know you will all join him in his moment of pride and courage when I tell you that John Lesbee will lead the crew that carries the hopes of man in this remote area of space. And now the others—"

He thereupon named seven of the nine persons with whom Lesbee had been conspiring to seize control of the ship.

Since the lifeboat would only hold eight persons, Lesbee recognized that Browne was dispatching as many of his enemies as he could. He listened with a developing dismay, as the commander ordered all persons on the ship to come to the recreation room. "Here I request that the crew of the lifeboat join me and the other officers on stage. Their instructions are to surrender themselves to any craft which seeks to intercept them. They will be equipped with instruments whereby we here can watch, and determine the stage of scientific attainments of the dominant race on the planet below."

Lesbee hurried to his room on the technicians' deck, hoping that perhaps Tellier or Cantlin would seek him out there. He felt himself in need of a council of war, however brief. He waited five minutes, but not one member of his conspiratorial group showed.

Nonetheless, he had time to grow calm. Peculiarly, it was the smell of the ship that soothed him most. From the earliest days of his life, the odor of energy and the scent of metal under stress had been perpetual companions. At the moment, with the ship in orbit, there was a letting up of stress. The smell was of old energies rather than new. But the effect was similar.

He sat in the chair he used for reading, eyes closed breathing in that complex of odors, product of so many titanic energies. Sitting there, he felt the fear leave his mind and body. He grew brave again, and strong.

Lesbee recognized soberly that his plan to seize power had involved risks. Worse, no one would question Browne's choice of him as the leader of the mission. " am," thought Lesbee, "probably the most highly trained technician ever to be on this ship." Browne Three had taken him when he was ten, and started him on the long grind of learning that led him, one after the other, to master the mechanical skills of all the various technical departments. And Browne Four had continued his training.

He was taught how to repair relay systems. He gradually came to understand the purposes of countless analogs. The time came when he could visualize the entire automation. Long ago, the colossal cobweb of electronic instruments within the walls had become almost an extension of his nervous system.

During those years of work and study, each daily apprenticeship chore left his slim body exhausted. After he came off duty, he sought a brief relaxation and usually retired to an early rest

He never did find the time to learn the intricate theory that underlay the ship's many operations.

His father, while he was alive, had made numerous attempts to pass his knowledge on to his son. But it was hard to teach complexities to a tired and sleepy boy. Lesbee even felt slightly relieved when his parent died. It took the pressure off him. Since then, however, he had come to realize that the Browne family, by forcing a lesser skill on the descendant of the original commander of the ship, had won their greatest victory.

As he headed finally for the recreation room, Lesbee found himself wondering: Had the Brownes trained him with the intention of preparing him for such a mission as this?

His eyes widened. If that was true, then his own conspiracy was merely an excuse. The decision to kill him might actually have been made more than a decade ago, and light years away . . .

As the lifeboat fell toward Alta III, Lesbee and Tellier sat in the twin control chairs and watched on the forward screen the vast, misty atmosphere of the planet.

Tellier was thin and intellectual, a descendant of the physicist Dr. Tellier who had made many speed experiments in the early days of the voyage. It had never been understood why spaceships could not attain even a good fraction of the speed of light, let alone velocities greater than light. When the scientist met his untimely death, there was no one with the training to carry on a testing program.

It was vaguely believed by the trained personnel who succeeded Tellier that the ship had run into one of the paradoxes implicit in the Lorenz-Fitzgerald Contraction theory.

Whatever the explanation, it was never solved.

Watching Tellier, Lesbee wondered if his companion and best friend felt as empty inside as he did. Incredibly, this was the first time he—or anyone—had been outside the big ship. "We're actually heading down," he thought, "to one of those great masses of land and water, a planet."

As he watched, fascinated, the massive ball grew visibly bigger.

They came in at a slant, a long, swift, angling approach, ready to jet away if any of the natural radiation belts proved too much for their defense systems. But as each stage of radiation registered in turn, the dials showed that the lifeboat machinery made the proper responses automatically.

The silence was shattered suddenly by an alarm bell.

Simultaneously, one of the screens focused on a point of rapidly moving light far below. The light darted toward them.

A missile!

Lesbee caught his breath.

But the shining projectile veered off, turned completely around, took up position several miles away, and began to fall with them.

His first thought was: "They'll never let us land," and he experienced an intense disappointment.

Another signal brrred from the control board.

"They're probing us," said Tellier, tensely.

An instant after the words were uttered, the lifeboat seemed to shudder and to stiffen under them. It was the unmistakable feel of a tractor beam. Its field clutched the lifeboat, drew it, held it.

The science of the Alta III inhabitants was already proving itself formidable.

Underneath him the lifeboat continued its movement.

The entire crew gathered around and watched as the point of brightness resolved into an object, which rapidly grew larger. It loomed up close, bigger than they.

152

There was a metallic bump. The lifeboat shuddered from stem to stern.

Even before the vibrations ceased Tellier said, "Notice they put our airlock against theirs."

Behind Lesbee, his companions began that peculiar joking of the threatened. It was a coarse comedy, but it had enough actual humor suddenly to break through his fear. Involuntarily he found himself laughing.

Then, momentarily free of anxiety, aware that Browne was watching and that there was no escape, he said, "Open the airlock! Let the aliens capture us as ordered."

## II

A few minutes after the outer airlock was opened, the airlock of the alien ship folded back also. Rubberized devices rolled out and contacted the Earth lifeboat, sealing off both entrances from the vacuum of space.

Air hissed into the interlocking passageway between the two craft. In the alien craft's lock, an inner door opened.

Again Lesbee held his breath.

There was a movement in the passageway. A creature ambled into view. The being came forward with complete assurance, and pounded with something he held at the end of one of his four leathery arms on the hull.

The creature had four legs and four arms, and a long thin body held straight up. It had almost no neck, yet the many skin folds between the head and the body indicated great flexibility was possible.

Even as Lesbee noted the details of its appearance, the being turned his head slightly, and its two large expressionless eyes gazed straight at the hidden wall receptor that was photographing the scene, and therefore straight into Lesbee's eyes.

Lesbee blinked at the creature, then tore his gaze away, swallowed hard, and nodded at Tellier. "Open up!" he commanded.

The moment the inner door of the Earth lifeboat opened, six more of the four-legged beings appeared one

153

after another in the passageway, and walked forward in the same confident way as had the first.

All seven creatures entered the open door of the lifeboat.

As they entered their thoughts came instantly into Lesbee's mind. . .

As Dzing and his boarding party trotted from the small Karn ship through the connecting airlock, his chief officer thought a message to him.

"Air pressure and oxygen content are within a tiny percentage of what exists at ground level on Karn. They can certainly live on our planet."

Dzing moved forward into the Earth ship, and realized that he was in the craft's control chamber. There, for the first time, he saw the men. He and his crew ceased their forward motion; and the two groups of beings—the humans and the Karn—gazed at each other.

The appearance of the two-legged beings did not surprise Dzing. Pulse viewers had, earlier, penetrated the metal walls of the lifeboat and had accurately photographed the shape and dimension of those aboard.

His first instruction to his crew was designed to test if the strangers were, in fact, surrendering. He commanded: "Convey to the prisoners that we require them as a precaution to remove their clothing."

. . . Until that direction was given, Lesbee was still uncertain as to whether or not these beings could receive human thoughts as he was receiving theirs. From the first moment, the aliens had conducted their mental conversations *as if* they were unaware of the thoughts of the human beings. Now he watched the Karn come forward. One tugged suggestively at his clothing. And there was no doubt.

The mental telepathy was a oneway flow only—from the Karn to the humans.

He was already savoring the implications of that as he hastily undressed. . . It was absolutely vital that Browne do not find it out.

Lesbee removed all his clothes; then, before laying them down, took out his notebook and pen. Standing there naked he wrote hurriedly:

154

"Don't let on that we can read the minds of these beings."

He handed the notebook around, and he felt a lot better as each of the men read it, and nodded at him silently.

Dzing communicated telepathically with someone on the ground. "These strangers," he reported, "clearly acted under command to surrender. The problem is, how can we now let them overcome us without arousing their suspicion that this is what we want them to do?"

Lesbee did not receive the answer directly. But he picked it up from Dzing's mind: "Start tearing the life-boat apart. See if that brings a reaction."

The members of the Karn boarding party went to work at once. Off came the control panels; floor plates were melted and ripped up. Soon instruments, wiring, controls were exposed for examination. Most interesting of all to the aliens were the numerous computers and their accessories.

Browne must have watched the destruction; for now, before the Karn could start wrecking the automatic machinery, his voice interjected:

"Watch out, you men! I'm going to shut your airlock and cause your boat to make a sharp right turn in exactly twenty seconds."

For Lesbee and Tellier that simply meant sitting down in their chairs, and turning them so that the acceleration pressure would press them against the backs. The other men sank to the ripped-up floor, and braced themselves.

Underneath Dzing, the ship swerved. The turn began slowly, but it propelled him and his fellows over to one wall of the control room. There he grabbed with his numerous hands at some handholds that had suddenly moved out from the smooth metal. By the time the turn grew sharper, he had his four short legs braced, and he took the rest of the wide swing around with every part of his long, sleek body taut. His companions did the same.

Presently, the awful pressure eased up, and he was able to estimate that their new direction was almost at right angles to what it had been.

155

He had reported what was happening while it was going on. Now, the answer came: "Keep on destroying. See what they do, and be prepared to succumb to anything that looks like a lethal attack."

Lesbee wrote quickly in his notebook: "Our method of capturing them doesn't have to be subtle. They'll make it easy for us—so we can't lose."

Lesbee waited tensely as the notebook was passed around. It was still hard for him to believe that no one else had noticed what he had about this boarding party.

Tellier added a note of his own: "It's obvious now that these beings were also instructed to consider themselves expendable."

And that settled it for Lesbee. The others hadn't noticed what he had. He sighed with relief at the false analysis, for it gave him that most perfect of all advantages: that which derived from his special education.

Apparently, he alone knew enough to have analyzed what these creatures were.

The proof was in the immense clarity of their thoughts. Long ago, on earth, it had been established that man had a faltering telepathic ability, which could be utilized consistently only by electronic amplification *outside* his brain. The amount of energy needed for the step-up process was enough to burn out brain nerves, if applied directly.

Since the Karn were utilizing it directly, they couldn't be living beings.

Therefore, Dzing and his fellows were an advanced robot type.

The true inhabitants of Alta III were not risking their own skins at all.

Far more important to Lesbee, he could see how he might use these marvellous mechanisms to defeat Browne, take over the *Hope of Man,* and start the long journey back to Earth.

# III

He had been watching the Karn at their work of destruction, while he had these thoughts. Now, he said aloud: "Hainker, Graves."

"Yes?" The two men spoke together.

"In a few moments I'm going to ask Captain Browne to turn the ship again. When he does, use our specimen gas guns!"

The men grinned with relief. "Consider it done," said Hainker.

Lesbee ordered the other four crewmen to be ready to use the specimen-holding devices at top speed. To Tellier he said, "You take charge if anything happens to me."

Then he wrote one more message in the notebook: "These beings will probably continue their mental intercommunication after they are apparently rendered unconscious. Pay no attention, and do not comment on it in any way."

He felt a lot better when that statement also had been read by the others, and the notebook was once more in his possession. Quickly, he spoke to the screen:

"Captain Browne! Make another turn, just enough to pin them."

And so they captured Dzing and his crew.

As he had expected, the Karn continued their telepathic conversation. Dzing reported to his ground contact: "I think we did that rather well."

There must have been an answering message from below, because he went on, "Yes, commander. We are now prisoners as per your instructions, and shall await events. . . The imprisoning method? Each of us is pinned down by a machine which has been placed astride us, with the main section adjusted to the contour of our bodies. A series of rigid metal appendages fasten our arms and legs. All these devices are electronically controlled, and we can of course escape at any time. Naturally, such action is for later. . ."

Lesbee was chilled by the analysis; but for expendables there was no turning back.

He ordered his men: "Get dressed. Then start repairing the ship. Put all the floor plates back except the section at G-8. They removed some of the analogs, and I'd better make sure myself that it all goes back all right."

When he had dressed, he reset the course of the lifeboat, and called Browne. The screen lit up after a moment, and there staring back at him was the unhappy countenance of the forty-year-old officer.

Browne said glumly: "I want to congratulate you and your crew on your accomplishments. It would seem that we have a small scientific superiority over this race, and that we can attempt a limited landing."

Since there would never be a landing on Alta III, Lesbee simply waited without comment as Browne seemed lost in thought.

The officer stirred finally. He still seemed uncertain. "Mr. Lesbee," he said, "as you must understand, this is an extremely dangerous situation for me—and—" he added hastily—"for this entire expedition."

What struck Lesbee, as he heard those words, was that Browne was not going to let him back on the ship. But he had to get aboard to accomplish his own purpose. He thought: "I'll have to bring this whole conspiracy out into the open, and apparently make a compromise offer."

He drew a deep breath, gazed straight into the eyes of Browne's image on the screen and said with the complete courage of a man for whom there is no turning back: "It seems to me, sir, that we have two alternatives. We can resolve all these personal problems either through a democratic election or by a joint captaincy, you being one of the captains and I being the other."

To any other person who might have been listening the remark must have seemed a complete non sequitur. Browne, however, understood its relevance. He said with a sneer, "So you're out in the open. Well, let me tell you, Mr. Lesbee, there was never any talk of elections when the Lesbees were in power. And for a very good reason. A spaceship requires a technical aristocracy to command it. As for a joint captaincy, it wouldn't work."

158

Lesbee urged his lie: "If we're going to stay here, we'll need at least two people of equal authority—one on the ground, one on the ship."

"I couldn't trust you on the ship!" said Browne flatly.

"Then you be on the ship," Lesbee proposed. "All such practical details can be arranged."

The older man must have been almost beside himself with the intensity of his own feelings on this subject. He flashed, "Your family has been out of power for over fifty years! How can you still feel that you have any rights?"

Lesbee countered, "How come you still know what I'm talking about?"

Browne said, a grinding rage in his tone, "The concept of inherited power was introduced by the first Lesbee. It was never planned."

"But here you are," said Lesbee, "yourself a beneficiary of inherited power."

Browne said from between clenched teeth: "It's absolutely ridiculous that the Earth government which was in power when the ship left—and every member of which has been long dead—should appoint somebody to a command position . . . and that now his descendant think that command post should be his, and his family's, for all time!"

Lesbee was silent, startled by the dark emotions he had uncovered in the man. He felt even more justified, if that were possible, and advanced his next suggestion without a qualm.

"Captain, this is a crisis. We should postpone our private struggle. Why don't we bring one of these prisoners aboard so that we can question him by use of films, or play acting? Later, we can discuss your situation and mine."

He saw from the look on Browne's face that the reasonableness of the suggestion, *and its potentialities,* were penetrating.

Browne said quickly, "Only you come aboard—and with one prisoner only. No one else!"

Lesbee felt a dizzying thrill as the man responded to his bait. He thought: "It's like an exercise in logic. He'll try to murder me as soon as he gets me alone and is satisfied

159

that he can attack without danger to himself. But that very scheme is what will get me aboard. And I've got to get on the ship to carry out *my* plan."

Browne was frowning. He said in a concerned tone: "Mr. Lesbee, can you think of any reason why we should not bring one of these beings aboard?"

Lesbee shook his head. "No reason, sir," he lied.

Browne seemed to come to a decision. "Very well. I'll see you shortly, and we can then discuss additional details."

Lesbee dared not say another word. He nodded, and broke the connection, shuddering, disturbed, uneasy.

"But," he thought, "what else can we do?"

He turned his attention to the part of the floor that had been left open for him. Quickly, he bent down and studied the codes on each of the programming units, as if he were seeking exactly the right ones that had originally been in those slots.

He found the series he wanted: an intricate system of cross-connected units that had originally been designed to program a remote-control landing system, an advanced Waldo mechanism capable of landing the craft on a planet and taking off again, all directed on the pulse level of human thought.

He slid each unit of the series into its sequential position and locked it in.

Then, that important task completed, he picked up the remote control attachment for the series and casually put it in his pocket.

He returned to the control board and spent several minutes examining the wiring and comparing it with a wall chart. A number of wires had been torn loose. These he now re-connected, and at the same time he managed with a twist of his pliers to short-circuit a key relay of the remote control pilot.

Lesbee replaced the panel itself loosely. There was no time to connect it properly. And, since he could easily justify his next move, he pulled a cage out of the storeroom. Into this he hoisted Dzing, manacles and all.

Before lowering the lid he rigged into the cage a simple resistor that would prevent the Karn from broadcasting

160

on the human thought level. The device was simple merely in that it was not selective. It had an on-off switch which triggered, or stopped, energy flow in the metal walls on the thought level.

When the device was installed, Lesbee slipped the tiny remote control for *it* into his other pocket. He did not activate the control. Not yet.

From the cage Dzing telepathed: "It is significant that these beings have selected me for this special attention. We might conclude that it is a matter of mathematical accident, or else that they are very observant and so noticed that I was the one who directed activities. Whatever the reason, it would be foolish to turn back now."

A bell began to ring. As Lesbee watched, a spot of light appeared high on one of the screens. It moved rapidly toward some crossed lines in the exact center of the screen. Inexorably, then, the *Hope of Man,* as represented by the light, and the lifeboat moved toward their fateful rendezvous.


## IV

Browne's instructions were: "Come to Control Room Below!"

Lesbee guided his powered dolly with the cage on it out of the big ship's airlock P—and saw that the man in the control room of the lock was Second Officer Selwyn. Heavy brass for such a routine task. Selwyn waved at him with a twisted smile as Lesbee wheeled his cargo along the silent corridor.

He saw no one else on his route. Other personnel had evidently been cleared from this part of the vessel. A little later, grim and determined, he set the cage down in the center of the big room and anchored it magnetically to the floor.

As Lesbee entered the captain's office, Browne looked up from one of the two control chairs and stepped down from the rubber-sheathed dais to the same level as Lesbee. He came forward, smiling, and held out his hand. He was a big man, as all the Brownes had been, bigger

161

by a head than Lesbee, good-looking in a clean-cut way. The two men were alone.

"I'm glad you were so frank," he said. "I doubt if I could have spoken so bluntly to you without your initiative as an example."

But as they shook hands, Lesbee was wary and suspicious. Lesbee thought: "He's trying to recover from the insanity of his reaction. I really blew him wide open."

Browne continued in the same hearty tone: "I've made up my mind. An election is out of the question. The ship is swarming with untrained dissident groups, most of which simply want to go back to Earth."

Lesbee, who had the same desire, was discreetly silent.

Browne said, "You'll be ground captain; I'll be ship captain. Why don't we sit down right now and work out a communique on which we can agree and that I can read over the intercom to the others?"

As Lesbee seated himself in the chair beside Browne, he was thinking: "What can be gained from publicly naming me ground captain?"

He concluded finally, cynically, that the older man could gain the confidence of John Lesbee—lull him, lead him on, delude him, destroy him.

Surreptitiously Lesbee examined the room. Control Room Below was a large square chamber adjoining the massive central engines. Its control board was a duplicate of the one on the bridge located at the top of the ship. The great vessel could be guided equally from either board, except that pre-emptive power was on the bridge. The officer of the watch was given the right to make Merit decisions in an emergency.

Lesbee made a quick mental calculation, and deduced that it was First Officer Miller's watch on the bridge. Miller was a staunch supporter of Browne. The man was probably watching them on one of his screens, ready to come to Browne's aid at a moment's notice.

A few minutes later, Lesbee listened thoughtfully as Browne read their joint communique over the intercom, designating him as ground captain. He found himself a little amazed, and considerably dismayed, at the absolute confidence the older man must feel about his own power

162

and position on the ship. It was a big step, naming his chief rival to so high a rank.

Browne's next act was equally surprising. While they were still on the viewers, Browne reached over, clapped Lesbee affectionately on the shoulders and said to the watching audience:

"As you all know, John is the only direct descendant of the original captain. No one knows exactly what happened half a hundred years ago when my grandfather first took command. But I remember the old man always felt that only he understood how things should be. I doubt if he had any confidence in *any* young whippersnapper over whom he did not have complete control. I often felt that my father was the victim rather than the beneficiary of my grandfather's temper and feelings of superiority."

Browne smiled engagingly. "Anyway, good people, though we can't unbreak the eggs that were broken then, we can certainly start healing the wounds, without—" his tone was suddenly firm—"negating the fact that my own training and experience make me the proper commander of the ship itself."

He broke off. "Captain Lesbee and I shall now jointly attempt to communicate with the captured intelligent life form from the planet below. You may watch, though we reserve the right to cut you off for good reason." He turned to Lesbee. "What do you think we should do first, John?"

Lesbee was in a dilemma. The first large doubt had come to him, the possibility that perhaps the other was sincere. The possibility was especially disturbing because in a few moments a part of his own plan would be revealed.

He sighed, and realized that there was no turning back at this stage. He thought: "We'll have to bring the entire madness out into the open, and only then can we begin to consider agreement as real."

Aloud, he said in a steady voice, "Why not bring the prisoner out where we can see him?"

As the tractor beam lifted Dzing out of the cage, and thus away from the energies that had suppressed his thought waves, the Karn telepathed to his contact on Alta III:

"Have been held in a confined space, the metal of which was energized against communication. I shall now attempt to perceive and evaluate the condition and performance of this ship—"

At that point, Browne reached over and clicked off the intercom. Having shut off the audience, he turned accusingly to Lesbee, and said, "Explain your failure to inform me that these beings communicated by telepathy."

The tone of his voice was threatening. There was a hint of angry color in his face.

It was the moment of discovery.

Lesbee hesitated, and then simply pointed out how precarious their relationship had been. He finished frankly, "I thought by keeping it a secret I might be able to stay alive a little longer, which was certainly not what you intended when you sent me out as an expendable."

Browne snapped, "But how did you hope to utilize?—" He stopped. "Never mind," he muttered.

Dzing was telepathing again:

"In many ways this is mechanically a very advanced type ship. Atomic energy drives are correctly installed. The automatic machinery performs magnificently. There is massive energy screen equipment, and they can put out a tractor beam to match anything we have that's mobile. But there is a wrongness in the energy flows of this ship, which I lack the experience to interpret. Let me furnish you some data. . ."

The data consisted of variable wave measurements, evidently—so Lesbee deduced—the wavelengths of the energy flows involved in the "wrongness."

He said in alarm at that point, "Better drop him into the cage while *we* analyze what he could be talking about."

Browne did so—as Dzing telepathed: "If what you suggest is true, then these beings are completely at our mercy—"

*Cut off!*

Browne was turning on the intercom. "Sorry I had to cut you good people off," he said. "You'll be interested

164

to know that we have managed to tune in on the thought pulses of the prisoner and have intercepted his calls to someone on the planet below. This gives us an advantage." He turned to Lesbee. "Don't you agree?"

Browne visibly showed no anxiety, whereas Dzing's final statement flabbergasted Lesbee. ". . . *completely at our mercy* . . ." surely meant exactly that. He was staggered that Browne could have missed the momentous meaning.

Browne addressed him enthusiastically, "I'm excited by this telepathy! It's a marvelous short-cut to communication, if we could build up our own thought pulses. Maybe we could use the principle of the remote-control landing device which, as you know, can project human thoughts on a simple, gross level, where ordinary energies get confused by the intense field needed for the landing."

What interested Lesbee in the suggestion was that he had in his pocket a remote control for precisely such mechanically produced thought pulses. Unfortunately, the control was for the lifeboat. It probably would be advisable to tune the control to the ship landing system also. It was a problem he had thought of earlier, and now Browne had opened the way for an easy solution.

He held his voice steady as he said, "Captain, let me program those landing analogs while you prepare the film communication project. That way we can be ready for him either way."

Browne seemed to be completely trusting, for he agreed at once.

At Browne's direction, a film projector was wheeled in. It was swiftly mounted on solid connections at one end of the room. The cameraman and Third Officer Mindel —who had come in with him—strapped themselves into two adjoining chairs attached to the projector, and were evidently ready.

While this was going on, Lesbee called various technical personnel. Only one technician protested. "But, John," he said, "that way we have a double control—with the lifeboat control having pre-emption over the ship. That's very unusual."

It was unusual. But it was the lifeboat control that was

165

in his pocket where he could reach it quickly; and so he said adamantly, "Do you want to talk to Captain Browne? Do you want his okay?"

"No, no." The technician's doubts seemed to subside. "I heard you being named joint captain. You're the boss. It shall be done."

Lesbee put down the closed-circuit phone into which he had been talking, and turned. It was then he saw that the film was ready to roll, and that Browne had his fingers on the controls of the tractor beam. The older man stared at him questioningly.

"Shall I go ahead?" he asked.

At this penultimate moment, Lesbee had a qualm.

Almost immediately he realized that the only alternative to what Browne planned was that he reveal his own secret knowledge.

He hesitated, torn by doubts. Then: "Will you turn that off?" He indicated the intercom.

Browne said to the audience, "We'll bring you in again on this in a minute, good people." He broke the connection and gazed questioningly at Lesbee.

Whereupon Lesbee said in a low voice, "Captain, I should inform you that I brought the Karn aboard in the hope of using him against you."

"Well, that is a frank and open admission," the officer replied very softly.

"I mention this," said Lesbee, "because if you had similar ulterior motives, we should clear the air completely before proceeding with this attempt at communication."

A blossom of color spread from Browne's neck over his face. At last he said slowly, "I don't know how I can convince you, but I had no schemes."

Lesbee gazed at Browne's open countenance, and suddenly he realized that the officer was sincere. Browne had accepted the compromise. The solution of a joint captaincy was agreeable to him.

Sitting there, Lesbee experienced an enormous joy. Seconds went by before he realized what underlay the intense pleasurable excitement. It was simply the discovery that—communication worked. You could tell your truth and get a hearing . . . if it made sense.

It seemed to him that his truth made a lot of sense. He was offering Browne peace aboard the ship. Peace at a price, of course; but still peace. And in this severe emergency Browne recognized the entire validity of the solution.

So it was now evident to Lesbee.

Without further hesitation he told Browne that the creatures who had boarded the lifeboat were robots— not alive at all.

Browne was nodding thoughtfully. Finally he said: "But I don't see how this could be utilized to take over the ship."

Lesbee said patiently, "As you know, sir, the remote landing control system includes five principal ideas which are projected very forcibly on the thought level. Three of these are for guidance—up, down and sideways. Intense magnetic fields, any one of which could partially jam a complex robot's thinking processes. The fourth and fifth are instructions to blast either up or down. The force of the blast depends on how far the control is turned on. Since the energy used is overwhelming those simple commands would take pre-emption over the robot. When that first one came aboard the lifeboat, I had a scan receiver—nondetectable—on him. This registered two power sources, one pointing forward, one backward, from the chest level. That's why I had him on his back when I brought him in here. But the fact is I could have had him tilted and pointing at a target, and activated either control four or five, thus destroying whatever was in the path of the resulting blast. Naturally, I took all possible precautions to make sure that this did not happen until you had indicated what you intended to do. One of these precautions would enable us to catch this creature's thoughts without—"

As he was speaking, he eagerly put his hand into his pocket, intending to show the older man the tiny on-off control device by which—when it was off—they would be able to read Dzing's thoughts without removing him from the cage.

He stopped short in his explanation, because an ugly expression had come suddenly into Browne's face.

The big man glanced at Third Officer Mindel. "Well, Dan," he said, "do you think that's it?"

Lesbee noticed with shock that Mindel had on sound amplifying earphones. He must have overheard every word that Browne and he had spoken to each other.

Mindel nodded. "Yes, Captain," he said. "I very definitely think he has now told us what we wanted to find out."

Lesbee grew aware that Browne had released himself from his acceleration safety belt and was stepping away from his seat. The officer turned and, standing very straight, said in a formal tone:

"Technician Lesbee, we have heard your admission of gross dereliction of duty, conspiracy to overthrow the lawful government of this ship, scheme to utilize alien creatures to destroy human beings, and confession of other unspeakable crimes. In this extremely dangerous situation, summary execution without formal trial is justified. I therefore sentence you to death and order Third Officer Dan Mindel to—"

He faltered, and came to a stop.

# V

Two things had been happening as he talked, Lesbee squeezed the "off" switch of the cage control, an entirely automatic gesture, convulsive, a spasmodic movement, result of his dismay. It was a mindless gesture. So far as he knew consciously, freeing Dzing's thoughts had no useful possibility for him. His only real hope—as he realized almost immediately—was to get his other hand into his remaining coat pocket and with it manipulate the remote-control landing device, the secret of which he had so naively revealed to Browne.

The second thing that happened was that Dzing, released from mental control, telepathed:

"Free again—and this time of course permanently! I have just now activated by remote control the relays that will in a few moments start the engines of this ship, and I have naturally re-set the mechanism for controlling the rate of acceleration—"

His thoughts must have impinged progressively on Browne, for it was at that point that the officer paused uncertainly.

Dzing continued: "I verified your analysis. This vessel does not have the internal energy flows of an interstellar ship. These two-legged beings have therefore failed to achieve the Light Speed Effect which alone makes possible trans-light velocities. I suspect they have taken many generations to make this journey, are far indeed from their home base, and I'm sure I can capture them all."

Lesbee reached over, tripped on the intercom and yelled at the screen: "All stations prepare for emergency acceleration! Grab anything!"

To Browne he shouted: "Get to your seat—*quick!*"

His actions were automatic responses to danger. Only after the words were spoken did it occur to him that he had no interest in the survival of Captain Browne. And that in fact the only reason the man was in danger was because he had stepped away from his safety belt, so that Mindel's blaster would kill Lesbee without damaging Browne.

Browne evidently understood his danger. He started toward the control chair from which he had released himself only moments before. His reaching hands were still a foot or more from it when the impact of Acceleration One stopped him. He stood there trembling like a man who had struck an invisible but palpable wall. The next instant Acceleration Two caught him and thrust him on his back to the floor. He began to slide toward the rear of the room, faster and faster, and because he was quick and understanding he pressed the palms of his hands and his rubber shoes hard against the floor and so tried to slow the movement of his body.

Lesbee was picturing other people elsewhere in the ship desperately trying to save themselves. He groaned, for the commander's failure was probably being duplicated everywhere.

Even as he had that thought, Acceleration Three caught Browne. Like a rock propelled by a catapult he shot toward the rear wall. It was cushioned to protect human beings, and so it reacted like rubber, bouncing him a little. But the stuff had only momentary resilience.

169

Acceleration Four pinned Browne halfway into the cushioned wall. From its imprisoning depths, he managed a strangled yell.

"Lesbee, put a tractor beam on me! Save me! I'll make it up to you. I—"

Acceleration Five choked off the words.

The man's appeal brought momentary wonder to Lesbee: He was amazed that Browne hoped for mercy . . . after what had happened.

Browne's anguished words did produce one effect in him. They reminded him that there was something he must do. He forced his hand and his arm to the control board and focussed a tractor beam that firmly captured Third Officer Mindel and the cameraman. His intense effort was barely in time. Acceleration followed acceleration, making movement impossible. The time between each surge of increased speed grew longer. The slow minutes lengthened into what seemed an hour, then many hours. Lesbee was held in his chair as if he were gripped by hands of steel. His eyes felt glassy; his body had long since lost all feeling.

He noticed something.

The rate of acceleration was different from what the original Tellier had prescribed long ago. The actual increase in forward pressure each time was less.

He realized something else. For a long time, no thoughts had come from the Karn.

Suddenly, he felt an odd shift in speed. A physical sensation of slight, very slight, angular movement accompanied the maneuver.

Slowly, the metal-like bands let go of his body. The numb feeling was replaced by the pricking as of thousands of tiny needles. Instead of muscle-compressing acceleration there was only a steady pressure.

It was the pressure that he had in the past equated with gravity.

Lesbee stirred hopefully, and when he felt himself move, realized what had happened. The artificial gravity had been shut off. Simultaneously, the ship had made a half turn within its outer shell. The drive power was now coming from below, a constant one gravity thrust.

At this late, late moment, he plunged his hand into the pocket which held the remote control for the pilotless landing mechanism—and activated it.

"That ought to turn on his thoughts," he told himself savagely.

But if Dzing was telepathing to his masters, it was no longer on the human thought level. So Lesbee concluded unhappily.

The ether was silent.

He now grew aware of something more. The ship smelled different: better, cleaner, purer.

Lesbee's gaze snapped over to the speed dials on the control board. The figures registering there were unbelievable. They indicated that the spaceship was traveling at a solid fraction of the speed of light.

Lesbee stared at the numbers incredulously. "We didn't have time!" he thought. "How could we go so fast so quickly—in hours only to near the speed of light!"

Sitting there, breathing hard, fighting to recover from the effects of that prolonged speed-up, he felt the fantastic reality of the universe. During all this slow century of flight through space, the *Hope of Man* had had the potential for this vastly greater velocity.

He visualized the acceleration series so expertly programmed by Dzing as having achieved a shift to a new state of matter in motion. The "light speed effect," the Karn robot had called it.

"And Tellier missed it," he thought.

All those experiments the physicist had performed so painstakingly, and left a record of, had missed the great discovery.

Missed it! And so a shipload of human beings had wandered for generations through the black deeps of interstellar space.

Across the room Browne was climbing groggily to his feet. He muttered, ". . . Better get back to . . . control chair."

He had taken only a few uncertain steps when a realization seemed to strike him. He looked up then, and stared wildly at Lesbee. "Oh!" he said. The sound came from the gut level, a gasp of horrified understanding.

As he slapped a complex of tractor beams on Browne,

171

Lesbee said, "That's right, you're looking at your enemy. Better start talking. We haven't much time."

Browne was pale now. But his mouth had been left free and so he was able to say huskily, "I did what any lawful government does in an emergency. I dealt with treason summarily, taking time only to find out what it consisted of."

Lesbee had had another thought, this time about Miller on the bridge. Hastily, he swung Browne over in front of him. "Hand me your blaster," he said. "Stock first."

He freed the other's arm, so that he could reach into the holster and take it out.

Lesbee felt a lot better when he had the weapon. But still another idea had come to him. He said harshly, "I want to lift you over to the cage, and I don't want First Officer Miller to interfere. Get that, *Mister* Miller!"

There was no answer from the screen.

Browne said uneasily, "Why over to the cage?"

Lesbee did not answer right away. Silently he manipulated the tractor beam control until Browne was in position. Having gotten him there, Lesbee hesitated. What bothered him was, why had the Karn's thought impulses ceased? He had an awful feeling that something was very wrong indeed.

He gulped, and said, "Raise the lid!"

Again, he freed Browne's arm. The big man reached over gingerly, unfastened the catch, and then drew back and glanced questioningly at Lesbee.

"Look inside!" Lesbee commanded.

Browne said scathingly, "You don't think for one second that—" He stopped, for he was peering into the cage. He uttered a cry: "He's gone!"


# VI

Lesbee discussed the disappearance with Browne.

It was an abrupt decision on his part to do so. The question of where Dzing might have got to was not something he should merely turn over in his own head.

He began by pointing at the dials from which the immense speed of the ship could be computed, and then, when that meaning was absorbed by the older man, said simply, "What happened? Where did he go? And how could we speed up to just under 186,000 miles a second in so short a time?"

He had lowered the big man to the floor, and now he took some of the tension from the tractor beam but did not release the power. Browne stood in apparent deep thought. Finally, he nodded. "All right," he said, "I know what happened."

"Tell me."

Browne changed the subject, said in a deliberate tone, "What are you going to do with me?"

Lesbee stared at him for a moment unbelievingly. "You're going to withhold this information?" he demanded.

Browne spread his hands. "What else can I do? Till I know my fate, I have nothing to lose."

Lesbee suppressed a strong impulse to rush over and strike his prisoner. He said finally, "In your judgment is this delay dangerous?"

Browne was silent, but a bead of sweat trickled down his cheek. "*I* have nothing to lose," he repeated.

The expression in Lesbee's face must have alarmed him, for he went on quickly, "Look, there's no need for you to conspire any more. What you really want is to go home, isn't it? Don't you see, with this new method of acceleration, we can make it to Earth in a few *months!*"

He stopped. He seemed momentarily uncertain.

Lesbee snapped angrily, "Who are you trying to fool? Months! We're a dozen light years in actual distance from Earth. You mean years, not months."

Browne hesitated then: "All right, a few years. But at least not a lifetime. So if you'll promise not to scheme against me further, I'll promise—"

"*You'll* promise!" Lesbee spoke savagely. He had been taken aback by Browne's instant attempt at blackmail. But the momentary sense of defeat was gone. He knew with a stubborn rage that he would stand for no nonsense.

He said in an uncompromising voice, "Mister Browne, twenty seconds after I stop speaking, you start talking. If you don't, I'll batter you against these walls. I mean it!"

Browne was pale. "Are you going to kill me? That's

173

all I want to know. Look—" his tone was urgent—"we don't have to fight any more. We can go home. Don't you see? The long madness is just about over. Nobody has to die."

Lesbee hesitated. What the big man said was at least partly true. There was an attempt here to make twelve years sound like twelve days, or at most twelve weeks. But the fact was, it *was* a short period compared to the century-long journey which, at one time, had been the only possibility.

He thought: "Am I going to kill him?"

It was hard to believe that he would, under the circumstances. All right. If not death, then what? He sat there uncertain. The vital seconds went by, and he could see no solution. He thought finally, in desperation: "I'll have to give in for the moment. Even a minute thinking about this is absolutely crazy."

He said aloud in utter frustration, "I'll promise you this. If you can figure out how I can feel safe in a ship commanded by you I'll give your plan consideration. And now, mister, start talking."

Browne nodded. "I accept that promise," he said. "What we've run into here is the Lorenz-Fitzgerald Contraction Theory. Only it's not a theory any more. We're living the reality of it."

Lesbee argued, "But it only took us a few hours to get to the speed of light."

Browne said, "As we approach light speed, space foreshortens and time compresses. What seemed like a few hours would be days in normal time and space."

What Browne explained then was different rather than difficult. Lesbee had to blink his mind to shut out the glare of his old ideas and habits of thought, so that the more subtle shades of super-speed phenomena could shine through into his awareness.

The time compression—as Browne explained it—was gradational. The rapid initial series of accelerations were obviously designed to pin down the personnel of the ship. Subsequent increments would be according to what was necessary to attain the ultra-speed finally achieved.

Since the drive was still on, it was clear that some

174

resistance was being encountered, perhaps from the fabric of space itself.

It was no time to discuss technical details. Lesbee accepted the remarkable reality and said quickly, "Yes, but where is Dzing?"

"My guess," said Browne, "is that he did not come along."

"How do you mean?"

"The space-time foreshortening did not affect him."

"But—" Lesbee began blankly.

"Look," said Browne harshly, "don't ask me how he did it. My picture is, he stayed in the cage till after the acceleration stopped. Then, in a leisurely fashion, he released himself from the electrically locked manacles, climbed out, and went off to some other part of the ship. He wouldn't have to hurry since by this time he was operating at a rate of, say, five hundred times faster than our living pace."

Lesbee said, "But that means he's been out there for hours—his time. What's he been up to?"

Browne admitted that he had no answer for that.

"But you can see," he pointed out anxiously, "that I meant what I said about going back to Earth. We have no business in this part of space. These beings are far ahead of us scientifically."

His purpose was obviously to persuade. Lesbee thought: "He's back to *our* fight. That's more important to him than any damage the real enemy is causing."

A vague recollection came of the things he had read about the struggle for power throughout Earth history. How men intrigued for supremacy while vast hordes of the invader battered down the gates. Browne was a true spiritual descendant of all those mad people.

Slowly, Lesbee turned and faced the big board. What was baffling to him was, what could you do against a being who moved five hundred times as fast as you did?

# VII

He had a sudden sense of awe, a picture . . . At any given instant Dzing was a blur. A spot of light. A movement

175

so rapid that, even as the gaze lighted on him, he was gone to the other end of the ship—and back.

Yet Lesbee knew it took time to traverse the great ship from end to end. Twenty, even twenty-five minutes, was normal walking time for a human being going along the corridor known as Center A.

It would take the Karn a full six seconds there and back. In its way that was a significant span of time, but after Lesbee had considered it for a moment he felt appalled.

What could they do against a creature who had so great a time differential in his favor?

From behind him, Browne said, "Why don't you use against him that remote landing control system that you set up with my permission?"

Lesbee confessed: "I did that, as soon as the acceleration ceased. But he must have been—back—in the faster time by then."

"That wouldn't make any difference," said Browne.

"Eh!" Lesbee was startled.

Browne parted his lips evidently intending to explain, and then he closed them again. Finally he said, "Make sure the intercom is off."

Lesbee did so. But he was realizing that Browne was up to something again. He said, and there was rage in his tone, "I don't get it, and you do. Is that right."

"Yes," said Browne. He spoke deliberately, but he was visibly suppressing excitement. "I know how to defeat this creature. That puts me in a bargaining position."

Lesbee's eyes were narrowed to slits. "Damn you, no bargain. Tell me, or else!"

Browne said, "I'm not really trying to be difficult. You either have to kill me, or come to some agreement. I want to know what that agreement is, because of course I'll do it."

Lesbee said, "I think we ought to have an election."

"I agree!" Browne spoke instantly. "You set it up." He broke off. "And now release me from these tractors and I'll show you the neatest spacetime trick you've ever seen, and that'll be the end of Dzing."

Lesbee gazed at the man's face, saw there the same openness of countenance, the same frank honesty that had

176

preceeded the execution order, and he thought, "What can he do?"

He considered many possibilities, and thought finally, desperately: "He's got the advantage over me of superior knowledge—the most undefeatable weapon in the world. The only thing I can really hope to use against it in the final issue is *my* knowledge of a multitude of technician-level details."

But—what could Browne do against Lesbee?

He said unhappily to the other, "Before I free you, I want to lift you over to Mindel. When I do, you get his blaster for me."

"Sure," said Browne casually.

A few moments later he handed Mindel's gun over to Lesbee. So that wasn't it.

Lesbee thought: "There's Miller on the bridge—can it be that Miller flashed him a ready signal when my back was turned to the board?"

Perhaps, like Browne, Miller had been temporarily incapacitated during the period of acceleration. It was vital that he find out Miller's present capability.

Lesbee tripped the intercom between the two boards. The rugged, lined face of the first officer showed large on the screen. Lesbee could see the outlines of the bridge behind the man and, beyond, the starry blackness of space. Lesbee said courteously, "Mr. Miller, how did you make out during the acceleration?"

"It caught me by surprise, Captain. I really got a battering. I think I was out for a while. But I'm all right now."

"Good," said Lesbee. "As you probably heard, Captain Browne and I have come to an agreement, and we are now going to destroy the creature that is loose on the ship. Stand by!"

Cynically, he broke the connection.

Miller was there all right, waiting. But the question was still, what could Miller do? The answer of course was that Miller could pre-empt. And—Lesbee asked himself—what could *that* do?

Abruptly, it seemed to him, he had the answer.

177

It was the technician's answer that he had been mentally straining for.

He now understood Browne's plan. They were waiting for Lesbee to let down his guard for a moment. Then Miller would pre-empt, cut off the tractor beam from Browne and seize Lesbee with it.

For the two officers it was vital that Lesbee not have time to fire the blaster at Browne. Lesbee thought: "It's the only thing they can be worried about. The truth is, there's nothing else to stop them."

The solution was, Lesbee realized with a savage glee, to let the two men achieve their desire. But first—

"Mr. Browne," he said quietly, "I think you should give your information. If I agree that it is indeed the correct solution, I shall release you and we shall have an election. You and I will stay right here till the election is over."

Browne said, "I accept your promise. The speed of light is a constant, and does not change in relation to moving objects. That would also apply to electromagnetic fields."

Lesbee said, "Then Dzing was affected by the remote-control device I turned on."

"Instantly," said Browne. "He never got a chance to do anything. How much power did you use?"

"Only first stage," said Lesbee. "But the machine-driven thought pulses in that would interfere with just about every magnetic field in his body. He couldn't do another coherent thing."

Browne said in a hushed tone, "It's got to me. He'll be out of control in one of the corridors, completely at our mercy." He grinned. "I told you I knew how to defeat him—because, of course, he was already defeated."

Lesbee considered that for a long moment, eyes narrowed. He realized that he accepted the explanation, but that he had preparations to make, and quickly—before Browne got suspicious of his delay.

He turned to the board and switched on the intercom. "People," he said, "strap yourselves in again. Help those who were injured to do the same. We may have another emergency. You have several minutes, I think, but don't waste any of them."

178

He cut off the intercom, and he activated the closed-circuit intercom of the technical stations. He said urgently, "Special instruction to Technical personnel. Report anything unusual, particularly if strange thought forms are going through your mind."

He had an answer to that within moments after he finished speaking. A man's twangy voice came over: "I keep thinking I'm somebody named Dzing, and I'm trying to report to my owners. Boy, am I incoherent!"

"Where is this?"

"D—4—19."

Lesbee punched the buttons that gave them a TV view of that particular ship location. Almost immediately he spotted a shimmer near the floor.

After a moment's survey he ordered a heavy-duty mobile blaster brought to the corridor. By the time its colossal energies ceased, Dzing was only a darkened area on the flat surface.

While these events were progressing, Lesbee had kept one eye on Browne and Mindel's blaster firmly gripped in his left hand. Now he said, "Well, sir, you certainly did what you promised. Wait a moment while I put this gun away, and then I'll carry out my part of the bargain."

He started to do so, then, out of pity, paused.

He had been thinking in the back of his mind about what Browne had said earlier: that the trip to Earth might only take a few months. The officer had backed away from that statement, but it had been bothering Lesbee ever since.

If it were true, then it was indeed a fact that nobody need die!

He said quickly, "What was your reason for saying that the journey home would only take—well—less than a year?"

"It's the tremendous time compression," Browne explained eagerly. "The distance as you pointed out is over 12 light-years. But with a time ratio of 3, 4, or 500 to one, we'll make it in less than a month. When I first started to say that, I could see that the figures were incomprehensible to you in your tense mood. In fact, I could scarcely believe them myself."

179

Lesbee said, staggered, "We can get back to Earth in a couple of weeks—my God!" He broke off, said urgently, "Look, I accept you as commander. We don't need an election. The status quo is good enough for any short period of time. Do you agree?"

"Of course," said Browne. "That's the point I've been trying to make."

As he spoke, his face was utterly guileless.

Lesbee gazed at that mask of innocence, and he thought hopelessly: "What's wrong? Why isn't he really agreeing? Is it because he doesn't want to lose his command so quickly?"

Sitting there, unhappily fighting for the other's life, he tried to place himself mentally in the position of the commander of a vessel, tried to look at the prospect of a return to view. It was hard to picture such a reality. But presently it seemed to him that he understood.

He said gently, feeling his way, "It would be kind of a shame to return without having made a successful landing anywhere. With this new speed, we could visit a dozen sun systems, and still get home in a year."

The look that came into Browne's face for a fleeting moment told Lesbee that he had penetrated to the thought in the man's mind.

The next instant, Browne was shaking his head vigorously. "This is no time for side excursions," he said. "We'll leave explorations of new star systems to future expeditions. The people of this ship have served their term. We go straight home."

Browne's face was now completely relaxed. His blue eyes shone with truth and sincerity.

There was nothing further that Lesbee could say. The gulf between Browne and himself could not be bridged.

The commander had to kill his rival, so that he might finally return to Earth and report that the mission of the *Hope of Man* was accomplished.


# VIII

In the most deliberate fashion Lesbee shoved the blaster into the inner pocket of his coat. Then, as if he were being careful, he used the tractor beam to push Browne about four feet away. There he set him down, released him from the beam, and—with the same deliberateness——drew his hand away from the tractor controls. Thus he made himself completely defenseless.

It was the moment of vulnerability.

Browne leaped at him, yelling: "Miller—pre-empt!"

First Officer Miller obeyed the command of his captain.

What happened then, only Lesbee, the technician with a thousand bits of detailed knowledge, expected.

For years it had been observed that when Control Room Below took over from Bridge, the ship speeded up slightly. And when Bridge took over from Control Room Below, the ship slowed instantly by the same amount—in each instance, something less than half a mile an hour.

The two boards were not completely synchronized. The technicians often joked about it, and Lesbee had once read an obscure technical explanation for the discrepancy. It had to do with the impossibility of ever getting two metals refined to the same precision of internal structure.

It was the age-old story of, no two objects in the universe are alike. But in times past, the differential had meant nothing. It was a technical curiosity, an interesting phenomenon of the science of metallurgy, a practical problem that caused machinists to curse good-naturedly when technicians like Lesbee required them to make a replacement part.

Unfortunately for Browne, the ship was now traveling near the speed of light.

His strong hands, reaching towards Lesbee's slighter body, were actually touching the latter's arm when the momentary deceleration occured as Bridge took over. The sudden slow-down was at a much faster rate than even Lesbee expected. The resistance of space to the forward movement of the ship must be using up more engine power than he had realized; it was taking a lot of thrust to maintain a one gravity acceleration.

The great vessel slowed about 150 miles per hour in the space of a second.

Lesbee took the blow of that deceleration partly against his back, partly against one side—for he had half-turned to defend himself from the bigger man's attack.

181

Browne, who had nothing to grab on to, was flung forward at the full 150 miles per hour. He struck the control board with an audible thud, stuck to it as if he were glued there; and then, when the adjustment was over—when the *Hope of Man* was again speeding along at one gravity—his body slid down the face of the board, and crumpled into a twisted position on the rubberized dais.

His uniform was discolored. As Lesbee watched, blood seeped through and dripped to the floor.

"Are you going to hold an election?" Tellier asked.

The big ship had turned back under Lesbee's command, and had picked up his friends. The life boat itself, with the remaining Karn still aboard, was put into an orbit around Alta III and abandoned.

The two young men were sitting now in the Captain's cabin.

After the question was asked, Lesbee leaned back in his chair, and closed his eyes. He didn't need to examine his total resistance to the suggestion. He had already savored the feeling that command brought.

Almost from the moment of Browne's death, he had observed himself having the same thoughts that Browne had voiced—among many others, the reasons why elections were not advisable aboard a spaceship. He waited now while Eleesa, one of his three wives—she being the younger of the two young widows of Browne—poured wine for them, and went softly out. Then he laughed grimly.

"My good friend," he said, "we're all lucky that time is so compressed at the speed of light. At 500-times compression, any further exploration we do will require only a few months, or years at most. And so I don't think we can afford to take the chance of defeating at an election the only person who understands the details of the new acceleration method. Until I decide exactly how much exploration we shall do, I shall keep our speed capabilities a secret. But I did, and do, think one other person should know where I have this information documented. Naturally, I selected First Officer Tellier."

"Thank you, sir," the youth said. But he was visibly thoughtful as he sipped his wine. He went on finally,

"Captain, I think you'd feel a lot better if you held an election. I'm sure you could win it."

Lesbee laughed tolerantly, shook his head. "I'm afraid you don't understand the dynamics of government," he said. "There's no record in history of a person who actually had control, handing it over."

He finished with the casual confidence of absolute power. "I'm not going to be presumptuous enough to fight a precedent like that!"

# HEIR UNAPPARENT

It was an uneasy, all-pervading sensation, a threat of pain to come combined with the beginning of the pain itself. The old man saw that Dr. Parker was looking at him startled.

"Good heavens, sir," the physician said. "You've been given Blackmail poison. This is incredible."

Arthur Clagg sat very still in the bed, his eyes narrowed, his thought a slow pattern of reception to impression. His gaze took in the chunky, red-faced Parker, the enormous bedroom, the shaded windows. At last, grimly, he shook his shaggy old head, and said:

"When will the crisis come in a man of my age?"

"About four days. The development is progressive, and the pain increases hour after hour by infinitesimal increments to a pitch of completely—"

The doctor broke off in a thin-lipped fury: "This is the worst crime in the history of the world. Poisoning a man ninety-four years of age. Why, it's—"

He must have noticed the scornful quality of Arthur Clagg's gaze. He stopped. He looked abashed. He said:

"I beg you pardon, sir."

Arthur Clagg said coldly: "I once defined you, doctor, as a person with an adult mind and the emotional capacity of a child. It still seems to fit."

He paused. He sat in the bed, cold-faced, thoughtful. He said finally in a precise, almost stately voice:

"You will refrain from informing anyone of what has happened, not even my great-granddaughter and her husband. No one! And—" A bleak smile touched his gray lips—"do not be too outraged by the crime. A man who dares to hold the reins of government is subject to all the risks of the trade, regardless of his age. In fact—"

He paused again. His smile twisted ironically as he went on:

"In fact, as is already apparent, the struggle for succession to the power of an old dictator is bound to be ferocious. A year ago a battery of doctors, including yourself, said I had at least fifteen more years of life ahead of me. That was very welcome news because I had, and have still, to decide who shall be my successor."

He smiled again, but there was a harshness in his voice as he went on:

"I now find that I have four days in which to make my decision. That is, *I think* I have four days. Is there anything in the news that will cut me down to even less time than that?"

The doctor was silent for a moment, as if he was organizing his mind; then:

"Your armies are still retreating, sir. Machine guns and rifles out of museums are almost useless against the forbidden atomic weapons of the rebel general, Garson. At their present rate of advance, the rebels should be here in six days. During the night they captured—"

Arthur Clagg scarcely heard. His mind was concentrating on the words "six days." That was it of course. His great-granddaughter Nadya, Merd Grayson her husband—the whole power group in the citadel wanted to force his hand before the arrival of the rebels. He grew aware again of the doctor's voice:

". . . Mr. Medgerow thinks that the fewness of their numbers prevents them from making a break-through. They—"

"Medgerow!" echoed Arthur Clagg, blankly. "Who's Medgerow? Oh, I remember. That's the inventor whose writings you once tried to bring to my attention. But, as you know, science no longer interests me."

185

Dr. Parker clicked his tongue apologetically. "I beg your pardon, sir. I used his name quite inadvertently."

The old man made a vague it-doesn't-matter movement. He said:

"Send in my valet, as you go out."

The doctor turned at the doorway. And a grim look crept over his thick face.

"Sir," he said, "I hope I will not seem presumptuous when I say that your friends and well-wishers will wait anxiously for you to turn *the* weapon on all your enemies."

He went out.


Arthur Clagg sat there, icily satiric. Fifty years, he thought, for fifty years the world has been educated against the use of weapons. For fifty years he had poured the wealth of the earth into the purest constructive channels, into social security, public works that *were* public and not mere political catchpolls.

The continents had been transformed; every conceivable idea for improvement within the bounds of scientific possibility had been subjected to the marvelous pressures of money and labor.

Green and fruitful in summer, gorgeously scientized in winter, peaceful and prosperous the year round, earth turned its made-over face towards its sun, a smiling, happy face. There was not an honest man alive who ought not to glory in the miracle that had been wrought during the brief span of half a century.

He had taken over a world devastated by atomic energy misused, and had changed it almost overnight into a dream of a billion wonders. And now—

Arthur Clagg suddenly felt his age. It seemed incredible that the first crisis could evoke the oldest evil impulse in human nature.

Kill! Destroy all your enemies. Be merciless. Bring out the irresistible weapon.

The surge of bitter thought quietened, as a discreet knock came at the door. Arthur Clagg sat heavy with his problem, as his valet entered. At last his mind calmed with the beginning of, not decision, but purpose.

The day passed. There was nothing to do but carry on

his routine and wait for his poisoners to come to him. They knew they had only four days in which to act. They wouldn't waste any time.

The intermediary would be Nadya or Merd.

It was like a thousand other days of his old age. All around him was movement, footsteps hurrying to and from his apartment, secretaries, department heads, police agents, an almost endless line of the people who kept him in touch with what was going on. A world of low voices telling him, telling him the monstrously many facts about a gigantic government whose every action was taken in his name.

The details only had to be left out. Except for that, everything absorbed him. Trouble in Chinese Manchuria —Renewed guerrilla activity in the virgin forest land of what had once been Germany—The cities controlled by the rebel general, Garson, were loosely held, and were not dangerous in themselves. "Very well. Go on sending them food—" Of all the government scientists, only a man called Medgerow had a wide acquaintance among important personages in the citadel.

"Hm-m-m," the old man mused aloud. "Medgerow! The name has already come up once today. What's he like?"

The chief of the State police shrugged. "Cultured conversationalist, abnormal though fascinating personality. But we've got nothing on him except that a lot of people go to see him. If I may ask, sir, why this interest in scientists?"

Arthur Clagg said slowly: "To my mind, no group either inside or outside the citadel would dare to act against me in this machine age, without a scientific adviser."

The police officer said matter-of-factly: "Shall I pick him up, and put on the pressure?"

"Don't be silly." Curtly. "If he's a good scientist, the simple little games you play with mechanical hypnotism and lie detectors won't catch him. But your action would have meantime served to warn the bigger game. You have given me the information I desire: So far as you know, there is no secret revolutionary force operating inside the citadel?"

"That is correct, sir."

When the police chief had gone, Arthur Clagg sat sunk

187

in thought. There no longer seemed any doubt. His first suspicion was correct. The poisoners were his own people.

It was the implication that was disturbing. Was it possible that, no matter how honorably a dictator might rule, his very existence kept *in* existence the violences of human power lusts, made bloodshed inevitable and, in its intensional structure, held the seeds of a far wider, greater chaos than the democracy which, for ten years, he had been considering restoring?

It seemed so; only—You couldn't bring back democracy with all *its* implications in three days.

The day dragged. At four o'clock Nadya, made up and glittering like a movie star, came in with a rustling of silk and a *clack-clack* of high heels. She brushed his cheek with her perfumed lips, then lighted a cigarette and flung herself onto a settee.

He thought: Nadya, poisoner. And felt a shock like fire. Earlier, the idea had been easy enough to accept, part of the life of intrigue that sinuated around him.

But *his* great-granddaughter! The last blood tie he had with the human race. All the rest, the noble Cecily, the quiet intellectual Peter, the first and loveliest Nadya, and the others, had slipped away into their graves, leaving him alone with this sanguinary betrayer and murderess.

The dark mood passed as swiftly as it had come, as Nadya said:

"Grandfather, you're impossible!"

Arthur Clagg studied her with abrupt but detached good humor. Nadya was twenty-eight. She had a pretty face, but her eyes were hard and bright, calculating rather than thoughtful.

She had once had great influence over him; and the old man realized with a cool objectivity why that had been so: Her youth! The vibrant purely animal spirits of a young girl had blinded him to the fact that she was just one more stranger not too cleverly out for what she could get.

That was over.

He waited; she went on earnestly:

"Grandfather, what is in your mind? Are you going to

188

permit the rebel Garson and that upstart parliament which is sponsoring him—are you going to let them shove you aside? Are you giving up without a fight, letting us all go down to ridicule and ruin because of your refusal to face the fact that human nature hasn't changed?"

Arthur Clagg said softly: "What would you do in my place, Nadya?"

It was not an answer to her tirade; it was designed purely and simply to draw her out. Up to a few years before, whenever he had given in to her wishes, that was the question that had always preceded the act of his yielding.

He saw from the way she was stiffening, that she recognized the phrase. A brilliant smile lighted her be-rouged face. Her eyes widened, grew eager. She said urgently:

"Grandfather, it is no exaggeration to say that you are probably the greatest man who has ever lived. In spite of your age, and the fact that you have delegated so many of your powers, your prestige is so great that, though there is gathering confusion resulting from the rebel march on the citadel, your world is holding together. But before you, and terribly near now, is the most important decision of your life:

"You have your tremendously potent weapon. For fifty years you have kept it hidden, but now you must bring it forth, and use it. With it you can decide what the future shall be. Medgerow says there is no record in history of a decision of such importance being defaulted because of the refusal of—"

"Medgerow!" ejaculated Arthur Clagg. He stopped himself. "Never mind. Go on."

Nadya was looking at him. "He's a horrible little man with a personality and an extraordinary self-confidence that makes him interesting in spite of his appearance. An inventor attached to the government science bureau, I believe."

She hesitated. She seemed to realize that the full force of her argument had to be rebuilt now that it had been interrupted. She said:

"Grandfather, in spite of all your repugnance to violence, the fact is that people have already died. If you don't kill the rebels, they will go on exterminating your

189

loyal army, and will eventually reach the citadel. I am going to suspend judgment as to what they will do to us when they get here. But it is a point that you ought to consider. You can't just leave it to blind chance."

She stopped; she drew a deep breath; then: "You have asked me for my opinion. As plainly as I can, I want to say that I think you should disarm the rebels, and then turn your weapon over to Merd. Only through him and me can your life work be saved from violent transformations. The laws of political accession are such that other groups would have to tear down at least part of the edifice you have so carefully built up. The world might even dissolve once more into separate contending states. The death toll *could* reach fantastic proportions.

"Can't you see—" She was so earnest that her voice trembled—"it is to our interest, and ours alone in all this wide world, to keep things as they are. Well," she finished with an unnatural casualness, "what do you say?"

It took a moment for the old man to realize that, for the time as least, she had finished.

After a moment, it struck him that he was not altogether displeased with her verbal picture. For all its cool bloodedness, it was a gentle solution to a deadly situation. For, as she had said, the choice was no longer between killing and not killing. Government soldiers had already died before the blast of atomic cannon, and, according to reports, mobile artillery had wrought havoc in the rebel ranks.

Death was definitely involved. Nevertheless—

Only a monstrosity of a man would hand a world and its helpless people over to a gang of poisoners.

He saw that Nadya, for all her return to casualness, was watching him anxiously. Arthur Clagg laughed, a silent, bitter laughter. He parted his lips, but before he could speak, the young woman said:

"Grandfather, I know you've hated me ever since I married Merd. You may not be aware of that dislike, but it's there; and the reason for it is emotional. I haven't dared mention it to you before, but this is an ultimate crisis. Within six days, atomic cannon will be burning at

190

this citadel; and in the fire of such a reality, not even the feelings of an old man can be spared."

"Hated you!" said Arthur Clagg.

It was not a reaction. It was a pure expression, a sound having no origin in thought. He did note in a remote part of his mind that she had said six days, not four. She apparently did not anticipate a crisis at the moment of his death. The implication, that she knew nothing of the poisoning, was startling.

She could, of course, have such firm mental control over herself that the seemingly unconscious reaction was actually deliberate. There was no time to think about that. Nadya was speaking:

"You've hated me in a perversion of love. I was all you had, and then I got married; and, naturally, thereafter Merd and the children came first. Grandfather, don't you see—that is why you hate me."

The gathered effects of the poison made thinking hard. The old man remained stiff, and, at first, hostile. He began to brace himself mentally. With a sudden, reaching effort, he threw off the queasy weight of his sickishness. Briefly, his mind drummed with energy. Thought came in the old, flashing way.

He relaxed finally, astounded. Why, you old fool, he thought. She's right. That *is* why you disliked her. Jealousy!

He studied her from under shaggy eyebrows, curious, conscious that earlier impressions were now subject to revision. In many ways Nadya's was a distinctive face, not so good-looking but definitely aristocratic. Funny how people got that way. He himself had always had a professorish sort of countenance and yet here was his great-granddaughter looking like a patrician.

Why was it that no one had ever educed the natural laws that would explain why the grandchildren of people who ruled all had the same expressions on their faces?

Arthur Clagg shook himself, and drew his mind back to Nadya. She had on, he decided after a moment, severely, too much make-up, almost as much as some of the hussies who fluttered around the citadel.

You could scarcely blame a woman though, for being in style.

The old man began to feel staggered. What was happening to his case against her?

Here she sat, a lean, aristocratic woman, anxious to retain her high position—who wouldn't in her place?—clever rather than intellectual, a little callous perhaps. But all people who commanded had to harden their hearts to individual suffering.

He who had lived in an age where a tornado of atomic energy killed a billion human beings *had* to have as successor a person who, in the final issue, was capable of exterminating anyone daring once more to precipitate such a holocaust. And now that there was doubt as to whether Nadya was a party to the poisoning, she was again eligible.

But if she and Merd weren't guilty, who was?

The old man sat shaken, uncertain. He might never find out, of course, in spite of the fact that the need to know was rapidly becoming an obsession. But he couldn't condemn anyone without proof. He said slowly:

"Leave me now, Nadya. You have presented your case well, but I have not decided. Tomorrow, I intend to—Never mind."

He waited till, with puzzled side glances, she had left. Then he picked up his private radio phone. It took a moment to establish the connection; then:

"Well?" said Arthur Clagg.

The police chief's voice came: "The arrangements are made. The meeting will take place in no man's land. He agrees to the presence of three bodyguards."

The officer broke off: "Sir, this is a most dangerous business. If anything should go wrong—"

The old man said curtly: "You are having the Mobile outfitted according to my instructions?"

"Yes, but—" Earnestly: "Sir, I ask again, what is your purpose in talking to General Garson?"

The old man only smiled tightly, and hung up. He had not one but two purposes in meeting Garson. It wouldn't do to tell anyone that his first purpose was to hear the case of the rebels. As for his second reason—

His smile deepened. No use broadcasting that either.

192

"Remember," said Arthur Clagg to his chief officer, "take no action till I tug at my ear."

The unpleasant part of the whole business was walking fifty feet from his Mobile to where the tables and chairs had been set up in the open meadow. Every step he took twisted his insides. Gasping, he sank into one of the chairs.

He was beginning to recover when a lanky individual in an all-fitting blue uniform descended the steps of the second Mobile, and strode across the grass. The man's movements had all the awkward freedom of the unrestrained extrovert.

Recognition was unmistakable. The lean, bony face with its lantern jaw had already stared at him several times from photographs. Even without the countenance, the nasal twanged voice, which had twice broadcast on the radio, would have made the identification inevitable. Rebel General Garson was photo and voco-genic. He said:

"Old Man, I hope you haven't got some slick schem up your sleeve."

It was loudly said, too loudly to be polite. But Arthur Clagg was too intent, too curious, to notice. Nor did he think immediately of replying. He was conscious of a genuine absorption in this man who dared to oppose the irresistible weapon.

Garson had brown eyes and uncombed, sandy hair. He sank into his chair, and stared unsmilingly at his aged opponent. Once more it was Garson who spoke, snappingly this time:

"Get to the point man."

Arthur Clagg hardly heard. Nor did the details of physical appearance interest him now. It was the man, his boldness in organizing a small army in a vast land, his defiance of death for an ideal, that almost, in itself, merited success for his enterprise.

Slowly, the old man straightened his anguished body, said with dignity:

"General Garson—as you will notice, I am recognizing your military title—to me you represent a trend of thought in the country. And as a result I might, if you can give me some dialectical arguments, allow parliament to

193

be re-established under your mentorship. I am not opposed to democracy, because, except for the disaster in which it involved itself half a century ago, it was a vigorous, marvelously growing organism. I have no doubt it can be so again. The danger is the free use of atomic energy—"

"Don't worry about that." Garson waved a gaunt hand. "My congress and I will keep it to ourselves."

"Eh!" Arthur Clagg stared across the table, not sure that he had heard correctly. He had the sudden, blank feeling that meaningless words had been projected at him.

"See here, Mr. Dictator Clagg, I don't know just what you had in mind, asking me to come over. I thought maybe you wanted to surrender, now that I've called your bluff. Here's my offer: I understand you've got some kind of estate down south. O.K. I'll let you an' your granddaughter and family live there under guard. If anybody starts somethin', naturally they get killed.

"My congress will set me up as president, and I'll just slip into your position as quickly as I can. In a few months everything'll be goin' along smooth as ever. That clear?"

The shock was greater. There seemed nothing to think. At last Arthur Clagg expostulated:

"But see here, you haven't got a congress yet. A congress is a governing body elected by secret ballot by the vote of all the people. Two hundred men can't just organize and call themselves congress. They—"

His voice trailed, as the implications penetrated of what he was saying. It seemed incredible but—was this man so ignorant of history that he didn't know what representative government was?

The old man tried to picture that. The psychology of it finally grew plausible. Like so many human beings, Garson was only dimly aware that there had been life before his own ego emerged from the mists of childhood.

To him, that pre-Garson period must be an unsubstantial hodge-podge. Somehow the words "congress" and "president" had come down to him. And he had made his own definitions.

With an effort Arthur Clagg drew his attention back to Garson. And the thought came finally: After all, it was the courage of this creature that was fascinating. A man who had the boldness to defy *the* weapon must be amenable to reason and to a partial re-education.

"Boy!" Garson's voice twanged. "You sure have been smart, Clagg. All these years pretending you had a super weapon, and fixing up books and motion pictures and things to make people think it all happened the way you said. You never fooled me though; and so now you've had your day. I'll sure carry on with that weapon game, though. It—"

His voice went on, but Arthur Clagg did not listen. He waited until the sound stopped; and then with a casual gesture tugged at his ear.

He saw Garson stiffen, as the mechanical hypnotic waves struck at him. The old man wasted no time.

"Garson," he intoned, "Garson, you will be glad to tell me, tell me, tell me who gave you the blueprints for atomic cannon. Garson, was it someone in the government? Garson, it is so easy to tell me."

"But I do not know." The man's voice was faraway somehow, and vaguely surprised. "They were given me by a man I do not know. He said he was an agent, an agent —"

"An agent for whom?" Arthur Clagg pressed.

"I do not know."

"But didn't you care? Didn't it worry you?"

"No, I figgered as soon as I had the cannon, the other guy would have to start worrying."

After three minutes, Arthur Clagg tugged at his ear again—and Garson came back to normal life. He looked a little startled, but the old man was not worried about the suspicions of so completely ignorant a man. He said icily:

"Since I gave you my word, mister, you may depart at once in perfect safety. I would advise you, however, to keep on traveling, because tomorrow no one in the vicinity of an atomic cannon will be alive.

"In any event I shall advise"—pause—"my son-in-law, my heir and successor, to hunt you down and have you brought to justice."

195

He was thinking as he finished: There was no time for further choice.

The house was one of a row of pleasant mansions that stood amid greenery in the shadow of the towering peak of building that was the citadel.

The outer door must have opened by remote control because, when Dr. Parker had gone through, he found himself in a narrow metal hallway. A tiny bulb in the ceiling shed a white glow upon a second door, which was all metal. The doctor stood motionless, then he called, shrilly:

"Medgerow, what's all this?"

There was a mechanical chuckle from one of the walls. "Don't get excited, doctor. As you know, the whole situation is now entering the critical stage, and I am taking no chances."

"B-but I've been here a hundred times before, and I've never seen any of this . . . this fortification."

"Good!" Medgerow's voice came again through the wall speaker. He sounded pleased. "It would take an atomic cannon or"—pause—"Arthur Clagg's Contradictory Force to blast me out of this. But come in."

The second door opened into a paneled hallway, and clanged behind Parker. A small man was waiting there for him. He chuckled as he saw Parker, then said curtly:

"Well, your report, man! You administered the poison substitute successfully?"

The doctor did not reply as he followed the other into the living room. These first moments in the presence of Medgerow always made him uneasy. Adjustment from normalness to unnormalness was a semi-involved process.

It wasn't so much, Parker realized bleakly for the hundredth time, that Medgerow's ugliness by itself was so jarring. A thousand males picked up at random from the streets outside would have yielded a dozen whose physical characteristics were less prepossessing.

Medgerow differed in that he exuded a curious, terrible aura of misshapen strength. His personality protruded with the concreteness of the hump of a hunchback. It seemed to make him not quite human.

196

Parker had discovered that, by letting only the corner of his eyes be aware of the man, he could stand his presence. That was what he did now. And said:

"Yes, I administered the substitute two nights ago. As I told you, the pain effects will be the same as with the real poison."

The image in the corner of the doctor's vision stood stock-still; then:

"He thinks he will die after four days?"

"Yes. And his reaction was to swear me to secrecy." He broke off anxiously: "Are you sure, are you absolutely sure that you can nullify his weapon long enough to seize control of it? How can you be positive that he will even use it?"

Medgerow clicked his tongue impatiently. "Of course I'm not sure. I am basing my estimations on the character of a man whose actions, speeches and writings I have studied for years. At this very moment, I'll warrant, the old man has practically decided to use the weapon in one way or another. In my opinion, he will use it to act against the rebels, and will then turn the weapon over to his son-in-law.

"This is all to the good. I want *him* to stamp out the rebel force before I move against him.

"In my opinion, the crisis will be tomorrow. If I read Arthur Clagg aright, he will by now have sought a meeting with General Garson, the rebel leader. He will have found a man who embodies the worst features of the demagogue. And, besides, Garson has dared to use atomic power. That, as I have told you, will balance in the old man's mind his suspicion that his great-granddaughter helped to poison him.

"Oh, yes, he'll use the weapon. And that"—the little monstrosity of a man chuckled—"is where I come in. Little did Arthur Clagg realize fifty years ago that he established a precedent, and became the first, not the last, of the scientist leaders. Now that men's minds accept such a possibility, scientists will begin to think in that direction, unconsciously molding their lives and their works with the hope of power in their minds. Such are the laws of dialectical materialism. But now I must—"

He broke off; his voice lost its sustained quality of intensity, grew quiet.

"Thanks for coming, doctor. As you know, we couldn't take the chance of a phone call being intercepted, particularly as the secret police have been making guarded inquiries about me."

As they shook hands, Medgerow, his blue eyes glistening, said:

"You have done well, Parker. I'm sorry you were too squeamish to use the real poison, but that can be remedied when I get into power. As it is, your assistance in helping me force the old man to bring out his weapon will gain you the reward you desire. Arthur Clagg's great-granddaughter, Nadya, will be *given* you in marriage as soon as her husband has been decently disposed of."

"Thank you," said Parker quietly.

Contemptuous-eyed the little man watched him go. He thought coldly:

Silly ass doctor! Couldn't he see that the public necessities of the situation required that the only legitimate heir of the *former* dictator marry the new ruler?

Pawns didn't take queens.

Speed was essential. He sent the invitations to Merd and Nadya for that afternoon. They arrived shortly after lunch. In spite of himself, the old man found himself staring searchingly at his son-in-law, seeking in the man's lean face reassurance that the colossal trust he was about to receive would not be misused.

He saw gray eyes, dark hair, a rather fine, sensitive face with stern lips—exactly the same physical characteristics, the same person, he had so violently disliked from the very first announcement of Nadya's betrothal. The body not the mind was visible.

It was not enough. The thought was a pain briefly greater than the agony of the poison. And yet, the decision was made. A man with two days to live couldn't think of anything but the easy solution. Arthur Clagg said curtly:

"Lock all the doors. We're going to uncover the weapon. It will require most of the afternoon."

Merd said explosively. "You mean, it's *here?*"

The old man ignored that. He went on drably:

"The weapon is mounted inside a plastic airplane, powered by four gas turbine jets and strato rockets. This machine is hidden in the east wing of the citadel which, as you perhaps know, was built by workers from every part of the world. The employment of men from far places who did not speak the same language made it possible to construct a hiding place without anyone guessing its true purpose."

He broke off, fumbled in his coat pocket, and produced a key.

"This will unlock a tool cupboard next to my bathroom. Bring the tools in here. You will need them all to uncover, and then activate the mechanical keys that will open the hidden chamber."

It took time, the two young people silent and intent on their unaccustomed work, carting machine saws, atomic drills, mobile planes into various indicated parts of the living room. When all the tools were gathered, the old man motioned them to the settee near him, and began:

"There has been a great deal of wild talk about the nature of my weapon. The speculation is quite unnecessary because many years ago I very foolishly gave out some of the theory in a series of articles published in the government science gazette. It was foolish, not because anyone will be able to duplicate the weapon but because—"

He broke off, frowning. "Never mind. I'll explain that later."

He went on, quietly: "The theory behind the Contradiction Force penetrates to the inner core of the meanings of life and of movement. Life, as you know, has been defined as orderly movement. There is movement also in inorganic matter, but this is a primitive version and is explained by the larger concept.

"What makes movement possible? Why does not matter, organic or inorganic, simply collapse into its basic components, and, thus inert, fulfill its apparently senseless destiny?

"You might answer that things are as they are because electrons whirl in orbits according to fixed laws, forming atoms which, in their turn, have a physically legal relationship to the larger structure of molecules, and so on. But that would be merely evading the issue.

"Movement occurs in an object because *in* it, in its very basic oneness, there is an antithesis, a contradiction. It is only because a thing contains a contradiction within itself that it moves and acquires impulse and activity.

"The theory by itself suggested the nature of the research: I found first what were the laws governing the contradiction in various types of matter, and I shall give you the mathematics in due course.

"The mechanical problem of practicalizing the theory, involved in its simplest functions the procuration of a force that would cause the contradiction in any given matter to operate, not in the orderly fashions that nature has laboriously evolved, but uncontrollably.

"Those who have not seen it in action cannot imagine how terrible the result is. It is not, has no relation to, atomic energy. As a destructive force, the hellish active area in the interior of a nova sun possibly equals it in violence, but such a sun cannot even theoretically surpass it.

"Fortunately, heat is not a byproduct, as would be the case if the force was related to atomic or electrical energy.

"It was only long after the weapon was an actuality that I discovered that I had hit on a billion-to-one chance, that my discovery was an accident that cannot be repeated in a million years.

"Tomorrow you will see it in action."

He paused and frowned, partly with pain, partly because—

"The weapon has only one aspect that is dangerous to us. It can be nullified by a simple, electrically induced magnetic flow in the object on which it is focused. That is why I was foolish in giving out the theory.

"Some day, somewhere, a smart scientist will discover the nullifying principle—and the weapon will cease to be a factor in world politics.

"I must confess I have worried about that in the dark watches of many nights. But now"—He straightened slowly—"let us get to work—"

200

Minute by minute, as the hours passed, his choice seemed more and more final.

The third day dawned cloudless. It was one of those brightly perfect spring mornings. The world below the plane was a gorgeous panorama of emerging green. Even now, with the anguish tearing at his body, it was hard for Arthur Clagg to realize that, in this setting of eternally youthful soil, his mortality was seeking its final ecstasy of expression.

They came to the rebel lines, and began to circle. The telescopes showed metal glinting among the trees below —and Arthur Clagg, with Nadya leaning over his shoulder, examined the maps the army had supplied.

"Climb higher," he ordered finally. And again, minutes later: "Higher."

After ten minutes more: *"Higher!"*

"But we're up about thirty-five miles," Merd protested. "We've already used up three quarters of our rocket fuel."

"Higher!" said the old man inexorably. "The problem at all times with this weapon is to remain clear of the explosion. When I first estimated mathematically its power, I hardly believed my figures. Fortunately, I had the sense to rig up a device that would cut off the force after one millionth of a second. If I do that now, and set this dial to 'METAL,' only the outermost rim of atoms on the one cannon below that I'm aiming at, will be affected."

He finished: "When you have five minutes fuel left, tell me."

Merd's voice came over the earphones. "Less than five minutes left now. I'll have to turn over to the jets."

"Steady!" said Arthur Clagg.

He had left the telescopic sights, and was swinging the gun around, locking it into place. Once more he looked through the sights. He pressed the trigger.

The ground below turned bluer than the sky. For a long moment, it looked like a placid lake in a glacier. Then the lake was gone. And where there had been trees and green beauty was a gray-black hole thirty miles in diameter.

Desert!

"Grandfather," Nadya cried. "The gun is swinging back. It'll hit you."

The old man did not move from the sights. The gun swung in a one hundred eighty degree arc, and clicked back into position just beside his head. He said, without looking up:

"It's all right, I made it that way."

A moment longer he looked, then he straightened. Awareness came that the plane was shuddering with speed, the jets whistling shrilly.

He sat down. He leaned back, weary, feeling strangely old. Slowly, he straightened, fighting the pain and the fatigue. Merd's voice came over the phones:

"Grandfather, there's news coming through from the citadel. Some idiot has started a revolution. Listen!"

A strange voice sounded: ". . . A rebellion in the air force . . . uprising in the citadel garrison, with fighting now going on in the gardens. A man named Medgerow has declared himself to be the new dictator—"

There was more, but Arthur Clagg's mind followed it no further. Medgerow. Funny, how the name had come up so often the last few days, almost like predestination. Nadya had mentioned him, and Dr. Parker and—"

The old man sagged a little. Parker—poison. For a moment, the connection seemed impossible. What could be the man's motive? Except for a tendency to lose control of his emotions, Parker was a timid, cautious fellow with a reasonably good mind.

Arthur Clagg sighed. There was no use thinking about it. Medgerow had precipitated a palace revolution before the arrival of Garson. Like Garson, the new usurper was apparently not taking the slightest notice of an old man and his mythical contradictory force.

Perhaps he should have announced in advance his intention to use it.

No use worrying about that now. The die was cast, and there were things to do. He straightened.

"Nadya."

"Yes, grandfather."

"Jump."

He had almost forgotten that people never disobeyed

him when he took that tone, that manner; it was so long since he had used it.

One measured look she gave him. Then she was running forward to Merd. She came back, tears in her eyes. Her lips touched his. She said:

"I shall join the children at the Lodge, and wait till I hear from you."

He watched her fall into the blue haze. It was five minutes later that Merd's voice came over the radio:

"There're some planes following us, grandfather. What —"

Three times Arthur Clagg pressed the trigger of the Contradictory Force weapon, but the planes came on, untouched, unharmed. At last, he whispered his defeat over the phone:

"Better obey their signal, Merd, and go down. There's nothing we can do."

They were actually landing before he realized he was still holding the weapon. He stared down grimly at the now useless double cone, and then let it slip clear of his fingers. He watched it swing back in its one hundred eighty degree arc, and click metallically into its rest position.

It lay in its cradle, still omnipotent under the right conditions. But by the time it was used again, Merd and he would be dead, and the law and order world he had created would be scrambled by the passions of men. And it would take a hundred years to put all the pieces to-gether again.

The devil of it, the irony, was that Medgerow had no reason to use it immediately. He felt the plane setting on its jets. Gently it touched the ground. Merd left the controls and came back to him immediately.

"They're signaling us to get off," he said quietly.

Arthur Clagg nodded. In silence they climbed to the ground. They were about a hundred feet away when the other planes began to disgorge men, most of whom carried tubes of rocket fuel to the big plane. One of the men, however, a tall chap in air force uniform, came over. He said insolently:

"The Medgerow orders that you be searched."

203

*The* Medgerow. Merd submitted stonily, but the old man watched the procedure with a bleak admiration for its thoroughness. When the man had finished, Arthur Clagg said:

"Satisfy my curiosity. Why did you rebel?"

The officer shrugged. "The—deadness—you created was killing my will to live. The Medgerow is going to release atomic energy. We're going to the planets, perhaps even the stars, in my lifetime."

When the officer had gone, Arthur Clagg turned to Merd, said:

"My desire for order grew out of the hideous misuse of atomic energy. But I always knew that man was the Contradictory Force of the organic universe, and that sooner or later, for better or worse, he must again be allowed to play with that ultimate fire. Apparently, the time has come."

A small man was climbing out of the nearest plane. He carried an atomic in one hand. He came forward briskly. And even though he had never seen Medgerow before, it seemed to Arthur Clagg that he would have recognized him anywhere, without any more description than he had already received by chance.

Merd was speaking distastefully: "I've discovered that by letting only the corner of my eyes be aware of him, I can stand his presence for a while."

It was an odd and altogether fascinating statement. The words drew the old man's attention briefly away from Medgerow. He felt momentarily absorbed by the insight they gave into Merd's character.

He found himself liking his son-in-law better.

There was no time to think about either Merd or his words.

Medgerow stood before them.

He looked unnormal. It wasn't so much, Arthur Clagg decided bleakly, that Medgerow's ugliness was jarring in itself. A thousand males picked at random would have yielded a dozen whose physical characteristics were less prepossessing.

Perhaps it was the triumphant smile on his face, with its frank and unashamed arrogance. It was hard to tell.

The man exuded a curious, terrible aura of misshapen strength. His personality protruded with the concreteness of the hump of a hunchback.

Gazing at him, old Arthur Clagg felt a chill, a sick consciousness of the extent of his failure. It seemed incredible that he had let himself be panicked into using his weapon, and had not once suspected that that was exactly what his hidden enemy was working for.

He thought: *The* Medgerow, heir of earth—the very idea was shattering.

Medgerow broke the silence, coolly: "In a moment I shall get into your plane and start climbing. As soon as I have reached a safe height, I shall fire at this"— he drew a strip of metal from his pocket, and tossed it onto the ground—"with your weapon. I like ironies like that."

For a moment, the old man could not believe that he had heard aright. The intention, so deliberately stated, was so far reaching in its implications, so unexpected, that it seemed impossible. He opened his mouth, then closed it again. The hope that came shook his very bones; it had no parallel in the long history of his career.

It was Merd who finally reacted vocally, Merd who said violently:

"But there's a city of fifty thousand over there about eight miles. You can't fire the weapon so near it."

Arthur Clagg fumbled at Merd's arm. He wanted to tell the young fool to stop arguing. Couldn't he see that Medgerow was playing into their hands?

But of course he couldn't. Merd didn't know the fear that had in the long ago made his great-grandfather-in-law install the weapon in the way that he had. Before he could decided how to stop Merd, Merd cried:

"Put a bullet through our brains, you murderer. You can't destroy a whole city, You *can't!*"

Once more, in a haze of anxiety now, Arthur Clagg parted his lips to utter words that would silence Merd. Just in time, he saw the look on Medgerow's face. And closed them again.

No words were needed. The best ally he had in this fateful moment was *the* Medgerow himself.

The little man stood, head flung back proudly. His eyes blazed with sardonic joy. He said:

"I shall not make the mistakes of the new princes of history. I have no desire to be dragged, as was Cromwell, out of my grave and hanged as a public spectacle. Nor shall I be so slow in starting my executions as were the early French revolutionists. And as for those talkative idiots Felix Pyat and Delescluze in 1871 Paris —it makes me sick just to think about them.

"Mussolini allowed himself to be caught in the same net. He permitted his potential destroyer and betrayers to remain alive. Hitler, of course, had half his work done for him when the Allies rid Germany of the Hohenzollern dynasty. He made only one mistake: Russia. Everybody's plans were naturally blown sky-high when atomic energy appeared on the scene."

Immeasurably savage grew his voice: "Force and terror—those are the weapons that win, when there are no undefeated armies extant to support opposition groups. I shall use the weapon on you because I have to test its operation anyway. I shall do this here and now because nothing will better convince the world of my unalterable determinations than the destruction of a city. So true is this that, if the city had not been to hand, it would have been necessary for me to transport all of us to its vicinity."

He finished cynically: "It will be a simple matter, once I am established, to propagandize people into believing that it was you, not I, who destroyed it."

"You can't do this," cried Merd wildly. "It's not human. It's—"

Firmly, this time, the old man caught his arm. "Merd," he said resonantly, "can't you see it's useless? We're dealing with a man who has a plan, a settled policy of conquest."

The remark seemed to please Medgerow. He said with satisfaction:

"That's right. Argument is useless. I never missed a bet in my strategy. You did everything exactly as I intended you to. Your decision had to be made too swiftly. You had no time to think."

"My foolishness," said Arthur Clagg quietly, "was in

thinking all these days and years that there was a decision to be made. I've just realized that, actually, I made my choice long and long ago. I chose, not self, but the good of all mankind, whereas you have chosen self."

"Eh!" Medgerow looked at him sharply, as if searching for a hidden meaning. Then he laughed. Then he said, arrogantly:

"Enough of this chatter. You ruined yourself twenty years ago, Arthur Clagg, when you ignored the letters sent you by a struggling science student, myself. I realize now you probably didn't even receive them. But that excuse doesn't apply to later years when powerful friends tried to draw my work to your attention; and you wouldn't even look at it."

He was suddenly livid with rage. He spat:

"Twenty years of obscurity—During the next twenty minutes, I'll let you think of what might have been if you had treated me from the beginning according to my merits."

He whirled away. The plane door clanged behind him. The gas turbines whinned. The jets hissed. Lightly, swiftly, the plane rose into the sky. It became a dot.

After a minute, the other planes took off and the two men were alone.

There was a long silence. At last, cold and contemptuous, Merd said:

"This creature cannot see that you are not, and never were, his type of dictator. The history of democracies teaches that in emergencies people will temporarily surrender their liberties. No greater emergency ever existed than the release of atomic energy. The period of control has been a long one, because the world had to be reorganized; and, like a new mold, allowed to set.

"In my considered opinion, the people are ready again to take over; and no one, not Medgerow, not me, not all the force anyone can possibly exert will stop them."

"Why, Merd," said Arthur Clagg, "I didn't know you felt like that. In fact, you have provided me with a whole series of pleasant shocks. Under pressure, you have showed a very great number of golden attributes.

Accordingly, I herewith commission you to begin re-establishing democracy as soon as we return to the citadel."

The young man was staring at him wildly. Then he swallowed hard. At last, shakily, he asked:

"W-what did you say? Back to the citadel—"

Arthur Clagg felt a sudden sympathy for his great-grandson-in-law, a sharp understanding of the agonized turmoil being experienced by a man who had geared himself to death, and now was confronted by the possibility of life.

It seemed curiously important that Merd suffer no more than he had to. The old man said grimly:

"I was terrified that some day the Contradictory Force would be set off accidentally. I therefore constructed the weapon so that its muzzle resembled its stock. I placed it so that it would swing around automatically after I had fired it, and point up towards the sky, or towards any stranger who might be impelled to fire it. *That is the position it is in this very moment, as Medgerow stands aiming it.*"

Old Arthur Clagg finished in a ringing tone: "Not with Medgerow, but in your hands, Merd, lies the destiny of mankind."

He did not know then that the poison inside him was only a substitute, and that he would be the wise old mentor of the new and lusty civilization of the stars.

# THE WEAPON SHOP

The village at night made a curiously timeless picture.
Fara walked contentedly beside his wife along the street.
The air was like wine; and he was thinking dimly of the
artist who had come up from Imperial City, and made
what the telestats called—he remembered the phrase
vividly—"a symbolic painting reminiscent of a scene in
the electrical age of seven thousand years ago."

Fara believed that utterly. The street before him with
its weedless, automatically tended gardens, its shops set
well back among the flowers, its perpetual hard, grassy
sidewalks, and its street lamps that glowed from every
pore of their structure—this was a restful paradise where
time had stood still.

And it was like being a part of life that the great artist's
picture of this quiet, peaceful scene before him was now
in the collection of the empress herself. She had praised it,
and naturally the thrice-blest artist had immediately and
humbly begged her to accept it.

What a joy it must be to be able to offer personal
homage to the glorious, the divine, the serenely gracious
and lovely Innelda Isher, one thousand one hundred
eightieth of her line.

As they walked, Fara half turned to his wife, In the
dim light of the nearest street lamp, her kindly, still youthful face was almost lost in shadow. He murmured softly,

instinctively muting his voice to harmonize with the pastel shades of night:

"She said—our empress said—that our little village of Glay seemed to her to have in it all the wholesomeness, the gentleness, that constitutes the finest qualities of her people. Wasn't that a wonderful thought, Creel? She must be a marvelously understanding woman. I—"

He stopped. They had come to a side street, and there was something about a hundred and fifty feet along it that—

"Look!" Fara said hoarsely.

He pointed with rigid arm and finger at a sign that glowed in the night, a sign that read:

## FINE WEAPONS
### THE RIGHT TO BUY WEAPONS IS THE RIGHT TO BE FREE

Fara had a strange, empty feeling as he stared at the blazing sign. He saw that other villagers were gathering. He said finally, huskily:

"I've heard of these shops. They're places of infamy, against which the government of the empress will act one of these days. They're built in hidden factories, and then transported whole to towns like ours and set up in gross defiance of property rights. That one wasn't there an hour ago."

Fara's face hardened. His voice had a harsh edge in it, as he said:

"Creel, go home."

Fara was surprised when Creel did not move off at once. All their married life, she had had a pleasing habit of obedience that had made cohabitation a wonderful thing. He saw that she was looking at him wide-eyed, and that it was a timid alarm that held her there. She said:

"Fara, what do you intend to do? You're not thinking of—"

"Go home!" Her fear brought out all the grim determination in his nature. "We're not going to let such a monstrous thing desecrate our village. Think of it"—his voice shivered before the appalling thought—"this fine,

210

old-fashioned community, which we had resolved always to keep exactly as the empress has it in her picture gallery, debauched now, ruined by this . . . this thing— But we won't have it; that's all there is to it."

Creel's voice came softly out of the half-darkness of the street corner, the timidity gone from it: "Don't do anything rash, Fara. Remember it is not the first new building to come into Glay——since the picture was painted."

Fara was silent. This was a quality of his wife of which he did not approve, this reminding him unnecessarily of unpleasant facts. He knew exactly what she meant. The gigantic, multitentacled corporation, Automatic Atomic Motor Repair Shops, Inc., had come in under the laws of the State with their flashy building, against the wishes of the village council—and had already taken half of Fara's repair business.

"That's different!" Fara growled finally. "In the first place people will discover in good time that these new automatic repairers do a poor job. In the second place its fair competition. But this weapon shop is a defiance of all the decencies that make life under the House of Isher such a joy. Look at the hypocritical sign: 'The right to buy weapons—' Aaaaahh!"

He broke off with: "Go home, Creel. We'll see to it that they sell no weapons in this town."

He watched the slender woman-shape move off into the shadows. She was halfway across the street when a thought occurred to Fara. He called:

"And if you see that son of ours hanging around some street corner, take him home. He's got to learn to stop staying out so late at night."

The shadowed figure of his wife did not turn; and after waching her for a moment moving along against the dim background of softly glowing street lights, Fara twisted on his heel, and walked swiftly toward the shop. The crowd was growing larger every minute, and the night pulsed with excited voices.

Beyond doubt, here was the biggest thing that had ever happened to the village of Glay.

The sign of the weapon shop was, he saw, a normal-illusion affair. No matter what his angle of view, he was always looking straight at it. When he paused finally in front of the great display window, the words had pressed back against the store front, and were staring unwinkingly down at him.

Fara sniffed once more at the meaning of the slogan, then forgot the simple thing. There was another sign in the window, which read:

## THE FINEST ENERGY WEAPONS IN THE KNOWN UNIVERSE

A spark of interest struck fire inside Fara. He gazed at that brilliant display of guns, fascinated in spite of himself. The weapons were of every size, ranging from tiny little finger pistols to express rifles. They were made of every one of the light, hard, ornamental substances: glittering glassein, the colorful but opaque Ordine plastic, viridescent magnesitic beryllium. And others.

It was the very deadly extent of the destructive display that brought a chill to Fara. So many weapons for the little village of Glay, where not more than two people to his knowledge had guns, and those only for hunting. Why, the thing was absurd, fantastically mischievous, utterly threatening.

Somewhere behind Fara, a man said: "It's right on Lan Harris' lot. Good joke on that old scoundrel. Will he raise a row!"

There was a faint titter from several men, that made an odd patch of sound on the warm, fresh air. And Fara saw that the man had spoken the truth. The weapon shop had a forty-foot frontage. And it occupied the very center of the green, gardenlike lot of tight-fisted, old Harris.

Fara frowned. The clever devils, the weapon-shop people, selecting the property of the most disliked man in town, coolly taking it over and giving everybody an agreeable titillation. But the very cunning of it made it vital that the trick shouldn't succeed.

He was still scowling anxiously when he saw the plump

212

figure of Mel Dale, the mayor. Fara edged toward him hurriedly, touched his hat respectfully, and said:

"Where's Jor?"

"Here." The village constable elbowed his way through a little bundle of men. "Any plans?" he said.

"There's only one plan," said Fara boldly. "Go in and arrest them."

To Fara's amazement, the two men looked at each other, then at the ground. It was the big constable who answered shortly:

"Door's locked. And nobody answers our pounding. I was just going to suggest we let the matter ride until morning."

"Nonsense!" His very astonishment made Fara impatient. "Get an ax and we'll break the door down. Delay will only encourage such riffraff to resist. We don't want their kind in our village for so much as a single night. Isn't that so?"

There was a hasty nod of agreement from everybody in his immediate vicinity. Too hasty. Fara looked around puzzled at eyes that lowered before his level gaze. He thought: "They are all scared. And unwilling." Before he could speak, Constable Jor said:

"I guess you haven't heard about those doors or these shops. From all account, you can't break into them."

It struck Fara with a sudden pang that it was he who would have to act here. He said, "I'll get my atomic cutting machine from my shop. That'll fix them. Have I your permission to do that, Mr. Mayor?"

In the glow of the weapon-shop window, the plump man was sweating visibly. He pulled out a handkerchief, and wiped his forehead. He said:

"Maybe I'd better call the commander of the Imperial garrison at Ferd, and ask them."

"No!" Fara recognized evasion when he saw it. He felt himself steel; the conviction came that all the strength in this village was in him. "We must act ourselves. Other communities have let these people get in because they took no decisive action. We've got to resist to the limit. Beginning now. This minute. Well?"

213

The mayor's "All right!" was scarcely more than a sigh of sound. But it was all Fara needed.

He called out his intention to the crowd; and then, as he pushed his way out of the mob, he saw his son standing with some other young men staring at the window display.

Fara called: "Cayle, come and help me with the machine."

Cayle did not even turn; and Fara hurried on, seething. That wretched boy! One of these days he, Fara, would have to take firm action there. Or he'd have a nogood on his hands.

The energy was soundless—and smooth. There was no sputter, no fireworks. It glowed with a soft, pure white light, almost caressing the metal panels of the door —but not even beginning to sear them.

Minute after minute, the dogged Fara refused to believe the incredible failure, and played the boundlessly potent energy on that resisting wall. When he finally shut off his machine, he was perspiring freely.

"I don't understand it," he gasped. "Why—no metal is supposed to stand up against a steady flood of atomic force. Even the hard metal plates used inside the blast chamber of a motor take the explosions in what is called infinite series, so that each one has unlimited rest. That's the theory, but actually steady running crystallizes the whole plate after a few months."

"It's as Jor told you," said the mayor. "These weapon shops are—big. They spread right through the empire, *and they don't recognize the empress.*"

Fara shifted his feet on the hard grass, disturbed. He didn't like this kind of talk. It sounded—sacrilegious. And besides it was nonsense. It must be. Before he could speak, a man said somewhere behind him:

"I've heard it said that that door will open only to those who cannot harm the people inside."

The words shocked Fara out of his daze. With a start, and for the first time, he saw that his failure had had a bad psychological effect. He said sharply:

"That's ridiculous! If there were doors like that, we'd all have them. We—"

The thought that stopped his words was the sudden

realization that he had not seen anybody try to open the door; and with all this reluctance around him it was quite possible that—

He stepped forward, grasped at the doorknob, and pulled. The door opened with an unnatural weightlessness that gave him the fleeting impression that the knob had come loose into his hand. With a gasp, Fara jerked the door wide open.

"Jor!" he yelled. "Get in!"

The constable made a distorted movement—distorted by what must have been a will to caution, followed by the instant realization that he could not hold back before so many. He leaped awkwardly toward the open door—and it closed in his face.

Fara stared stupidly at his hand, which was still clenched. And then, slowly, a hideous thrill coursed along his nerves. The knob had—withdrawn. It had twisted, become viscous, and slipped amorphously from his straining fingers. Even the memory of that brief sensation gave him a feeling of unnormal things.

He grew aware that the crowd was watching with a silent intentness. Fara reached again for the knob, not quite so eagerly this time; and it was only a sudden realization of his reluctance that made him angry when the handle neither turned nor yielded in any way.

Determination returned in full force, and with it came a thought. He motioned to the constable. "Go back, Jor, while I pull."

The man retreated, but it did no good. And tugging did not help. The door would not open. Somewhere in the crowd, a man said darkly:

"It decided to let you in, then it changed its mind."

"What foolishness are you talking!" Fara spoke violently. "*It* changed its mind. Are you crazy? A door has no sense."

But a surge of fear put a half-quaver into his voice. It was the sudden alarm that made him bold beyond all his normal caution. With a jerk of his body, Fara faced the shop.

The building loomed there under the night sky, in itself bright as day, huge in width and length, and alien, men-

215

acing, no longer easily conquerable. The dim queasy wonder came as to what the soldiers of the empress would do if they were invited to act. And suddenly—a bare, flashing glimpse of grim possibility—the feeling grew that even they would be able to do nothing.

Abruptly, Fara was conscious of horror that such an idea could enter his mind. He shut his brain tight, said wildly:

"The door opened for me once. It will open again."

It did. Quite simply it did. Gently, without resistance, *with* that same sensation of weightlessness, the strange, sensitive door followed the tug of his fingers. Beyond the threshold was dimness, a wide, darkened alcove. He heard the voice of Mel Dale behind him, the mayor saying:

"Fara, don't be a fool. What will you do inside?"

Fara was vaguely amazed to realize that he had stepped across the threshold. He turned, startled, and stared at the blur of faces. "Why—" he began blankly; then he brightened; he said, "Why, I'll buy a gun, of course."

The brilliance of his reply, the cunning implicit in it, dazzled Fara for half a minute longer. The mood yielded slowly, as he found himself in the dimly lighted interior of the weapon shop.

It was preternaturally quiet inside. Not a sound penetrated from the night from which he had come; and the startled thought came that the people of the shop might actually be unaware that there was a crowd outside.

Fara walked gingerly on a rugged floor that muffled his footsteps utterly. After a moment, his eyes accustomed themselves to the soft lighting, which came like a reflection from the walls and ceilings. In a vague way, he had expected ultranormalness; and the ordinariness of the atomic lighting acted like a tonic to his tensed nerves.

He shook himself angrily. Why should there be anything really superior? He was getting as bad as those credulous idiots out in the street.

He glanced around with gathering confidence. The place looked quite common. It was a shop, almost scantily furnished. There were showcases on the walls and on the floor, glitteringly lovely things, but nothing unusual, and

216

not many of them—a few dozens. There was in addition a double, ornate door leading to a back room—

Fara tried to keep one eye on that door, as he examined several showcases, each with three or four weapons either mounted or arranged in boxes or holsters.

Abruptly, the weapons began to excite him. He forgot to watch the door, as the wild thought struck that he ought to grab one of those guns from a case, and then the moment someone came, force him outside where Jor would perform the arrest and—

Behind him, a man said quietly: "You wish to buy a gun?"

Fara turned with a jump. Brief rage flooded him at the way his plan had been wrecked by the arrival of the clerk.

The anger died as he saw that the intruder was a fine-looking, silver-haired man, older than himself. That was immeasurably disconcerting. Fara had an immense and almost automatic respect for age, and for a long second he could only stand there gaping. He said at last, lamely: "Yes, yes, a gun."

"For what purpose?" said the man in his quiet voice.

Fara could only look at him blankly. It was too fast. He wanted to get mad. He wanted to tell these people what he thought of them. But the age of this representative locked his tongue, tangled his emotions. He managed speech only by an effort of will:

"For hunting." The plausible word stiffened his mind. "Yes, definitely for hunting. There is a lake to the north of here," he went on more fulsomely, glibly, "and—"

He stopped, scowling, startled at the extent of his dishonesty. He was not prepared to go so deeply into prevarication. He said curtly:

"For hunting."

Fara was himself again. Abruptly, he hated the man for having put him so completely at a disadvantage. With smoldering eyes he watched the old fellow click open a showcase, and take out a green-shining rifle.

As the man faced him, weapon in hand, Fara was thinking grimly, "Pretty clever, having an old man as a front." It was the same kind of cunning that had made

217

them choose the property of Miser Harris. Icily furious, taut with his purpose, Fara reached for the gun; but the man held it out of his reach, saying:

"Before I can even let you test this, I am compelled by the by-laws of the weapon shops to inform you under what circumstances you may purchase a gun."

So they had private regulations. What a system of psychological tricks to impress gullible fools. Well, let the old scoundrel talk. As soon as he, Fara, got hold of the rifle, he'd put an end to hypocrisy.

"We weapons makers," the clerk was saying mildly, "have evolved guns that can, in their particular ranges, destroy any machine or object made of what is called matter. Thus whoever possesses one of our weapons is the equal and more of any soldier of the empress. I say more because each gun is the center of a field of force which acts as a perfect screen against immaterial destructive forces. That screen offers no resistance to clubs or spears or bullets, or other material substances, but it would require a small atomic cannon to penetrate the superb barrier it creates around its owner.

"You will readily comprehend," the man went on, "that such a potent weapon could not be allowed to fall, unmodified, into irresponsible hands. Accordingly, no gun purchased from us may be used for aggression or murder. In the case of the hunting rifle, only such specified game birds and animals as we may from time to time list in our display windows may be shot. Finally, no weapon can be resold without our approval. Is that clear?"

Fara nodded dumbly. For the moment, speech was impossible to him. The incredible, fantastically stupid words were still going round and around in his head. He wondered if he ought to laugh out loud, or curse the man for daring to insult his intelligence so tremendously.

So the gun mustn't be used for murder or robbery. So only certain birds and animals could be shot. And as for reselling it, suppose—suppose he bought this thing, took a trip of a thousand miles, and offered it to some wealthy stranger for two credits—who would ever know?

Or suppose he held up the stranger. Or shot him. How would the weapon shop ever find out? The thing was so ridiculous that—

He grew aware that the gun was being held out to him stock first. He took it eagerly, and had to fight the impulse to turn the muzzle directly on the old man. Mustn't rush this, he thought tautly. He said:

"How does it work?"

"You simply aim it, and pull the trigger. Perhaps you would like to try it on a target we have."

Fara swung the gun up. "Yes," he said triumphantly, "and you're it. Now, just get over there to the front door, and then outside."

He raised his voice: "And if anybody's thinking of coming through the back door, I've got that covered, too."

He motioned jerkily at the clerk. "Quick now, move! I'll shoot! I swear I will."

The man was cool, unflustered. "I have no doubt you would. When we decided to attune the door so that you could enter despite your hostility, we assumed the capacity for homicide. However, this is our party. You had better adjust yourself accordingly, and look behind you—"

There was silence. Finger on trigger, Fara stood moveless. Dim thoughts came of all the *half-things* he had heard in his days about the weapon shops: that they had secret supporters in every district, that they had a private and ruthless hidden government, and that once you got into their clutches, the only way out was death and—

But what finally came clear was a mind picture of himself, Fara Clark, family man, faithful subject of the empress, standing here in this dimly lighted store, deliberately fighting an organization so vast and menacing that— He must have been mad.

Only—here he was. He forced courage into his sagging muscles. He said:

"You can't fool me with pretending there's someone behind me. Now, get to that door. And *fast!*"

The firm eyes of the old man were looking past him. The man said quietly: "Well, Rad, have you all the data?"

219

"Enough for a primary," said a young man's baritone voice behind Fara. "Type A-7 conservative. Good average intelligence, but a Monaric development peculiar to small towns. One-sided outlook fostered by the Imperial schools present in exaggerated form. Extremely honest. Reason would be useless. Emotional approach would require extended treatment. I see no reason why we should bother. Let him live his life as it suits him."

"If you think," Fara said shakily, "that that trick is going to make me turn, you're crazy. That's the left wall of the building. I know there's no one there."

"I'm all in favor, Rad," said the old man, "of letting him live his life. But he was the prime mover of the crowd outside. I think he should be discouraged."

"We'll advertise his presence," said Rad. "He'll spend the rest of his life denying the charge."

Fara's confidence in the gun had faded so far that, as he listened in puzzled uneasiness to the incomprehensible conversation, he forgot it completely. He parted his lips, but before he could speak, the old man cut in, persistently:

"I think a little emotion might have a long-run effect. Show him the palace."

Palace! The startling word tore Fara out of his brief paralysis. "See here," he began, "I can see now that you lied to me. This gun isn't loaded at all. It's—"

His voice failed him. Every muscle in his body went rigid. He stared like a madman. *There was no gun in his hands.*

"Why, you—" he began wildly. And stopped again. His mind heaved with imbalance. With a terrible effort he fought off the spinning sensation, thought finally, tremblingly: Somebody must have sneaked the gun from him. That meant—there was someone behind him. The voice was no mechanical thing. Somehow, they had—

He started to turn—and couldn't. What in the name of— He struggled, pushing with his muscles. And couldn't move, couldn't budge, couldn't even—

The room was growing curiously dark. He had difficulty seeing the old man and— He would have shrieked then if he could. Because the weapon shop was gone. He was—

He was standing in the sky above an immense city.

In the sky, and nothing beneath him, nothing around him but air, and blue summer heaven, and the city a mile, two miles below.

Nothing, nothing— He would have shrieked, but his breath seemed solidly embedded in his lungs. Sanity came back as the remote awareness impinged upon his terrified mind that he was actually standing on a hard floor, and that the city must be a picture somehow focused directly into his eyes.

For the first time, with a start, Fara recognized the metropolis below. It was the city of dreams, Imperial City, capital of the glorious Empress Isher— From his great height, he could see the gardens, the gorgeous grounds of the silver palace, the official Imperial residence itself—

The last tendrils of his fear were fading now before a gathering fascination and wonder; they vanished utterly as he recognized with a ghastly thrill of uncertain expectancy that the palace was drawing nearer at great speed.

"Show him the palace," they had said. Did that mean, could it mean—

That spray of tense thoughts splattered into nonexistence, as the glittering roof flashed straight at his face. He gulped, as the solid metal of it passed through him, and then other walls and ceilings.

His first sense of imminent and mind-shaking desecration came as the picture paused in a great room where a score of men sat around a table at the head of which sat—a young woman.

The inexorable, sacrilegious, limitlessly powered cameras that were taking the picture swung across the table, and caught the woman full face.

It was a handsome face, but there was passion and fury twisting it now, and a very blaze of fire in her eyes, as she leaned forward, and said in a voice at once familiar—how often Fara had heard its calm, measured ones on the telestats—and distorted. Utterly distorted by anger and an insolent certainty of command. That caricature of a beloved voice slashed across the silence as clearly as if he, Fara was there in that room:

"I want that skunk killed, do you understand? I don't

care how you do it, but I want to hear by tomorrow night that he's dead."

The picture snapped off and instantly—it was as swift as that—Fara was back in the weapon shop. He stood for a moment, swaying, fighting to accustom his eyes to the dimness; and then—

His first emotion was contempt at the simpleness of the trickery—a motion picture. What kind of a fool did they think he was, to swallow something as transparently unreal as that? He'd—

Abruptly, the appalling lechery of the scheme, the indescribable wickedness of what was being attempted here brought red rage.

"Why, you scum!" he flared. "So you've got somebody to act the part of the empress, trying to pretend that— Why, you—"

"That will do," said the voice of Rad; and Fara shook as a big young man walked into his line of vision. The alarmed thought came that people who would besmirch so vilely the character of her imperial majesty would not hesitate to do physical damage to Fara Clark. The young man went on in a steely tone:

"We do not pretend that what you saw was taking place this instant in the palace. That would be too much of a coincidence. But it was taken two weeks ago; the woman *is* the empress. The man whose death she ordered is one of her many former lovers. He was found murdered two weeks ago; his name, if you care to look it up in the news files, is Banton McCreddie. However, let that pass. We're finished with you now and—"

"But I'm not finished," Fara said in a thick voice. "I've never heard or seen so much infamy in all my life. If you think this town is through with you, you're crazy. We'll have a guard on this place day and night, and nobody will get in or out. We'll—"

"That will do." It was the silver-haired man; and Fara stopped out of respect for age, before he thought. The old man went on: "The examination has been most interesting. As an honest man, you may call on us if you are ever in trouble. That is all. Leave through the side door."

It *was* all. Impalpable forces grabbed him, and he was

222

shoved at a door that appeared miraculously in the wall, where seconds before the palace had been.

He found himself standing dazedly in a flower bed, and there was a swarm of men to his left. He recognized his fellow townsmen and that he was—outside.

The incredible nightmare was over.

"Where's the gun?" said Creel, as he entered the house half an hour later.

"The gun?" Fara stared at his wife.

"It said over the radio a few minutes ago that you were the first customer of the new weapon shop. I thought it was queer, but—"

He was eerily conscious of her voice going on for several words longer, but it was the purest jumble. The shock was so great that he had the horrible sensation of being on the edge of an abyss.

So that was what the young man had meant: "Advertise! We'll advertise his presence and—"

Fara thought: His reputation! Not that his was a great name, but he had long believed with a quiet pride that Fara Clark's motor repair shop was widely known in the community and countryside.

First, his private humiliation inside the shop. And now this—lying—to people who didn't know why he had gone into the store. Diabolical.

His paralysis ended, as a frantic determination to rectify the base charge drove him to the telestat. After a moment, the plump, sleepy face of Mayor Mel Dale appeared on the plate. Fara's voice made a barrage of sound, but his hopes dashed, as the man said:

"I'm sorry, Fara. I don't see how you can have free time on the telestat. You'll have to pay for it. They did."

"They did!" Fara wondered vaguely if he sounded as empty as he felt.

"And they've just paid Lan Harris for his lot. The old man asked top price, and got it. He just phoned me to transfer the title."

"Oh!" The world was shattering. "You mean nobody's going to do anything. What about the Imperial garrison at Ferd?"

Dimly, Fara was aware of the mayor mumbling some-

223

thing about the empress' soldiers refusing to interfere in civilian matters.

"Civilian matters!" Fara exploded. "You mean these people are just going to be allowed to come here whether we want them or not, illegally forcing the sale of lots by first taking possession of them?"

A sudden thought struck him breathless. "Look, you haven't changed your mind about having Jor keep guard in front of the shop?"

With a start, he saw that the plump face in the telestat plate had grown impatient. "Now, see here, Fara," came the pompous words, "let the constituted authorities handle this matter."

"But you're going to keep Jor there," Fara said doggedly.

The mayor looked annoyed, said finally peevishly: "I promised, didn't I? So he'll be there. And now—do you want to buy time on the telestat? It's fifteen credits for one minute. Mind you, as a friend, I think you're wasting your money. No one has ever caught up with a false statement."

Fara said grimly: "Put two on, one in the morning, one in the evening."

"All right. We'll deny it completely. Good night."

The telestat went blank; and Fara sat there. A new thought hardened his face. "That boy of ours—there's going to be a showdown. He either works in my shop, or he gets no more allowance."

Creel said: "You've handled him wrong. He's twenty-three, and you treat him like a child. Remember, at twenty-three, you were a married man."

"That was different," said Fara. "I had a sense of responsibility. Do you know what he did tonight?"

He didn't quite catch her answer. For the moment, he thought she said: "No; in what way did you humiliate him first?"

Fara felt too impatient to verify the impossible words. He rushed on: "He refused in front of the whole village to give me help. He's a bad one, all bad."

"Yes," said Creel in a bitter tone, "he is all bad. I'm sure you don't realize how bad. He's as cold as steel, but without steel's strength or integrity. He took a long time,

224

but he hates even me now, because I stood up for your side so long, knowing you were wrong."

"What's that?" said Fara, startled; then gruffly: "Come, come, my dear, we're both upset. Let's go to bed."

He slept poorly.

There were days then when the conviction that this was a personal fight between himself and the weapon shop lay heavily on Fara. Grimly, though it was out of his way, he made a point of walking past the weapon shop, always pausing to speak to Constable Jor and—

On the fourth day, the policeman wasn't there.

Fara waited patiently at first, then angrily; then he walked hastily to his shop, and called Jor's house. No, Jor wasn't home. He was guarding the weapon store.

Fara hesitated. His own shop was piled with work, and he had a guilty sense of having neglected his customers for the first time in his life. It would be simple to call up the mayor and report Jor's dereliction. And yet—

He didn't want to get the man into trouble—

Out in the street, he saw that a large crowd was gathering in front of the weapon shop. Fara hurried. A man he knew greeted him excitedly:

"Jor's been murdered, Fara!"

"Murdered!" Fara stood stock-still, and at first he was not clearly conscious of the grisly thought that was in his mind: Satisfaction! A flaming satisfaction. Now, he thought, even the soldiers would have to act. They—

With a gasp, he realized the ghastly tenor of his thoughts. He shivered, but finally pushed the sense of shame out of his mind. He said slowly:

"Where's the body?"

"Inside."

"You mean, those . . . scum—" In spite of himself, he hesitated over the epithet; even now, it was difficult to think of the fine-faced, silver-haired old man in such terms. Abruptly, his mind hardened; he flared: "You mean those scum actually killed him, then pulled his body inside?"

"Nobody saw the killing," said a second man beside Fara, "but he's gone, hasn't been seen for three hours. The mayor got the weapon shop on the telestat, but they claim they don't know anything. They've done away with him, that's what, and now they're pretending innocence. Well, they won't get out of it as easily as that. Mayor's gone to phone the soldiers at Ferd to bring up some big guns and—"

Something of the intense excitement that was in the crowd surged through Fara, the feeling of big things brewing. It was the most delicious sensation that had ever tingled along his nerves, and it was all mixed with a strange pride that he had been so right about this, that he at least had never doubted that here was evil.

He did not recognize the emotion as the full-flowering joy that comes to a member of a mob. But his voice shook, as he said:

"Guns? Yes, that will be the answer, and the soldiers will have to come, of course."

Fara nodded to himself in the immensity of his certainty that the Imperial soldiers would now have no excuse for not acting. He started to say something dark about what the empress would do if she found out that a man had lost his life because the soldiers had shirked their duty, but the words were drowned in a shout:

"Here comes the mayor! Hey, Mr. Mayor, when are the atomic cannons due?"

There was more of the same general meaning, as the mayor's sleek, all-purpose car landed lightly. Some of the questions must have reached his honor, for he stood up in the open two-seater, and held up his hand for silence.

To Fara's astonishment, the plump-faced man looked at him with accusing eyes. The thing seemed so impossible that, quite instinctively, Fara looked behind him. But he was almost alone; everybody else had crowded forward.

Fara shook his head, puzzled by that glare; and then, astoundingly, Mayor Dale pointed a finger at him, and said in a voice that trembled:

"There's the man who's responsible for the trouble that's come upon us. Stand forward, Fara Clark, and show yourself. You've cost this town seven hundred credits that we could ill afford to spend."

Fara couldn't have moved or spoken to save his life. He

just stood there in a maze of dumb bewilderment. Before he could even think, the mayor went on, and there was quivering self-pity in his tone:

"We've all known that it wasn't wise to interfere with these weapon shops. So long as the Imperial government leaves them alone, what right have we to set up guards, or act against them? That's what I've thought from the beginning, but this man . . . this . . . this Fara Clark kept after all of us, forcing us to move against our wills, and so now we've got a seven-hundred-credit bill to meet and—"

He broke off with: "I might as well make it brief. When I called the garrison, the commander just laughed and said that Jor would turn up. And I had barely disconnected when there was a money call from Jor. He's on Mars."

He waited for the shouts of amazement to die down. "It'll take three weeks for him to come back by ship, and we've got to pay for it, and Fara Clark is responsible. He—"

The shock was over. Fara stood cold, his mind hard. He said finally, scathingly: "So you're giving up, and trying to blame me all in one breath. I say you're all fools."

As he turned away, he heard Mayor Dale saying something about the situation not being completely lost, as he had learned that the weapon shop had been set up in Glay because the village was equidistant from four cities, and that it was the city business the shop was after. This would mean tourists, and accessory trade for the village stores and—

Fara heard no more. Head high, he walked back toward his shop. There were one or two catcalls from the mob, but he ignored them.

He had no sense of approaching disaster, simply a gathering fury against the weapon shop, which had brought him to this miserable status among his neighbors.

The worst of it, as the days passed, was the realization that the people of the weapon shop had no personal interest in him. They were remote, superior, undefeatable. That unconquerableness was a dim, suppressed awareness inside Fara.

227

When he thought of it, he felt a vague fear at the way they had transferred Jor to Mars in a period of less than three hours, when all the world knew that the trip by fastest spaceship required nearly three weeks.

Fara did not go to the express station to see Jor arrive home. He had heard that the council had decided to charge Jor with half of the expense of the trip, on the threat of losing his job if he made a fuss.

On the second night after Jor's return, Fara slipped down to the constable's house, and handed the officer one hundred seventy-five credits. It wasn't that he was responsible, he told Jor, but—

The man was only too eager to grant the disclaimer, provided the money went with it. Fara returned home with a clearer conscience.

It was on the third day after that that the door of his shop banged open and a man came in. Fara frowned as he saw who it was: Castler, a village hanger-on. The man was grinning:

"Thought you might be interested, Fara. Somebody came out of the weapon shop today."

Fara strained deliberately at the connecting bolt of a hard plate of the atomic motor he was fixing. He waited with a gathering annoyance that the man did not volunteer further information. Asking questions would be a form of recognition of the worthless fellow. A developing curiosity made him say finally, grudgingly:

"I suppose the constable promptly picked him up."

He supposed nothing of the kind, but it was an opening.

"It wasn't a man. It was a girl."

Fara knitted his brows. He didn't like the idea of making trouble for women. But—the cunning devils! Using a girl, just as they had used an old man as a clerk. It was a trick that deserved to fail, the girl probably a tough one who needed rough treatment. Fara said harshly:

"Well, what's happened?"

"She's still out, bold as you please. Pretty thing, too."

The bolt off, Fara took the hard plate over to the polisher, and began patiently the long, careful task of smoothing away the crystals that heat had seared on

228

the once shining metal. The soft throb of the polisher made the background to his next words:

"Has anything been done?"

"Nope. The constable's been told, but he says he doesn't fancy being away from his family for another three weeks, and paying the cost into the bargain."

Fara contemplated that darkly for a minute, as the polisher throbbed on. His voice shook with suppressed fury, when he said finally:

"So they're letting them get away with it. It's all been as clever as hell. Can't they see that they mustn't give an inch before these . . . these transgressors. It's like giving countenance to sin."

From the corner of his eye, he noticed that there was a curious grin on the face of the other. It struck Fara suddenly that the man was enjoying his anger. And there was something else in that grin; something—a secret knowledge.

Fara pulled the engine plate away from the polisher. He faced the ne'er-do-well, scathed at him:

"Naturally, that sin part wouldn't worry you much."

"Oh," said the man nonchalantly, "the hard knocks of life make people tolerant. For instance, after you know the girl better, you yourself will probably come to realize that there's good in all of us."

It was not so much the words, as the curious I've-got-secret-information tone that made Fara snap:

"What do you mean—if I get to know the girl better! I won't even speak to the brazen creature."

"One can't always choose," the other said with enormous casualness. "Suppose he brings her home."

"Suppose who brings who home?" Fara spoke irritably. "Castler, you——"

He stopped; a dead weight of dismay plumped into his stomach; his whole being sagged. "You mean—" he said.

"I mean," replied Castler with a triumphant leer, "that the boys aren't letting a beauty like her be lonesome. And, naturally, your son was the first to speak to her."

He finished: "They're walkin' together now on Second Avenue, comin' this way, so——"

229

"Get out of here!" Fara roared. "And stay away from me with your gloating. Get out!"

The man hadn't expected such an ignominious ending. He flushed scarlet, then went out, slamming the door.

Fara stood for a moment, every muscle stiff; then, with an abrupt, jerky movement, he shut off his power, and went out into the street.

The time to put a stop to that kind of thing was—now!

He had no clear plan, just that violent determination to put an immediate end to an impossible situation. And it was all mixed up with his anger against Cayle. How could he have had such a worthless son, he who paid his debts and worked hard, and tried to be decent and to live up to the highest standards of the empress?

A brief, dark thought came to Fara that maybe there was some bad blood on Creel's side. Not from her mother, of course—Fara added the mental thought hastily. *There* was a fine, hard-working woman, who hung on to her money, and who would leave Creel a tidy sum one of these days.

But Creel's father had disappeared when Creel was only a child, and there had been some vague scandal about him having taken up with a telestat actress.

And now Cayle with this weapon-shop girl. A girl who had let herself be picked up—

He saw them, as he turned the corner onto Second Avenue. They were walking a hundred feet distant, and heading away from Fara. The girl was tall and slender, almost as big as Cayle, and, as Fara came up, she was saying:

"You have the wrong idea about us. A person like you can't get a job in our organization. You belong in the Imperial Service, where they can use young men of good education, good appearance and no scruples. I—"

Fara grasped only dimly that Cayle must have been trying to get a job with these people. It was not clear; and his own mind was too intent on his purpose for it to mean anything at the moment. He said harshly:

"Cayle!"

The couple turned, Cayle with the measured unhurriedness of a young man who has gone a long way on the

230

road to steellike nerves; the girl was quicker, but withal dignified.

Fara had a vague, terrified feeling that his anger was too great, self-destroying, but the very violence of his emotions ended that thought even as it came. He said thickly:

"Cayle, get home—at once."

Fara was aware of the girl looking at him curiously from strange, gray-green eyes. No shame, he thought, and his rage mounted several degrees, driving away the alarm that came at the sight of the flush that crept into Cayle's cheeks.

The flush faded into a pale, tight-lipped anger; Cayle half-turned to the girl, said:

"This is the childish old fool I've got to put up with. Fortunately, we seldom see each other; we don't even eat together. What do you think of him?"

The girl smiled impersonally: "Oh, we know Fara Clark; he's the backbone of the empress in Glay."

"Yes," the boy sneered. "You ought to hear him. He thinks we're living in heaven; and the empress is the divine power. The worst part of it is that there's no chance of his ever getting that stuffy look wiped off his face."

They walked off; and Fara stood there. The very extent of what had happened had drained anger from him as if it had never been. There was the realization that he had made a mistake so great that—

He couldn't grasp it. For long, long now, since Cayle had refused to work in his shop, he had felt this building up to a climax. Suddenly, his own uncontrollable ferocity stood revealed as a partial product of that—deeper—problem.

Only, now that the smash was here, he didn't want to face it—

All through the day in his shop, he kept pushing it out of his mind, kept thinking:

Would this go on now, as before, Cayle and he living in the same house, not even looking at each other when they met, going to bed at different times, getting up, Fara at 6:30, Cayle at noon? Would *that* go on through all the days and years to come?

231

When he arrived home, Creel was waiting for him. She said:

"Fara, he wants you to loan him five hundred credits, so that he can go to Imperial City."

Fara nodded wordlessly. He brought the money back to the house the next morning, and gave it to Creel, who took it into the bedroom.

She came out a minute later. "He says to tell you good-by."

When Fara came home that evening, Cayle was gone. He wondered whether he ought to feel relieved or—what?

The days passed. Fara worked. He had nothing else to do, and the gray thought was often in his mind that now he would be doing it till the day he died. Except—

Fool that he was—he told himself a thousand times how big a fool—he kept hoping that Cayle would walk into the shop and say:

"Father, I've learned my lesson. If you can ever forgive me, teach me the business, and then you retire to a well-earned rest."

It was exactly a month to a day after Cayle's departure that the telestat clicked on just after Fara had finished lunch. "Money call," it sighed, "money call."

Fara and Creel looked at each other. "Eh," said Fara finally, "money call for us."

He could see from the gray look in Creel's face the thought that was in her mind. He said under his breath: "Damn that boy!"

But he felt relieved. Amazingly, relieved! Cayle was beginning to appreciate the value of parents and—

He switched on the viewer. "Come and collect," he said.

The face that came on the screen was heavy-jowled, beetle-browed—and strange. The man said:

"This is Clerk Pearton of the Fifth Bank of Ferd. We have received a sight draft on you for ten thousand credits. With carrying charges and government tax, the sum required will be twelve thousand one hundred credits. Will you pay it now or will you come in this afternoon and pay it?"

"B-but . . . b-but—" said Fara. "W-who—"

He stopped, conscious of the stupidity of the question, dimly conscious of the heavy-faced man saying something about the money having been paid out to one Cayle Clark, that morning, in Imperial City. At last, Fara found his voice:

"But the bank had no right," he expostulated, "to pay out the money without my authority. I—"

The voice cut him off coldly: "Are we then to inform our central that the money was obtained under false pretenses? Naturally, an order will be issued immediately for the arrest of your son."

"Wait . . . wait—" Fara spoke blindly. He was aware of Creel beside him, shaking her head at him. She was as white as a sheet, and her voice was a sick, stricken thing, as she said:

"Fara, let him go. He's through with us. We must be as hard—let him go."

The words rang senselessly in Fara's ears. They didn't fit into any normal pattern. He was saying:

"I . . . I haven't got— How about my paying . . . installments? I—"

"If you wish a loan," said Clerk Pearton, "naturally we will be happy to go into the matter. I might say that when the draft arrived, we checked up on your status, and we are prepared to loan you eleven thousand credits on indefinite call with your shop as security. I have the form here, and if you are agreeable, we will switch this call through the registered circuit, and you can sign at once."

"Fara, no."

The clerk went on: "The other eleven hundred credits will have to be paid in cash. Is that agreeable?"

"Yes, yes, of course, I've got twenty-five hund—" He stopped his chattering tongue with a gulp; then: "Yes, that's satisfactory."

The deal completed, Fara whirled on his wife. Out of the depths of his hurt and bewilderment, he raged:

"What do you mean, standing there and talking about not paying it? You said several times that I was responsible for him being what he is. Besides, we don't know why he needed the money. He—"

Creel said in a low, dead tone: "In one hour, he's stripped us of our life work. He did it deliberately, thinking of us as two old fools, who wouldn't know any better than to pay it."

Before he could speak, she went on: "Oh, I know I blamed you, but in the final issue, I knew it was he. He was always cold and calculating, but I was weak, and I was sure that if you handled him in a different . . . and besides I didn't want to see his faults for a long time. He—"

"All I see," Fara interrupted doggedly, "is that I have saved our name from disgrace."

His high sense of duty rightly done lasted until mid-afternoon, when the bailiff from Ferd came to take over the shop.

"But what—" Fara began.

The bailiff said: "The Automatic Atomic Repair Shops, Limited, took over your loan from the bank, and are foreclosing. Have you anything to say?"

"It's unfair," said Fara. "I'll take it to court. I'll—"

He was thinking dazedly: "If the empress ever learned of this, she'd . . . she'd—"

The courthouse was a big, gray building; and Fara felt emptier and colder every second, as he walked along the gray corridors. In Glay, his decision not to give himself into the hands of a bloodsucker of a lawyer had seemed a wise act. Here, in these enormous halls and palatial rooms, it seemed the sheerest folly.

He managed, nevertheless, to give an articulate account of the criminal act of the bank in first giving Cayle the money, then turning over the note to his chief competitor, apparently within minutes of his signing it. He finished with:

"I'm sure, sir, the empress would not approve of such goings-on against honest citizens. I—"

"How dare you," said the cold-voiced creature on the bench, "use the name of her holy majesty in support of your own gross self-interest?"

234

Fara shivered. The sense of being intimately a member of the empress' great human family yielded to a sudden chill and a vast mind-picture of the ten million icy courts like this, and the myriad malevolent and heartless men—*like this*—who stood between the empress and her loyal subject, Fara.

He thought passionately: If the empress knew what was happening here, how unjustly he was being treated she would—

Or would she?

He pushed the crowding, terrible doubt out of his mind—came out of his hard reverie with a start, to hear the Cadi saying:

"Plaintiff's appeal dismissed, with costs assessed at seven hundred credits, to be divided between the court and the defense solicitor in the ratio of five to two. See to it that the appellant does not leave till the costs are paid. Next case—"

Fara went alone the next day to see Creel's mother. He called first at "Farmer's Restaurant" at the outskirts of the village. The place was, he noted with satisfaction in the thought of the steady stream of money flowing in, half full, though it was only midmorning. But madame wasn't there. Try the feed store.

He found her in the back of the feed store, overseeing the weighing out of grain into cloth measures. The hard-faced old woman heard his story without a word. She said finally, curtly:

"Nothing doing, Fara. I'm one who has to make loans often from the bank to swing deals. If I tried to set you up in business, I'd find the Automatic Atomic Repair people getting after me. Besides, I'd be a fool to turn money over to a man who lets a bad son squeeze a fortune out of him. Such a man has no sense about worldly things.

"And I won't give you a job because I don't hire relatives in my business." She finished: "Tell Creel to come and live at my house. I won't support a man, though. That's all."

He watched her disconsolately for a while, as she went on calmly superintending the clerks who were manipulating the old, no longer accurate measuring machines.

Twice her voice echoed through the dust-filled interior, each time with a sharp: "That's overweight, a gram at least. Watch your machine."

Though her back was turned, Fara knew by her posture that she was still aware of his presence. She turned at last with an abrupt movement, and said:

"Why don't you go to the weapon shop? You haven't anything to lose, and you can't go on like this."

Fara went out, then, a little blindly. At first the suggestion that he buy a gun and commit suicide had no real personal application. But he felt immeasurably hurt that his mother-in-law should have made it.

Kill himself? Why, it was ridiculous. He was still only a young man, going on fifty. Given the proper chance, with his skilled hands, he could wrest a good living even in a world where automatic machines were encroaching everywhere. There was always room for a man who did a good job. His whole life had been based on that credo.

Kill himself—

He went home to find Creel packing. "It's the common sense thing to do," she said. "We'll rent the house and move into rooms."

He told her about her mother's offer to take her in, watching her face as he spoke. Creel shrugged.

"I told her 'No' yesterday," she said thoughtfully. "I wonder why she mentioned it to you."

Fara walked swiftly over to the great front window overlooking the garden, with its flowers, its pool, its rockery. He tried to think of Creel away from this garden of hers, this home of two thirds a lifetime, Creel living in rooms—and knew what her mother had meant. There was one more hope—

He waited till Creel went upstairs, then called Mel Dale on the telestat. The mayor's plump face took on an uneasy expression as he saw who it it was.

But he listened pontifically, said finally: "Sorry, the council does not loan money; and I might as well tell you, Fara—I have nothing to do with this, mind you—but you can't get a license for a shop any more."

"W-what?"

"I'm sorry!" The mayor lowered his voice. "Listen,

236

Fara, take my advice and go to the weapon shop. These places have their uses."

There was a click, and Fara sat staring at the blank face of the viewing screen.

So it was to be—death!

He waited until the street was empty of human beings, then slipped across the boulevard, past a design of flower gardens, and so to the door of the shop. The brief fear came that the door wouldn't open, but it did, effortlessly.

As he emerged from the dimness of the alcove into the shop proper, he saw the silver-haired old man sitting in a corner chair, reading under a softly bright light. The old man looked up, put aside his book, then rose to his feet.

"It's Mr. Clark," he said quietly. "What can we do for you?"

A faint flush crept into Fara's cheeks. In a dim fashion, he had hoped that he would not suffer the humiliation of being recognized; but now that his fear was realized, he stood his ground stubbornly. The important thing about killing himself was that there be no body for Creel to bury at great expense. Neither knife nor poison would satisfy that basic requirement.

"I want a gun," said Fara, "that can be adjusted to disintegrate a body six feet in diameter in a single shot. Have you that kind?"

Without a word, the old man turned to a showcase, and brought forth a sturdy gem of a revolver that glinted with all the soft colors of the inimitable Ordine plastic. The man said in a precise voice:

"Notice the flanges on this barrel are little more than bulges. This makes the model ideal for carrying in a shoulder holster under the coat; it can be drawn very swiftly because, when properly attuned, it will leap toward the reaching hand of its owner. At the moment it is attuned to me. Watch while I replace it in its holster and—"

The speed of the draw was absolutely amazing. The old man's fingers moved; and the gun, four feet away, was in them. There was no blur of movement. It was

237

like the door the night that it had slipped from Fara's grasp, and slammed noiselessly in Constable Jor's face. *Instantaneous!*

Fara, who had parted his lips as the old man was explaining, to protest the utter needlessness of illustrating any quality of the weapon except what he had asked for, closed them again. He stared in a brief, dazed fascination; and something of the wonder that was here held his mind and his body.

He had seen and handled the guns of soldiers, and they were simply ordinary metal or plastic things that one used clumsily like any other material substance, not like this at all, not possessed of a dazzling life of their own, leaping with an intimate eagerness to assist with all their superb power the will of their master. They—

With a start, Fara remembered his purpose. He smiled wryly, and said:

"All this is very interesting. But what about the beam that can fan out?"

The old man said calmly: "At pencil thickness, this beam will pierce any body except certain alloys of lead up to four hundred yards. With proper adjustment of the firing nozzle, you can disintegrate a six-foot object at fifty yards or less. This screw is the adjustor."

He indicated a tiny device in the muzzle itself. "Turn it to the left to spread the beam, to the right to close it."

Fara said. "I'll take the gun. How much is it?"

He saw that the old man was looking at him thoughtfully; the oldster said finally, slowly: "I have previously explained our regulations to you, Mr. Clark. You recall them, of course?"

"Eh!" said Fara, and stopped, wide-eyed. It wasn't that he didn't remember them. It was simply—

"You mean," he gasped, "those things actually apply. They're not—"

With a terrible effort, he caught his spinning brain and blurring voice. Tense and cold, he said:

"All I want is a gun that will shoot in self-defense, but which I can turn on myself if I have to or—want to."

"Oh, suicide!" said the old man. He looked as if a great understanding had suddenly dawned on him. "My dear sir, we have no objection to you killing yourself at any time. That is your personal privilege in a world where privileges grow scanter every year. As for the price of this revolver, it's four credits."

"Four cre . . . only four credits!" said Fara.

He stood, absolutely astounded, his whole mind snatched from its dark purpose. Why, the plastic alone was—and the whole gun with its fine, intricate workmanship—twenty-five credits would have been dirt cheap.

He felt a brief thrall of utter interest; the mystery of the weapon shops suddenly loomed as vast and important as his own black destiny. But the old man was speaking again:

"And now, if you will remove your coat, we can put on the holster—"

Quite automatically, Fara complied. It was vaguely startling to realize that, in a few seconds, he would be walking out of here, equipped for self-murder, and that there was now not a single obstacle to his death.

Curiously, he was disappointed. He couldn't explain it, but somehow there had been in the back of his mind a hope that these shops might, just might—what?

What indeed? Fara sighed wearily—and grew aware again of the old man's voice, saying:

"Perhaps you would prefer to step out of our side door. It is less conspicuous than the front."

There was no resistance in Fara. He was dimly conscious of the man's fingers on his arm, half guiding him; and then the old man pressed one of several buttons on the wall—so that's how it was done—and there was the door.

He could see flowers beyond the opening; without a word he walked toward them. He was outside almost before he realized it.

Fara stood for a moment in the neat little pathway, striving to grasp the finality of his situation. But nothing would come except a curious awareness of many men around him; for a long second, his brain was like a log drifting along a stream at night.

Through that darkness grew a consciousness of some-

239

thing wrong; the wrongness was there in the back of his mind, as he turned leftward to go to the front of the weapon store.

Vagueness transformed to a shocked, startled sound. For—he was not in Glay, and the weapon shop *wasn't* where it had been. In its place—

A dozen men brushed past Fara to join a long line of men farther along. But Fara was immune to their presence, their strangeness. His whole mind, his whole vision, his very being was concentrating on the section of machine that stood where the weapon shop had been.

A machine, oh, a machine—

His brain lifted up, up in his effort to grasp the tremendousness of the dull-metaled immensity of what was spread here under a summer sun beneath a sky as blue as a remote southern sea.

The machine towered into the heavens, five great tiers of metal, each a hundred feet high; and the superbly streamlined five hundred feet ended in a peak of light, a gorgeous spire that tilted straight up a sheer two hundred feet farther, and matched the very sun for brightness.

And it *was* a machine, not a building, because the whole lower tier was alive with shimmering lights, mostly green, but sprinkled colorfully with red and occasionally a blue and yellow. Twice, as Fara watched, green lights directly in front of him flashed unscintillatingly into red.

The second tier was alive with white and red lights, although there were only a fraction as many lights as on the lowest tier. The third section had on its dull-metal surface only blue and yellow lights; they twinkled softly here and there over the vast area.

The fourth tier was a series of signs, that brought the beginning of comprehension. The whole sign was:

WHITE        —    BIRTHS
RED          —    DEATHS
GREEN        —    LIVING
BLUE         —    IMMIGRATION TO EARTH
YELLOW       —    EMIGRATION

The fifth tier was also all sign, finally explaining:

## POPULATIONS

| | |
|---|---|
| SOLAR SYSTEM | 19,174,463,747 |
| EARTH | 11,193,247,361 |
| MARS | 1,097,298,604 |
| VENUS | 5,141,053,811 |
| MOONS | 1,742,863,971 |

The numbers changed, even as he looked at them, leaping up and down, shifting below and above what they had first been. People were dying, being born, moving to Mars, to Venus, to the moons of Jupiter, to Earth's moon, and others coming back again, landing minute by minute in the thousands of spaceports. Life went on in its gigantic fashion—and here was the stupendous record. Here was—

"Better get in line," said a friendly voice beside Fara. "It takes quite a while to put through an individual case, I understand."

Fara stared at the man. He had the distinct impression of having had senseless words flung at him. "In line?" he started—and stopped himself with a jerk that hurt his throat.

He was moving forward, blindly, ahead of the younger man, thinking a curious jumble about that this must have been how Constable Jor was transported to Mars—when another of the man's words penetrated.

"Case?" said Fara violently. "Individual case!"

The man, a heavy-faced, blue-eyed young chap of around thirty-five, looked at him curiously: "You must know why you're here," he said. "Surely, you wouldn't have been sent through here unless you had a problem of some kind that the weapon shop courts will solve for you; there's no other reason for coming to Information Center."

Fara walked on because he was in the line now, a fast moving line that curved him inexorably around the machine; and seemed to be heading him toward a door that led into the interior of the great metal structure.

So it was a building as well as a machine.

A problem, he was thinking, why, of course, he had a problem, a hopeless, insoluble, completely tangled problem, so deeply rooted in the basic structure of Imperial civilization that the whole world would have to be overturned to make it right.

With a start, he saw that he was at the entrance. And the awed thought came: In seconds he would be committed irrevocably to—what?

Inside was a long, shining corridor, with scores of completely transparent hallways leading off the main corridor. Behind Fara, the young man's voice said:

"There's one, practically empty. Let's go."

Fara walked ahead; and suddenly he was trembling. He had already noticed that at the end of each side hallway were some dozen young women sitting at desks, interviewing men and . . . and, good heavens, was it possible that all this meant—

He grew aware that he had stopped in front of one of the girls.

She was older than she had looked from a distance, over thirty, but good-looking, alert. She smiled pleasantly, but impersonally, and said:

"Your name, please?"

He gave it before he thought and added a mumble about being from the village of Glay. The woman said:

"Thank you. It will take a few minutes to get your file. Won't you sit down?"

He hadn't noticed the chair. He sank into it; and his heart was beating so wildly that he felt choked. The strange thing was that there was scarcely a thought in his head, nor a real hope; only an intense, almost mindwrecking excitement.

With a jerk, he realized that the girl was speaking again, but only snatches of her voice came through that screen of tension in his mind:

"—Information Center is . . . in effect . . . a bureau of statistics. Every person born . . . registered here . . . their education, change of address . . . occupation . . . and the highlights of their life. The whole is maintained by . . . combination of . . . Imperial Chamber of Statistics and . . . through medium of agents . . . in every community—"

242

It seemed to Fara that he was missing vital information, and that if he could only force his attention and hear more— He strained, but it was no use; his nerves were jumping madly and—

Before he could speak, there was a click, and a thin, dark plate slid onto the woman's desk. She took it up, and examined it. After a moment, she said something into a mouthpiece, and in a short time two more plates precipitated out of the empty air onto her desk. She studied them impassively, looked up finally.

"You will be interested to know," she said, "that your son, Cayle, bribed himself into a commission in the Imperial army with five thousand credits."

"Eh?" said Fara. He half rose from his chair, but before he could say anything, the young woman was speaking again, firmly:

"I must inform you that the weapon shops take no action against individuals. Your son can have his job, the money he stole; we are not concerned with moral correction. That must come naturally from the individual, and from the people as a whole—and now if you will give me a brief account of your problem for the record and the court."

Sweating, Fara sank back into his seat; his mind was heaving; most desperately, he wanted more information about Cayle. He began:

"But . . . but what . . . how—" He caught himself; and in a low voice described what had happened. When he finished, the girl said:

"You will proceed now to the Name Room; watch for your name, and when it appears go straight to Room 474. Remember, 474—and now, the line is waiting, if you please—"

She smiled politely, and Fara was moving off almost before he realized it. He half turned to ask another question, but an old man was sinking into his chair. Fara hurried on, along a great corridor, conscious of curious blasts of sound coming from ahead.

Eagerly, he opened the door; and the sound crashed at him with all the impact of a sledge hammer blow.

It was such a colossal, incredible sound that he stopped

243

short, just inside the door, shrinking back. He stood then trying to blink sense into a visual confusion that rivaled in magnitude that incredible tornado of noise.

Men, men, men everywhere; men by the thousands in a long, broad auditorium, packed into rows of seats, pacing with an abandon of restlessness up and down aisles, and all of them staring with a frantic interest at a long board marked off into squares, each square lettered from the alphabet, from A, B, C and so on to Z. The tremendous board with its lists of names ran the full length of the immense room.

The Name Room, Fara was thinking shakily, as he sank into a seat—and his name would come up in the C's, and then—

It was like sitting in at a no-limit poker game, watching the jewel-precious cards turn up. It was like playing the exchange with all the world at stake during a stock crash. It was nerve-racking, dazzling, exhausting, fascinating, terrible, mind-destroying, stupendous. It was—

It was like nothing else on the face of the earth.

New names kept flashing on to the twenty-six squares; and men would shout like insane beings and some fainted, and the uproar was absolutely shattering; the pandemonium raged on, one continuous, unbelievable sound.

And every few minutes a great sign would flash along the board, telling everyone:

"WATCH YOUR OWN INITIALS."

Fara watched, trembling in every limb. Each second it seemed to him that he couldn't stand it an instant longer. He wanted to scream at the room to be silent; he wanted to jump up to pace the floor, but others who did that were yelled at hysterically, threatened wildly, hated with a mad, murderous ferocity.

Abruptly, the blind savagery of it scared Fara. He thought unsteadily: "I'm not going to make a fool of myself. I—"

"Clark, Fara—" winked the board. "Clark, Fara—"

With a shout that nearly tore off the top of his head, Fara leaped to his feet. "That's me!" he shrieked. "Me!"

No one turned; no one paid the slightest attention. Shamed, he slunk across the room where an endless line of men kept crowding into a corridor beyond.

The silence in the long corridor was almost as shattering as the mind-destroying noise it replaced. It was hard to concentrate on the idea of a number—474.

It was completely impossible to imagine what could lie beyond—474.

The room was small. It was furnished with a small, business-type table and two chairs. On the table were seven neat piles of folders, each pile a different color. The piles were arranged in a row in front of a large, milky-white globe, that began to glow with a soft light. Out of its depths, a man's baritone voice said:

"Fara Clark?"

"Yes," said Fara.

"Before the verdict is rendered in your case," the voice went on quietly, "I want you to take a folder from the blue pile. The list will show the Fifth Interplanetary Bank in its proper relation to yourself and the world, and it will be explained to you in due course."

The list, Fara saw, was simply that, a list of the names of companies. The names ran from A to Z, and there were about five hundred of them. The folder carried no explanation; and Fara slipped it automatically into his side pocket, as the voice came again from the shining globe:

"It has been established," the words came precisely, "that the Fifth Interplanetary Bank perpetrated upon you a gross swindle, and that it is further guilty of practicing scavengery, deception, blackmail and was accessory in a criminal conspiracy.

"The bank made contact with your son, Cayle, through what is quite properly known as a scavenger, that is an employee who exists by finding young men and women who are morally capable of drawing drafts on their parents or other victims. The scavenger obtains for this service a commission of eight percent, which is always paid by the person making the loan, in this case your son.

"The bank practiced deception in that its authorized agents deceived you in the most culpable fashion by pretending that it had already paid out the ten thousand credits to your son, whereas the money was not paid over until your signature had been obtained.

245

"The blackmail guilt arises out of the threat to have your son arrested for falsely obtaining a loan, a threat made at a time when no money had exchanged hands. The conspiracy consists of the action whereby your note was promptly turned over to your competitor.

"The bank is accordingly triple-fined, thirty-six thousand three hundred credits. It is not in our interest, Fara Clark, for you to know how this money is obtained. Suffice to know that the bank pays it, and that of the fine the weapon shops allocate to their own treasury a total of one half. The other half—"

There was a *plop;* a neatly packaged pile of bills fell onto the table. "For you," said the voice; and Fara, with trembling fingers, slipped the package into his coat pocket. It required the purest mental and physical effort for him to concentrate on the next words that came:

"You must not assume that your troubles are over. The re-establishment of your motor repair shop in Glay will require force and courage. Be discreet, brave and determined, and you cannot fail. Do not hesitate to use the gun you have purchased in defense of your rights. The plan will be explained to you. And now, proceed through the door facing you—"

Fara braced himself with an effort, opened the door and walked through.

It was a dim, familiar room that he stepped into, and there was a silver-haired, fine-faced man who rose from a reading chair, and came forward in the dimness, smiling gravely.

The stupendous, fantastic, exhilarating adventure was over; and he was back in the weapon shop of Glay.

He couldn't get over the wonder of it—this great and fascinating organization established here in the very heart of a ruthless civilization, a civilization that had in a few brief weeks stripped him of everything he possessed.

With a deliberate will, he stopped that glowing flow of thought. A dark frown wrinkled his solidly built face; he said:

"The . . . judge—" Fara hesitated over the name, frowned again, annoyed at himself, then went on: "The judge said that, to re-establish myself I would have to—"

246

"Before we go into that," said the old man quietly, "I want you to examine the blue folder you brought with you."

"Folder?" Fara echoed blankly. It took a long moment to remember that he had picked up a folder from the table in Room 474.

He studied the list of company names with a gathering puzzlement, noting that the name Automatic Atomic Motor Repair Shops was well down among the A's, and the Fifth Interplanetary Bank only one of several great banks included. Fara looked up finally:

"I don't understand," he said; "are these the companies you have had to act against?"

The silver-haired man smiled grimly, shook his head. "That is not what I mean. These firms constitute only a fraction of the eight hundred thousand companies that are constantly in our books."

He smiled again, humorlessly: "These companies all know that, because of us, their profits on paper bear no relation to their assets. What they don't know is how great the difference really is; and, as we want a general improvement in business morals, not merely more skillful scheming to outwit us, we prefer them to remain in ignorance."

He paused, and this time he gave Fara a searching glance, said at last: "The unique feature of the companies on this particular list is that they are every one wholly owned by Empress Isher."

He finished swiftly: "In view of your past opinions on that subject, I do not expect you to believe me."

Fara stood as still as death, for—he did believe with unquestioning conviction, completely, finally. The amazing, the unforgivable thing was that all his life he had watched the march of ruined men into the oblivion of poverty and disgrace—and blamed *them*.

Fara groaned. "I've been like a madman," he said. "Everything the empress and her officials did was right. No friendship, no personal relationship could survive with me that did not include belief in things as they were. I suppose if I started to talk against the empress I would receive equally short shrift."

"Under no circumstances," said the old man grimly, "must you say anything against her majesty. The weapon shops will not countenance any such words, and will give no further aid to anyone who is so indiscreet. The reason is that, for the moment, we have reached an uneasy state of peace with the Imperial government. We wish to keep it that way; beyond that I will not enlarge on our policy.

"I am permitted to say that the last great attempt to destroy the weapon shops was made seven years ago, when the glorious Innelda Isher was twenty-five years old. That was a secret attempt, based on a new invention; and failed by purest accident because of our sacrifice of a man from seven thousand years in the past. That may sound mysterious to you, but I will not explain.

"The worst period was reached some forty years ago when every person who was discovered receiving aid from us was murdered in some fashion. You may be surprised to know that your father-in-law was among those assassinated at that time."

"Creel's father!" Fara gasped. "But—"

He stopped. His brain was reeling; there was such a rush of blood to his head that for an instant he could hardly see.

"But," he managed at last, "it was reported that he ran away with another woman."

"They always spread a vicious story of some kind," the old man said; and Fara was silent, stunned.

The other went on: "We finally put a stop to their murders by killing the three men from the top down, *excluding* the royal family, who gave the order for the particular execution involved. But we do not again want that kind of bloody murder.

"Nor are we interested in any criticism of our toleration of so much that is evil. It is important to understand that *we do not interfere in the main stream of human existence*. We right wrongs; we act as a barrier between the people and their more ruthless exploiters. Generally speaking, we help only honest men; that is not to say that we do not give assistance to the less scrupulous, but only to the extent of selling them guns—which is a very great aid indeed, and which is one of the reasons why the government is relying almost exclusively for its power on an economic chicanery.

"In the four thousand years since the brilliant genius,

Walter S. DeLany invented the vibration process that made the weapon shops possible, and laid down the first principles of weapon shop political philosophy, we have watched the tide of government swing backward and forward between democracy under a limited monarchy to complete tyranny. And we have discovered one thing:

*"People always have the kind of government they want.* When they want change, they must change it. As always we shall remain an incorruptible core—and I mean that literally; we have a psychological machine that never lies about a man's character—I repeat, an incorruptible core of human idealism, devoted to relieving the ills that arise inevitably under any form of government.

"But now—your problem. It is very simple, really. You must fight, as all men have fought since the beginning of time for what they valued, for their just rights. As you know the Automatic Repair people removed all your machinery and tools within an hour of foreclosing on your shop. This material was taken to Ferd, and then shipped to a great warehouse on the coast.

"We recovered it, and with our special means of transportation have now replaced the machines in your shop. You will accordingly go there and—"

Fara listened with a gathering grimness to the instructions, nodded finally, his jaw clamped tight.

"You can count on me," he said curtly. "I've been a stubborn man in my time; and though I've changed sides, I haven't changed *that*."

Going outside was like returning from life to—death; from hope to—reality.

Fara walked along the quiet streets of Glay at darkest night. For the first time it struck him that the weapon shop Information Center must be halfway around the world, for it had been day, brilliant day.

The picture vanished as if it had never existed, and he grew aware again, preternaturally aware of the village of Glay asleep all around him. Silent, peaceful—yet ugly, he thought, ugly with the ugliness of evil enthroned.

He thought: The right to buy weapons—and his heart swelled into his throat; the tears came to his eyes.

249

He wiped his vision clear with the back of his hand, thought of Creel's long dead father, and strode on, without shame. Tears were good for an angry man.

The shop was the same, but the hard, metal padlock yielded before the tiny, blazing, supernal power of the revolver. One flick of fire; the metal dissolved—and he was inside.

It was dark, too dark to see, but Fara did not turn on the lights immediately. He fumbled across to the window control, turned the windows to darkness vibration, and then clicked on the lights.

He gulped with awful relief. For the machines, his precious tools that he had seen carted away within hours after the bailiff's arrival, were here again, ready for use.

Shaky from the pressure of his emotion, Fara called Creel on the telestat. It took a little while for her to appear; and she was in her dressing robe. When she saw who it was she turned a dead white.

"Fara, oh, Fara, I thought—"

He cut her off grimly: "Creel, I've been to the weapon shop. I want you to do this: go straight to your mother. I'm here at my shop. I'm going to stay here day and night until it's settled that I *stay*. . . . I shall go home later for some food and clothing, but I want you to be gone by then. Is that clear?"

Color was coming back into her lean, handsome face. She said: "Don't you bother coming home, Fara. I'll do everything necessary. I'll pack all that's needed into the carplane including a folding bed. We'll sleep in the back room at the shop."

Morning came palely, but it was ten o'clock before a shadow darkened the open door; and Constable Jor came in. He looked shamefaced.

"I've got an order here for your arrest," he said.

"Tell those who sent you," Fara replied deliberately, "that I resisted arrest—with a gun."

The deed followed the words with such rapidity that Jor blinked. He stood like that for a moment, a big, sleepy-looking man, staring at that gleaming, magical revolver; then:

"I have a summons here ordering you to appear at

the great court of Ferd this afternoon. Will you accept
it?"

"Certainly."

"Then you will be there?"

"I'll send my lawyer," said Fara. "Just drop the summons on the floor there. Tell them I took it."

The weapon shop man had said: "Do not ridicule by
word any legal measure of the Imperial authorities. Simply
disobey them."

Jor went out, and seemed relieved. It took an hour
before Mayor Mel Dale came pompously through the
door.

"See here, Fara Clark," he bellowed from the doorway. "You can't get away with this. This is defiance of
the law."

Fara was silent as his honor waddled farther into
the building. It was puzzling, almost amazing, that Mayor
Dale would risk his plump, treasured body. Puzzlement
ended as the mayor said in a low voice:

"Good work, Fara; I knew you had it in you. There's
dozens of us in Glay behind you, so stick it out. I had
to yell at you just now, because there's a crowd outside.
Yell back at me, will you? Let's have a real name calling. But, first, a word of warning: the manager of the
Automatic Repair shop is on his way here with his bodyguards, two of them—"

Shakily, Fara watched the mayor go out. The crisis
was at hand. He braced himself, thought: "Let them
come, let them—"

It was easier than he had thought—for the men who
entered the shop turned pale when they saw the holstered
revolver. There was a violence of blustering, nevertheless,
that narrowed finally down to:

"Look here," the man said, "we've got your note for
twelve thousand one hundred credits. You're not going
to deny you owe that money."

"I'll buy it back," said Fara in a stony voice, "for
exactly half, not a cent more."

The strong-jawed young man looked at him for a
long time. "We'll take it," he said finally, curtly.

Fara said: "I've got the agreement here—"

His first customer was old man Miser Lan Harris.

251

Fara stared at the long-faced oldster with a vast surmise, and his first, amazed comprehension came of how the weapon shop must have settled on Harris' lot—by arrangement.

It was an hour after Harris had gone that Creel's mother stamped into the shop. She closed the door.

"Well," she said, "you did it, eh? Good work. I'm sorry if I seemed rough with you when you came to my place, but we weapon-shop supporters can't afford to take risks for those who are not on our side.

"But never mind that. I've come to take Creel home. The important thing is to return everything to normal as quickly as possible."

It was over; incredibly it was over. Twice, as he walked home that night, Fara stopped in midstride, and wondered if it had not all been a dream. The air was like wine. The little world of Glay spread before him, green and gracious, a peaceful paradise where time had stood still.

*You Will Also Want To Read . . .*

# QUARK/

*A Quarterly of Speculative Fiction*
Selected and Edited by Samuel R. Delany and
Marilyn Hacker

In these new quarterlies of speculative literature and
graphics, the editors have tried to display the finest
work of both new and established authors, whatever its
imaginative substance, structure, or texture.

## QUARK/1

includes stories by:

* Adam * Bailey * Benford * Bernott * Boucher *
* Bryant * Delany * Disch * Dozois * Eklund *
* Hickey * Lafferty * Le Guin * Link * Priest *
* Russ * Stanley * van Vogt *

(66-480, $1.25)

## QUARK/2

includes stories by:

* Bernott * Brunner * Bryant * Cohen * Disch *
* Dorman * Emshwiller * Farmer * Fitzgerald *
* Frost * Hacker * Keilty * Lieber * Obtulowicz *
* Panshin * Penney * Sallis * Sladek * Stoney *
* Yep *

(66-530, $1.25)

# THE GLORY THAT WAS

by L. Sprague de Camp

*with an introduction by Robert A. Heinlein*

*The Glory That Was . . . what?*

Isolated from the rest of the world by a force wall, 27th century Greece is a mystery—which two men are determined to solve. Wiyem Flin, a classical scholar, believes his missing wife Thalia has been taken there. Knut Bulnes, a magazine editor, goes with Flin for the sake of adventure and an exclusive story. When they penetrate the force barrier they find that they have been thrown back in time 3000 years to classical Greece. At least, it looks, smells, and sounds like classical Greece ought to. But if it's the real thing, what's Thalia doing there . . . as Euripides' wife?

(63-542, 60¢)

Science Fiction

## MONSTERS

by A. E. van Vogt

A brilliant, exciting collection of vintage van Vogt—eight stories of cosmic horror in strange worlds of time and space.

(63-406, 60¢)

---

## THE PROXY INTELLIGENCE AND OTHER MIND BENDERS

by A. E. van Vogt

A. E. van Vogt "seems equally at home with all the richest themes of the genre; the mathematics and physics of space travel, the strange mutations and symbiosis of imagined life in other stellar systems, cybernetics and the robot, and the vast possibilities of extra-sensory perception. To this he adds a subtle political sense with an ardent humanistic ethic."

—*Angus Wilson*

(64-512, 75¢)

## THE HOUSE THAT STOOD STILL

by A. E. van Vogt

Earth is threatened with destruction from enemy forces lurking in the galaxy. Only the strange powers of the masked immortals in THE HOUSE THAT STOOD STILL could save the earth—and they would rather flee than fight.

(64-603, 75¢)

------------------------------------------------

If you are unable to obtain these books from your local dealer, they may be ordered directly from the publisher. Please allow 4 weeks for delivery.

PAPERBACK LIBRARY
Department B
315 Park Avenue South
New York, N.Y. 10010

Please send me the books I have checked.
I am enclosing payment plus 10¢ per copy to cover postage and handling.

Name ...........................................................................

Address .......................................................................

City .......................................... State ............ Zip ............

................Please send me your free mail order catalog